The Least of These

Endorsements

Clarice James continues her winning streak with *The Least of These*, tackling the issues of *whistleblowing* and medical malpractice with insight, humor, and suspense. She does a good job developing her young heroine, showing both her resolve and her fears. James deftly portrays a small New England town, its gossip, and goodness. This is a strong addition to James's body of work and to anyone's women's fiction collection.

—**Kathleen D. Bailey**, award-winning author of *Westward Hope, Settlers' Hope, and Redemption's Hope* (Western Dream Series)

Suspense, sweet and endearing romance, and a cast of appealingly genuine characters. As for the setting—I want to visit Andover, Maine, population 821, for Olde Home Days to eat sausages with fresh-out-of-the-garden peppers and onions, and to cheer on the drivers in the tractor race. Ms. James's touches of humor made me chuckle many times. A delightful read that left me with wistfully pleasant memories.

—**Susan F. Craft**, author of *The Chamomile, Laurel*, and *Cassia* (The Women of the American Revolution Series)

Clarice James never fails to grab me on the first page and hold me to the last. Her latest, *The Least of These*, is no exception. From Bolivia to Kentucky, Pennsylvania, and Maine, this expertly crafted story is populated with characters who won my heart and inspired me. James toggles seamlessly from one locale and character—not to mention generation—to another, and her subtle humor adds just the right lighthearted touch. From intergenerational relationships, to romance and mystery, this story is James's best yet.

—**Linda Brooks Davis**, award-winning author of *The Calling of Ella McFarland, The Mending of Lillian Cathleen,* and *The Awakening of Miss Adelaide* (The Women of Rock Creek Series)

Clarice James has again delighted her readers with *The Least of These*, a tender tale with a powerful spiritual truth woven through it. It's filled with engaging characters who will make you laugh and touch your heart. *The Least of These* has mystery, romance, and some unexpected plot twists that will keep the reader turning the pages, and sad to see it end.

—**Janet Grunst**, award-winning author of *A Heart Set Free, A Heart for Freedom*, and *Setting Two Hearts Free* (Revolutionary War Series)

Clarice James is a talented writer, and *The Least of These* is her best book yet. A solid five stars. It begins with a vulnerable young woman hiding out in a small town reminiscent of Jan Karon's beloved Mitford. All the characters are well drawn, even the minor ones; the plot threads are neatly woven together; and the ending surprised me. Humor is scattered throughout. I do hope Mrs. James is planning one or more sequels.

—**Carol Raj**, author of *The Curious Prayer Life of Muriel Smith* and *Charlotte Masterson Gets a Life*

The moment I met Carley, I was intrigued. When Geneva made her entrance, I tossed my to-do list and wrapped myself up in a story that captivated my heart and inspired me to be my best self- no matter what life throws my way. I'm confident you too will soon be packing a bag and catching the next bus to Andover. Brace your heart to be changed by two women at the intersection of family, faith, and fertilizer.

—**Lori Roeleveld**, blogger, speaker, coach, and author of *The Art of Hard Conversations: Biblical Tools for the Tough Talks that Matter*

Clarice James's captivating characters never fail to make me chuckle at their traits, chafe over their tragedies, and cheer for their triumphs. After reading *The Least of These*, I'm convinced I could pick them out of the crowd at Olde Home Days in Andover, Maine. I'd tell them in person how inspiring their stories are, how somebody ought to put them into a book. Oh, wait ...

—**Terrie Todd**, award-winning author of *The Silver Suitcase*, *Maggie's War*, *Bleak Landing*, and *Rose Among Thornes*

Clarice James artfully weaves wit and humor throughout her latest book, *The Least of These*. Her skilled ability to develop each character's personality kept me interested and invested in the story. I admired Geneva's wisdom, generosity, and practicality. Carley's life includes a bit of suspense, but she gracefully matures through her struggles.

—**Konnie Viner**, author of *Rested Soul, Resilient Heart: Finding Hope in the Storms of Abuse and Betrayal* (nonfiction) and *Amaryllis Journey*, a novel

The Least of These

Clarice G. James

ELK LAKE PUBLISHING INC
PUBLISHING THE POSITIVE
Plymouth, Massachusetts

COPYRIGHT

This book is a work of fiction. Characters are the product of the author's imagination. Any resemblance to actual events or persons, living or dead, is entirely coincidental. The legal names of Maine residents, Leo Camire, Esau Cooper, Rylee Cooper, Cynthia Giroux, Frank Gregoire, Linda Gregoire, Martha O'Leary, and Mary Salatino have been used with their permission, but all events related to their names in this book are fictional.

Scripture taken from the King James Version and the Darby Translation of the Holy Bible, both in Public Domain.

Cover Design: Derinda Babcock

Editor(s): Judy Hagey, Deb Haggerty

PUBLISHED BY: Elk Lake Publishing, Inc., 35 Dogwood Dr., Plymouth, MA 02360, 2021

Library Cataloging Data

Names: James, Clarice G. (Clarice G. James)

The Least of These, Clarice G. James

358 p. 23 cm x 15 cm (9 in x 6 in)

Identifiers: ISBN 13: 978-1-64949-250-0 (paperback) | 978-1-64949-251-7 (trade paperback) | 978-1-64949-252-4 (e-book)

Key Words: Medicare fraud; whistleblower; anonymous giving; God's calling; jump to conclusions; Andover, Maine; hiding in a small town

Library of Congress Control Number: 2021938903 Fiction

DEDICATION

With love and thanks to my brother Frank Gregoire and his wife Linda who introduced me to the curious, crazy, hardworking, and wonderful people of Andover, Maine, population 821.

ACKNOWLEDGMENTS

While researching settings for this novel, my husband David and I visited Andover, Maine, where my brother Frank Gregoire and his wife, Linda, have a vacation home. We connected with some of their friends and neighbors at the Little Red Hen Diner & Bakery, the Knotty Moose Tavern, and the Liar's Table at Mills Market. We even joined the good people at Calvary Bible Church for a serendipitous potluck luncheon after attending their Sunday service. Everyone we met in town seemed to have a story to tell, which gave me plenty of material for *this* one.

In alphabetical order, I'd like to thank Leo Camire, Esau Cooper and his daughter, Rylee, Cynthia Giroux, Frank and Linda Gregoire, Martha O'Leary, and Mary Salatino for their invaluable help during my visit and for answering all my follow-up questions.

Leo filled me in on the ambulance service, the Appalachian Trail, and Andover Olde Home Days. Mary and Martha, having both worked at the town hall for years, shared their wealth of information and knowledge of the town's history. Cynthia answered questions and added background information via social media. Esau's colorful account of the lawn tractor race made me add that scene to my book. Esau's daughter, Rylee, though younger than my character, agreed to let me use her name. [Note: With their permission, I used the names of the people above in my story, but most of the actions attributed to the characters are pure fiction.]

As with my previous four novels, the input from my critique group members was invaluable. Thanks Mike Anderson, David James, Cricket Lomicka, Bob Paige, and Jeremiah Peters.

Thanks to my beta readers, Debra Bock and Susan Loud, for their thoughtful suggestions. Thanks also to my fellow authors who went through the complete manuscript, many with a fine-point red pen: Kathleen D. Bailey, Susan F. Craft, Linda B. Davis, Janet Grunst, Carol Raj, Lori Roeleveld, Terrie Todd, and Konnie Viner. [Their endorsements are included in the front of the book.]

I am most grateful for the encouragement and input of publisher Deb Haggerty of Elk Lake Publishing, Inc. and her team of professionals, including editor Judy Hagey and cover designer Derinda Babcock.

On a personal note, I don't know how I would have managed to finish this story if not for the love, support, and input of my husband David. For almost two years, he listened to me yammer on about the story, the town, and its characters, all the while enduring serious health issues and hospital stays. He is my hero.

Finally, thank you, Lord, for putting all these people in my life and for making good use of the gifts and talents you have given me.

PROLOGUE

CARLEY: SEVEN YEARS OLD

NEW HOPE, PENNSYLVANIA

Seven-year-old Carley Rae Jantzen tidied up the pretend hospital ward in her pink and purple bedroom. Daddy's size fourteen shoeboxes made the bestest hospital beds. She could fill up a whole ward with stuffed-animal patients if only he'd buy more shoes.

Carley was sure the oatmeal box she'd wrapped in silver tape looked like a real MRI machine ... not that she'd ever seen one before 'cept on TV. Using Daddy's duct tape was a good idea. She'd never seen him wrap a duck or even a chicken before and hoped she never did, 'cuz that tape was really, really sticky.

"Taco, I need to see if your insides are coming apart. *Cierra los ojos.* Close your eyes now and don't make a peep." She shoved her plush Chihuahua into one end of her make-believe scanner, then pulled the puppy out the other. "Now that didn't hurt a bit, did it?"

Carley tucked the terrycloth hand towel blankets around Suzy and Sandy, her baby-doll patients. Though Sandy was brown and Suzy pink, she figured adopting them on the same day, from the same yard sale, for the same two dollars meant they had to be twins.

She shook a plastic thermometer and put it in Suzy's mouth. After a minute, she checked it. "No fever. Good. Now let me get you dressed. This yellow bonnet and sweater will look so pretty on you."

Her dad knocked on her half-open bedroom door. "Nurse Carley, how are your patients doing this morning?"

She buttoned the baby-doll's sweater. "Some are getting better, but I need more bandages."

"Didn't I give you a box a couple weeks ago?"

She nodded. "Yes, but I used them all up at school. Kids keep getting hurt at recess."

"Am I aiding and abetting you to compete with the school nurse?"

She put both hands on her waist. "*Daddy*, remember? Nurse Bertie made me her 'sistant."

He flat handed the side of his head. "How could I forget something so important?"

"That's okay." She snugged up close to him. "If I don't take my allowance this week, can you get me the bandages with cartoons on them? And some stickers? Kids feel way better when you give them a sticker."

"What happened to lollipops?"

"Nurse Bertie doesn't give out candy 'cuz some kids are 'lergic, like Braden. He turns red and puffy."

"Poor Braden." He kissed the top of her head. "Okay, I'll see what I can do."

She grasped the handle of her rolling Looney Tunes suitcase.

He glanced back at her. "Are you running away from home or something?"

"This is my show and tell stuff, remember?"

"Right, show and tell. What time is that again?"

Does Daddy ever listen to me?

She made her way to the kitchen and pointed to the notice stuck to the refrigerator by a frog magnet. "Miss Joseph said I'm up right after lunch."

"I wouldn't miss it." He motioned to her suitcase. "So, what's your presentation about?"

She gave him a look. "I a'ready told you. It's a surprise."

"I remember now." He straightened her ponytail. "Did you put your lunch in your backpack?"

"Yup."

He groaned when he lifted her pack off the counter. "Is it me, or does this get heavier every day?"

Carley shrugged and hoped he wouldn't check inside. "Just lunch and stuff." She'd packed extra to share with her friends 'cuz all Selena ever had was beans and rice, and lots o' times Tammy had no lunch at all. She headed for the back door. "Hurry, Daddy, or we'll be late."

He shook his head. "You're sounding more and more like your mother every day."

Carley smiled 'cuz she liked when he said that.

After lunch, Miss Joseph clapped her hands to get everyone settled in their seats—including the parents. "Carley, come on up. Class, let's give her a round of applause."

Carley walked to the front and gave a little bow before she unzipped her suitcase and set everything out on the desk. She stood up straight, like she'd practiced, and cleared her throat.

"My name is Carley Rae Jantzen. I was named after my mother." She reached for the gold-framed photo of her mother in her wedding gown and turned the picture to face the class. "This is my mom on the day she married my dad."

3

The kids—mostly the girls—oohed and aahed over the picture. She knew they would. Her mother looked like a movie star.

Selena leaned in closer. "I think you look like her."

"Very much so," Miss Joseph said.

Tammy pointed to her mother's dark, shiny hair. "Your hair is the 'xact same color."

Everything they said made Carley feel warm and fuzzy inside.

She unfolded her mom's wedding veil and placed it on her head. "Maybe one day when I get married, I can wear this."

Braden sang out, "Carley's getting married! Carley's getting married!"

Miss Joseph shushed him before she helped Carley tack up her huge map of South America on the bulletin board.

"My mom and dad both came from Kentucky, but they first met in Bolivia on a mission trip." She pointed to a spot on the map. "Right here. Dad helped build huts and dig wells and stuff like that. Mom was a nurse. She gave patients shots."

She scooted back to the desk. "Bolivian people speak Spanish. My dad is fluid in Spanish. He's teaching me for when I go to Bolivia someday. Cómo estás means 'How are you?' ¿Trajiste a tu hamer? means 'Did you bring a hammer?' And Esto picará un poco means 'This will sting a little.'"

Carley handed a photo album to a boy in the front row. "These are pictures of my parents with all their Bolivian friends. You can pass it around."

Next, she held up one of her mother's most important nursing tools. "This is my mom's theth-es-scope. She used this to listen to patients' hearts and lungs. I can't pass it around 'cuz it's not a toy."

Braden grumbled. "We won't break it. Come on, give it here."

Carley made believe she didn't hear him and picked up her baby doll Suzy.

"Carley's got a baby! Carley's got a baby!"

Sheesh. Mr. Bully-Big-Mouth Braden again.

Miss Joseph stepped to the side of Braden's desk, like she always did when he got "out of hand," as she'd say.

"When my mom was waiting for me to be born, she knitted the sweater and bonnet my doll is wearing. My dad said she picked yellow because she didn't know if I was going to be a boy or a girl. See, aren't the puppy buttons cute?" She brought the sweater up to her cheek. "The yarn is so soft. I must have loved wearing this when I was little."

Uh, oh. Miss Joseph is clearing her throat. Does she want me to hurry?

The last thing Carley showed the class was the Bible verse pillow. "My great-grandmother made this pillow for my mom when she moved away from Kentucky. Daddy says this sewing is called m-broidery." She read the verse out loud slowly to make sure she got all the words right. "Verily ... I say unto you ... inasmuch as ye have done it unto ... one of the least of these ... my brethren ... ye have done it unto me. Matthew 25:40."

Braden wisecracked, "This is *show* and tell not *talk* and tell. Where's your mother? She's supposed to be here."

Why can't he be quiet? Carley wanted to punch him.

Miss Joseph placed her hand on Braden's shoulder. "We apologize, Carley. Braden will not interrupt you again, will you, Braden?"

He mumbled something that sounded like "Sorry," but Carley didn't believe him.

She straightened her shoulders again. "My mom won't be here. She died two days after I was born. My dad says it wasn't my fault; it was just her time."

Kids whispered until the teacher made them stop. Selena sniffled a little, and Tammy's eyes got teary.

Carley took a deep breath. "Some kids think I don't have a mom, but I do." She put her hand on her heart and felt it beating. "She's inside here. My dad says I'm a lot like her. When I grow up, I'm gonna be a nurse and a missionary like her too. One day when I get to heaven, I'll know who she is right away."

Carley paused for a second to make sure she hadn't left anything out. She packed up her things and took another bow. "The end."

Miss Joseph clapped on her way to the front of the room. All the kids did too—even Braden.

Why is Daddy wiping his eyes?

Carley scooted to the back row. "Are you okay?"

"I'm more than okay." He hugged her and whispered, "Best show and tell in the whole history of all show and tells." He handed her a paper bag. "And you can keep your allowance. You earned it."

She peeked inside. "Superhero bandages ... and stickers! Thanks!" Carley hugged him back. "You're my favorite."

He high fived her. "I'd better be."

The next day at recess, Braden cut himself while wrestling on the blacktop with another boy.

Carley heard him crying and raced over with her backpack. "Where does it hurt?"

"My elbow's bleeding!"

Carley tilted her head to examine his bloody scrape. "You'll be okay. Nurse Bertie is on her way."

The school nurse checked him out. "Nothing broken. I cleaned the area. Carley, can you handle it from here?"

She nodded. "Yes, ma'am." Carley pulled out a pack of bandages. "Which one do you want?"

6

He stopped whining. "Superhero bandages? Where'd you get these?"

"My dad got them for me."

"As a prize for doing a good show and tell?"

Is he teasing me again? She looked in his eyes. *I don't think so.*

She shrugged. "Maybe."

No surprise, Braden chose The Hulk bandage.

She stuck it to his elbow. "There. You're all set."

"Cool." He grinned. "Ya know, you said something wrong in your show and tell yesterday."

God, please make Mr. Bully-Big-Mouth be nice.

"You won't *be* a good nurse. You *are* a good nurse already."

Carley's face warmed. "Um, thanks."

By the end of recess, Braden had a full row of stickers and two extra bandages.

Well, you did make him nice, God.

Chapter One

Carley: Present Day

Philadelphia, Pennsylvania

Carley Rae Jantzen's only connection to her extended and distant family was a great-aunt named Geneva Kellerman on her mother's side. Since she'd barely heard of this sixty-two-year-old woman, never mind met her, she didn't feel indebted to her at all. Carley had only agreed to the live-in position with this elderly relative for two reasons: she needed a job and a place to hide. Maine was as fine a place as any.

Her aunt's attorney, Vern Beckham, had tracked her down through an online ancestry program. The timing of his proposition was pure serendipity—at least for Carley. She couldn't speak for the older woman. Nevertheless, she'd answered before another of Geneva's relatives could jump at the offer.

To secure Mr. Beckham's approval, Carley had had to share some of her secret with him. He was agreeable enough to accept her condition: Other than him, no one—not even her aunt—was to know her real name or why she was there.

Now, for an alias ... She refilled her water bottle and got comfortable in front of her laptop.

Over the past week, she'd tried on a few monikers for size, but they'd itched. Her new name needed to be simple enough to be believable, yet not too plain or cool as to sound fake. Tonight, a quick search of "Andover, Maine families" brought her to the surname *Merrill*. Surely, the town residents couldn't argue with that.

Before she could decide on a first name, her phone rang. By now the number was familiar—Attorney Beckham.

In his smooth baritone he said, "Hello, Carley. I'm calling to confirm your arrival next week."

She surveyed her furnished apartment. Her personal items were packed in boxes, bags, and her three-piece luggage set, a high school graduation gift from her dad. "I'm leaving early Monday morning. Can I call you when I see how the trip goes?"

"No problem. One more thing, what name should I give your aunt?"

Scanning the scribblings on her pad for a name, she decided to stick with something she couldn't mess up. "Carley. Carley Merrill."

"Very good, Ms. *Merrill*. See you soon."

On Friday, Carley's final day of work at Key State Family Medical, she logged onto a travel club's website to download and print directions to keep her on the scenic backroads and off the highways. Covering the five hundred miles from Philadelphia to Andover, Maine—population 821 in its last census—would take her at least ten hours. No way did she want to depend solely on GPS.

Carley was diligent to delete her browsing history.

Of course, she had no reason to believe she'd be tracked by Dr. Full-of-Himself. He'd accepted an invitation to speak at an exclusive medical conference in Los Angeles that week. By the time he got back, Carley *Merrill* would be ensconced in a new life.

Her fraud case attorney had cautioned her to keep quiet and not to trust a soul. Of course, Carley would have made an exception for her dad if she could have reached him in Bolivia. She waffled about confiding in Roxanne Ingram, Key State's office administrator *and* her best friend in Philly. They'd become even closer while babysitting Roxy's four-year-old nephew every Friday to give his parents a date night. Carley would miss the little guy's bright eyes and crooked smile. In the end, she decided not to tell anyone, so they wouldn't have to worry or lie.

After weeks of watching detective shows and reading mystery novels, Carley's "going on the lam" to-do list became a bit unwieldy. *Trade my car in. Disconnect the new car's GPS. Get a burner phone. Get a fake ID. Dye my hair red. Pay in cash. Avoid street cameras.*

In the end, she had no choice but to pare down the list.

Her plan to trade in her two-year-old red VW Beetle convertible for a twelve-year-old Hyundai hatchback went south when the questionable Cash & Dash car dealer offered her an insulting amount of cash. No trade meant no GPS to disconnect.

Carley did buy a prepaid phone with an untraceable number. Instead of dying her dark brown hair red, she lopped her locks off with pinking shears for a more natural look. She had no idea how to get a fake ID, so her fake last name would have to suffice. As for street cameras ... she'd wing it.

Besides, who will be looking for me if they don't think I'm missing?

Early Monday morning, the last thing she did before cutting off her old cell service was leave Roxy and Dr. Nichols the same message: "Sorry. There's an emergency with my father in La Paz. Not sure when I'll be back." Since everyone at work knew her father was a missionary in Bolivia, her excuse would sound plausible. Besides, she hadn't exactly lied. There was always an emergency in La Paz.

Hours of driving gave her plenty of time to get used to her last name. Over and over, she recited, "Carley Merrill, Carley Merrill, Carley Merrill" until the name rolled off her tongue with ease.

Somewhere along the way, paranoia set in and picked up a couple of hitchhikers—loneliness and fear. Around the halfway mark of her trip, she skirted a heavy rainstorm and found a two-star B&B in a small town in Massachusetts, one that accepted cash. After a solid night's sleep and a breakfast hearty enough to satisfy her until supper, she was back on the road.

I can do this ... because I have no choice.

ANDOVER, MAINE

Tree lines thickened and roads narrowed the further north Carley drove. Rustic camps, log cabins, and new builds were interspersed among sprawling homesteads. Junk piles and heavy-duty plastic garages adorned yards. One or two vehicles with no license plate seemed to be parked at every fifth house. Accustomed to an urban environment, she wasn't used to all the yard clutter. Did the neighbors ever complain about one another?

Maybe Mainers mind their own business ... or do they call themselves Mainites or Mainiacs?

She reached South Main Street in Andover proper around two o'clock. Banners welcoming bikers, cyclists, campers, and Appalachian Trail hikers were posted all around town. A sign outside the fire department read, "Volunteers Needed."

The parking spaces at Sawmill Market & Tagging Station were filled. Across the street, the Red Rooster Diner and Bakery boasted of homemade kale soup and fresh rhubarb pie. She stopped at Andover Country Store to refill her water bottle. *Lame excuse.* The truth was, she was close and needed a bit more time to compose herself.

While waiting in line behind a couple of hunters bragging about the wild turkeys they'd bagged a few weeks back, she spotted a well-used phone directory on the counter near a pay phone. *Do they still have working payphones?* She thumbed to the M's, where she found a half page filled with the name *Merrill*. Satisfied, she smiled and closed the book.

A short middle-aged man approached her—his torso almost the length of his legs. He stroked his scrubby chin. "Hope ya don't mind me askin', are you Miss Geneva's niece comin' to visit?"

She nodded. "I am."

Okay, so maybe Mainers are nosey like everyone else.

"I 'spected so." He stuck out his hand. "Name's Dubbah Polaski. Welcome to Andovah."

She shook his hand. "Carley Merrill."

"Merrill, huh? Any relation to the Merrills 'round these parts?"

She tilted her head as if she were thinking. "I don't think so, but you never know." She was pleased with her answer.

"Anyway, we got us a nice town. People's real good to each other, 'specially Miss G."

She made a move to leave. "Well, I'd better get going before my aunt thinks I got lost."

"You say hi to her for me. Tell her me and Warren'll come by anytime to take one of those ol' John Deeres off her hands in trade when's she's ready."

"I'll do that."

South Main Street turned into North Andover Road. An old, white New England church sat adjacent to a quaint village common complete with a gazebo. Carley found South Arm Road easy enough, but with all its twists and turns and hills and valleys, she almost missed the driveway.

A good-sized, well-kept farmhouse and two-car garage sat at least a hundred feet back. Two substantial greenhouses and a large barn stood off to the side on the large parcel of land. A few smaller outbuildings, too.

Not outhouses, I hope.

She had called ahead to give attorney Beckham her guesstimated time of arrival. Other than a golf cart, hers was the only vehicle in sight. *Oh, well, I've introduced myself to new patients before.* Though moving in with one was not quite the same.

She exited her car. The most noticeable thing about the campestral setting was the panoramic mountain backdrop. Having lived in the city the last ten years, she couldn't help but stare. Carley had promised herself once she paid off her student loans, she would vacation in places like this. Places where brooks babbled, wind whistled through trees, and the sun dropped behind mountains in the evening.

But her fifty-plus-hour work weeks never left her the time—an excuse she'd repeated so often she even believed it herself. Now, depending on Aunt Geneva's health and disposition, this might not be so bad.

The farmhouse and its wraparound screened-in front porch looked freshly painted. Evergreens served as a backdrop to a collection of colorful perennials. Did hired help or kindly neighbors pitch in to keep the place up?

"Hidey-ho!"

Carley spun around to see where the voice came from.

"Up here!" A slight figure dressed in jeans and a straw hat, holding a long pole with a curved blade on the end, called from a ladder. "I've got to cut the branches back to keep the squirrels out of my chimney."

"*Your* chimney? Oh, I'm so sorry. I thought this was the Kellerman house."

"Last time I checked, it was." The woman climbed down a few rungs. "You must be Carley Merrill, my long-lost niece, the one Vern found."

Carley stumbled over her words, "Yes, um, I thought ... I mean ... you're on a ladder."

"Observant, I see." The woman chuckled. "As long as I'm able and have no one to boss me, I pretty much do as I please." She squinted at her. "Is that what you think you're here for? To boss me around?"

"No, not at all." She fidgeted with her handbag strap. "I was told, well ... I thought ... you see, I'm a nurse practitioner."

"Did Vern lead you to believe I was an invalid?" She stepped off the last rung.

Mr. Beckham's words flashed before her. *Getting on in years ... not as agile as she used to be ... could use some help.* "Um, uh, not in so many words. More like I was needed, I assumed, in my capacity as an NP."

"That old worrywart is a sneaky one." She removed a garden glove and extended her hand. "I'm Geneva Kellerman, your aunt on your mother's side. My brother Waylon was your mother's father. Most folks call me Miss Neva. If you're comfortable, feel free to do the same."

"Miss Neva, sure." The familial ring of "Auntie Geneva" seemed off-key anyway.

"Now, how about we get your luggage out of your car and settle you in your room? You can rest a bit, or we can sit on the front porch and enjoy the blueberry lemonade I fixed this morning."

"Blueberry lemonade sounds nice." Not that she'd ever had any before. Carley had a more pressing question. *Why am I here if not to nurse this woman into 'the sweet by and by?'*

Chapter Two

Carley: Present Day

Andover, Maine

The front porch wrapped around to a side entrance which was brightened by a dandelion-yellow door. Carley followed Miss Neva inside to a mudroom. The creamy-white walls, warm-gray floor tiles, and dark-green cubbies fit well with the style.

Her aunt hung her straw hat on a hook. "This cubby here is yours."

"Thanks." She hung a few jackets and stashed her boots. She'd unpack the rest of her things once she learned more.

And if you don't like what you learn, what then? She shook the question out of her head—again.

The living room, dining room, and kitchen were open post and beam construction with vaulted ceilings and wide plank pine floors. The furnishings seemed more comfy than fussy, more traditional than modern, though the artwork seemed different enough to be original.

You didn't need a doormat to read *welcome* in this home.

The fieldstone fireplace reached the full height of the room. Carley ran her fingers over a well-worn rifle hanging below a high mantel made from a rough-hewn beam.

"Just so you know, I keep my weapons loaded. That Winchester you're admirin' there as well as the bolt action Remington I carry in my truck."

Carley pulled her hand back.

"Never know what you might run into around here." Her aunt rubbed her hands together. "Now, for the grand tour." She motioned to a spacious room off the living room. "I call this the library, mainly because *library* sounds way more relaxing than *office*. I do my work in there. Feel free to peruse the shelves for something to read."

"Thanks." Carley took a quick peek before she followed her down the hall.

Miss Neva pointed. "Powder room, my bedroom, and another guest bedroom across the hall."

Mentally, she had prepared herself for a sick old lady's cramped, cluttered, sour-smelling house. She was amused by the irony—her apartment in Philadelphia had been more cramped and cluttered than this place.

"Would you rather upstairs or down? All my guest rooms have their own bath. Personally, I'm partial to the view upstairs at the back of the house."

Carley thought over the situation. "Perhaps I should take the room closest to yours."

"Never you mind about that. As I said, I'm not in need of a nurse."

"If I were nearby, and you did need something—"

"Upstairs it is!" As if to prove her point, the woman took the steps at a trot. "You'll love the view."

Her aunt was right. The view from the balcony off the bedroom was like nothing she'd ever seen in Philly. Not another house in sight. The pale expanse of sky, a brook running through miles of rolling green acres, all in the shadow of a mountain range. Without turning from the peaceful scene, Carley asked, "How long have you been blessed to live here?"

"Bought this property some thirty years ago. The landscape reminded me of my home back in Kentucky—minus the underground fires, gaseous vapors, and orange toxic water."

The question in Carley's expression may have prompted the explanation from her aunt. "I spent my first fifteen years in Appalachian Mountain coal country, not far from where your mother was born."

There had to be more to her story, but Carley dared not ask. What if her hostess had questions of her own?

Miss Neva fluffed a pillow on a bedside chair. "Now how about that lemonade?"

"Sure."

Leading the way, her aunt checked her watch. "Besides, rocking on the porch always helps me decide what critter to shoot for dinner."

Carley tripped over the threshold on her way out of the room.

The two women sat on the porch with a pitcher and glasses on the table between them.

Carley quenched her thirst with the tart concoction. "This *is* tasty."

"Did you think I'd lie?"

"Well, no." *Why? Do you think I would?*

No sooner had they synchronized their rocking when a silver SUV pulled up the driveway. A tall, fit man, maybe around her aunt's age, got out. "Afternoon, ladies. Thought I'd stop by and introduce myself to your niece."

Miss Neva waved him over. "Afternoon, Vern. Come on up."

He mounted the steps. "You must be Carley."

She shook the hand he offered. "Yes, nice to meet you in person, Mr. Beckham."

"Call me Vern, please."

Miss Neva poured him some lemonade and gave him a hard stare. "So, what nonsense have you been feeding my niece?"

He lowered himself onto a porch swing. "No nonsense at all. I told the young lady you were seeking someone to assist you."

Her aunt huffed. "In my *old* age?"

Carley started to feel bad for him. "He didn't say that exactly."

"Vern, did you neglect to mention you're a year *older* than me?"

Pushing lightly off the deck with one foot, he began to swing. "Now, Neva, no matter what a person's age, they can always use a little help." He sipped his drink. "Isn't that what you're always telling folks?"

She squinted. "You better be sweet if you expect to be invited to supper."

A slow smile appeared on his face. "By the way, when I stopped for gas, T-bone told me your pickup passed inspection without a hitch. Dubber and Warren were there. They offered to drive the truck home for you, but I took the liberty of declining their assistance."

"Heavens, why? Could've saved me a trip."

"You see, they'd just come back from gathering up a load of manure from Esau Cooper's place. And from what I could make out"—he tapped his nose—"the load was fresh."

Her aunt grimaced. "You just earned your supper."

Carley slowed her chair. "Dubber? I forgot. I met him at the country store on my way in. He said to call him when you want to get rid of one of your John Deere tractors."

She shook her head. "Those two will never give up."

He chuckled. "They probably promised Esau they'd mow his field with their *new* acquisition in trade for the load."

"They'll add that manure to their compost pile and have the best black gold fertilizer on the market. They dickered with me last month for a load in exchange for my old truck tires."

A smile played across Vern's features. "For something fun to do, you should take Carley by their yard o' treasures, maybe peruse their portfolio of available goods and services for trade."

Geneva wagged her finger at him. "You scoff, but those boys are more industrious than most—even if their inventory consists of loose ends and spare parts."

He drained his glass. "Can't argue with you there."

Her aunt pushed herself up. "Well, I'd best figure out what I'm cooking for supper."

Daring to call her aunt's bluff, Carley asked, "Miss Neva, would you like me to get your rifle for you?"

The woman didn't hesitate as she walked toward the door. "No, I'd blow that squirrel to smithereens using a rifle. I use a shotgun for small'uns, then all I have to do is pick out the shot."

Before Carley could panic, she spied the mirth in the creases around Vern's eyes.

Miss Neva turned back. "Vern, check my greenhouse, will you? You might find something ripe for the pickin'. You know where I keep the basket. Carley, maybe you could help me set the table?"

The three of them sat together in the country kitchen at a long wooden table with plenty of history in its nicks and bruises.

Miss Neva folded her hands and bowed her head. "Lord, we welcome your presence in this home. Thank you for my niece, Carley, safe and sound here with us. Please bless our time together and this food to our bodies in Jesus's name. Amen."

The prayer caught Carley by surprise. She and her aunt might have more in common than she'd thought. She began to relax, partly because the "critter" on her plate looked and smelled a lot like chicken.

Her ease was short-lived when Miss Neva asked, "So, where did you attend nursing school?"

Having imagined a doddering or maybe semi-senile patient, Carley hadn't concocted answers to everyday questions. She belabored a mouthful of peas and decided the truth would be simpler. "I got my Bachelor of Science degree in nursing at the University of Pennsylvania. Later, at Bloomsburg, my accreditation as an Adult-Gerontology Primary Care Nurse Practitioner."

Miss Neva's eyes grew wide. "Gerontology? You mean old people?"

Carley shook her head. "Actually, adult-gerontology means healthcare for adults from adolescence on up."

"I see." She refilled their glasses. "I was fifteen when I moved up north. Your mama was only a little tyke. Years later, mines shut down and miners moved north. Is that how your family ended up in Pennsylvania? Were you raised there?"

"Dad and I lived in all kinds of cities ... and towns and, um, states. I don't recall him saying why he left Kentucky." Carley avoided making eye contact with Vern. "My mother died a few days after giving birth to me."

"That is so sad. Since my brother Waylon and his wife had passed years prior, I had no idea what'd happened to your mother or that I even had a niece until Vern searched my ancestry."

"I'm glad he found me." She smiled. "How about you? What made you leave Kentucky and come to Maine?"

Her aunt rested her utensils on her plate. "I was born in a coal town where the mortality rate was the only thing that thrived. Where the children often draw rivers and creeks with an orange crayon because of the underground coal fires. Even President Johnson's visit in 1964 to declare an 'unconditional war on poverty in America' didn't change things.

"On his deathbed, Daddy made Mama promise to get me out before coal dust or a husband got the best of me. She found me a job as a mother's helper up north. Me? I thought I was going to Cincinnati."

Vern chuckled. "Still remember the very day Otto and I caught sight of you. All gangly, with big blue eyes full of fear and awe."

"You should talk. You and Otto were quite the Mutt and Jeff duo back then. Him with his stocky build and quiet way and you, tall and skinny and all mouth."

He laughed. "I especially remember how you tried to act so brave."

She waved his remark away with the back of her hand. "Enough of that now."

Carley asked, "Who's Otto?"

Her aunt rested her arms on the table. "Otto Kellerman was a good man and my husband for thirty-five years. He passed four and a half years ago from a ruptured aortic aneurysm. 'Quick and sudden,' the doctor said."

"I'm so sorry." Carley always hated not knowing what to say.

Vern put his napkin on the table. "I couldn't have had a better friend."

A respectful silence fell over the room, which Carley chose not to break.

When her aunt began to clear the table, she moved to help her.

"No, you relax, dear. Whipping the cream for the apple crisp will only take me a few minutes."

"Once you've tasted Neva's desserts, you'll never go back to store bought." After her aunt left the room, he whispered, "You can trust her, you know. Please think about telling her your story."

"I can't take the chance." She caught his eye. "And you promised, remember?"

"Oh, I'll keep my word, all right. Trouble is, Carley, you're not a very accomplished liar."

Before his assertion could be further proved or dessert could be served, a truck pulled into the yard with a loud honk.

He rose from his seat. "That'd be Dubber and Warren dropping off my chainsaw. I told them I'd be here."

"Wait a minute," Miss Neva came out with a covered plastic container. "Give them this crisp to take home and tell them I don't expect anything in return."

Coffee and dessert were on the table when he got back.

True to Vern's review, the apple crisp was so good Carley didn't have to say another word or tell another lie for the rest of the meal.

Later that night, under sheets smelling of pine boughs and mountain air—or fabric softener, she wasn't sure which—Carley pondered the speed at which the pace of her life had escalated. For over two years, she'd been an invaluable nurse practitioner in a well-established medical practice in Philadelphia. Now, she was reduced to a whistleblower hiding in the backwoods of Maine.

Part of her brain couldn't ... or didn't want to? ... compute those facts. After all, this mess involved a man she'd highly respected and could have ... cared for. *Loved* didn't seem like the appropriate word to use—especially after what she knew now.

Carley tossed and turned over regrets and recriminations for another half hour, pounding her pillow into submission. *How could I have been so naïve? What took me so long to figure things out? Did he suspect how I felt? I'm pathetic! The man I fell for never even existed!*

Finally, she got up, opened the French doors, and stepped onto the balcony. A light breeze cooled her anger. Sounds of nature soothed her jittering nerves. The stars above and around reminded her of the majesty of God.

By the time she returned to bed, Carley was convinced this town, this home, was as safe a place as any to be on the lam. She curled up under the covers and smiled. Sleeping late, a luxury her six a.m. alarm clock had denied her for years, was now made possible by her aunt's good health.

"Wakey, wakey, eggs and bakey!"

"Huh?" Carley dragged herself up on one elbow. Trying to focus, she reached for her phone. "Six thirty?" She flopped back down and groaned. Why was she surprised? This was the same woman she'd found up on a ladder, trimming trees yesterday—not exactly a lay-about.

She ran a washcloth across her face and a brush through her hair and then threw on some jeans, a tank top, and hoodie. While she hurried down the steps, the aroma of bacon and coffee woke a few more of her brain cells. "Morning, Miss Neva. Breakfast sure smells good."

"Mornin'. After your long trip, I hope you don't mind me letting you sleep in a little."

Sleep in? Carley noticed the table was already set. "How can I help?"

"Mind getting the paper off the porch?"

Expecting to find something like the *Gazebo Gazette* or *Andover Snitch* on the stoop, she was surprised to see *The Wall Street Journal*. Carley scolded herself for another of her quick-draw judgments. By now, she should've known people are not always who or what they seemed to be.

She bent to pick up the paper. *What is that awful smell?* She sniffed the air. Miss Neva's clean, empty food container was on the top step with a sticky note that read, "Dee-lish! Thanks, Miss G. Here's a little something for your trouble. D + W."

A pail of what smelled like manure sat on the bottom step.

Her aunt chuckled when Carley told her about their olfactory offering. "Figured they'd leave something. Those two can't abide owing anybody for more than a day." She plated the eggs, bacon, home fries, and English muffins. "Don't expect me to cook like this every morning. I'm more of a juice, coffee, and oatmeal person."

Carley pantomimed wiping sweat from her brow. "Phew! I was worried how I'd work off all the calories."

"No need to worry. Burning calories is never a problem when you garden."

Over breakfast, she learned that Bountiful Acres, the Kellermans' business, was situated in more than one town in Oxford County. Early on in their marriage, Miss Neva and her husband had started a tree farm in Rumford. Blueberries soon followed in Bethel. Up until Otto died, their Andover acreage had supplied fruits and vegetables to retail and wholesale customers throughout the county. The high tunnel system, or hoop house, Otto put in place had extended their growing season by a month on both ends.

"Otto only had a few passions in life. Farming was one of them. Thankfully, he found a soulmate in Norm Fournier, who he later promoted to tree farm manager. The year after

Otto died, I sold the cornfields and the heavy machinery. The following year, the blueberry farm. I also cut the garden way back. Now I only plant enough for myself and the neighbors."

"You said your husband had 'a few passions.' What were his others?"

She lowered her cup to its saucer. "Our marriage and his friendship with Vern ... in that order."

Stilled by this intimate detail, Carley wondered if she'd ever find a man like that. Her mind was drawn back to Philly and the temptation of Dr. Harrison Nichols and his contagious smile and mesmerizing eyes. She stopped herself before she got stuck in the muck and the mire of emotions. A proverb she'd memorized to warn herself away from him came to mind: *Like a dog that returns to his vomit is a fool who repeats his folly.*

Her aunt interrupted her thoughts. "We've got an easy day today. After we tidy up here, we need to do a little weeding. Vern said there were plenty more peas to pick. We can bring a few pounds over to my friend Faith at the diner. Don't let me forget to stop at T-bone's to get my truck."

Carley pushed the idea of taking a stroll around the neighborhood aside. She'd need to help out around here if she didn't want to wear out her welcome. "Where do we start?"

"I'll wash. You dry."

Once the kitchen was back in order, they headed outside. Miss Neva snapped up the pail of fertilizer and set it in the back of the golf cart. "Hop in."

Earlier, when her aunt had said she'd cut back on farming, Carley had imagined an eight-by-ten-foot patch, not a garden twice as large flanked by two greenhouses on a parcel of land the size of two football fields. This put a whole new spin on the phrase "do a little weeding."

Miss Neva drove at a quick pace. "Otto was one of the first to master four-season techniques, so we grow year-round. Only difference now is I only use one of the greenhouses. The county homeschool co-op uses the other. You'll see the children around here a couple times a week." She pulled to a stop. "So, have you ever gardened before?"

"No. I'm not even sure I can tell the difference between a good plant and a bad."

"Then maybe I'll start you at this front section." She handed her the pail. "Only place I didn't fertilize, and I need to seed there soon."

Carley held the stinky bucket as far away from her nose as possible. "How do I spread it?"

"For this small area, by hand." Her aunt stepped inside one of the small outbuildings.

Carley swallowed hard, determined not to act like a tenderfoot. Besides, hadn't she dealt with worse when she'd worked at the hospital? She reached in, grabbed a fistful, and started flinging the stinky contents across the bare soil.

Miss Neva exited the shed and joined her. "That's one way of doing it, but I thought you might like to use these rubber gloves and garden trowel."

"Oh, sure." *Idiot.*

"Once that pail's empty, you can pick some peas." She winked. "Might be best if you washed your hands first. There's a sink in the greenhouse."

Carley picked and shelled for over two hours until she had an acceptable offering to bring to the diner. Her tank top was drenched, her hair matted, and she smelled more than a little funky. She cleaned up as best she could in the five-minute heads-up Miss Neva gave her.

"Don't worry, we're not fancy around here. Besides, no use taking a shower until after we finish the rest of the weeding this afternoon."

This afternoon?

28

Chapter Three

Geneva: Fifteen Years Old

Bethel, Maine

Tired, hungry, and scared, fifteen-year-old Geneva Newell stepped off the bus in Augusta on her journey to Bethel, Maine. From truck to bus to train and back to bus again, three days'd passed since she'd left her home in Kingdom Come, Kentucky. Every mile behind her, Daddy's reason for sending her away made less and less sense. Was she really in danger of getting black lung disease like him? She'd never worked a day of her life in a mine.

Geneva dropped her bags and sat on a bench to reread the travel directions from her employer. Someone was s'posed to pick her up in Augusta and drive her to Bethel. "Less than two hours away," they'd said.

If they show up.

She shivered and pulled her oversized cranberry blazer closed against the biting wind. Maine sure was a lot colder than Kentucky in September.

Geneva'd been hired as a mother's helper. Mama'd arranged the whole thing through Brother Vinter's sister-in-law, Mrs. Lankford, who'd moved to Maine seven years back to work as a cook for the Emerson family. Why couldn't Geneva stay home and help her own mother instead of someone else's a million miles away? Maybe it had something to do with her brother Waylon being twenty-two years older than her. She'd been what Mama always called "a late blessing."

When no one in sight seemed to be lookin' for her, Geneva darted inside the station to use the ladies' room. *Mercy!* Her reflection in the mirror was a fright. The blue plaid cotton dress Mama'd begged her to wear now clung to her thin body in wrinkles. That hand-me-down was the nicest thing she owned. She washed her face and hands and brushed her dark-as-coal hair, as Daddy'd called it. She smoothed her eyebrows, licked her lips, and pinched color back into her cheeks. When she came out, the station was near empty.

Oh, Lord, what do I do now?

Another fifteen minutes ticked by before a gray-haired man, dressed in a fancy jacket with brass buttons, tipped his cap to her. "Excuse me, might you be Miss Geneva Newell?"

She stood. "Yes, sir, that'd be me." Even though everyone back home called her Neva.

"I'm Upton, driver for the Emerson family. I apologize if I kept you waiting. I'm afraid I got a little turned around in Augusta. Don't often get to the capital city. Allow me to take your bags."

"Yes, thank you, sir, Mr. Upton." She stumbled behind him on the way to a white station wagon, the kind with the fancy wood panels on the side. The chrome plated name on the front panel read Town & Country. She'd only ever seen a car like this in magazines at the hospital where Daddy was.

Mr. Upton put her luggage in the back, then opened the front passenger door for her. A picnic basket sat on the tan leather seat between them. He lifted the cover. "Mrs. Emerson thought you might be hungry after your long trip, so she had Mrs. Lankford pack a snack. Help yourself, miss. Dinner won't be served until seven."

Mercy. Who eats supper at seven o'clock at night? That's near bedtime.

A shiny red apple, a loaf of some kinda bread, and a big lump of cheese were packed inside. There were two stubby insulated bottles, too, like Daddy used to take to the mines. One held hot soup, the other cold milk. This "snack" was the best meal she'd eaten in months.

Mr. Upton told her about the family she'd be livin' with. Besides havin' a driver, Mr. and Mrs. Emerson had a maid, a cook, and a gardener. Geneva's job was to help with the children—Eliza, ten, Noah, eight, and Daniel, five.

What kind of people can't take care of their own selves and their young'uns?

The clock on the dashboard told Geneva the trip from Augusta to Bethel took over an hour and a half. With every minute of the drive, her stomach tightened. At least it was full, and for that she was grateful.

Her mouth fell open as they pulled into a half-moon driveway in front of a gigantic white building. Nothing in Kingdom Come—or the whole of Letcher County, for that matter—was ever this white, even when it started out that way. Coal dust made its way into everything, not just Daddy's lungs.

Mama, what have you gotten me into?

Mr. Upton opened the car door for her. Not that she was needin' him to, but she'd froze up at the sight of the three-story house. The middle section was as wide as the biggest tree felled in Letcher County was long. (Geneva knew 'cause she'd seen the pictures on the front of *The Mountain Eagle* newspaper.) Two smaller houses sat on either side. She counted at least four brick chimneys sticking out the rooftop.

Probably need at least that many fireplaces to heat a place this big. Mercy!

She got up her nerve to ask, "Mr. Upton, what's that building over there, the one with the four barn doors?"

"That is where the family garages their vehicles. You'll find horses out back in the barn."

Horses? All they'd ever had back home was a half dozen chickens and a goat that got eaten by a big cat.

She trailed behind him as he carried her bags up the steps and through the heavy double doors. An older woman and a girl around her age stood in the entryway.

Mr. Upton gestured, "Miss Geneva, this is Mrs. Lankford, the cook for the family, and this is her daughter, Faith."

Mrs. Lankford was the woman Mama'd said got her the job. Geneva did a half-curtsey—at least she tried.

Mrs. Lankford said, "Welcome," but Geneva wasn't sure she meant it.

Faith smiled and reached for one of her bags. "Hi! You and I will be sharing a room together. Come on, I'll show you the way."

Mrs. Lankford called after them. "Don't be long. The family will be home after Eliza's dance recital. They'll want to meet the girl."

"*The girl?* You mean Geneva?"

Mrs. Lankford put her hands on her hips. "Don't sass me, girl. You know what I mean."

When they reached the third-floor landing, Faith turned left and walked to the end of the hall. She opened the door to a large airy room. "Home sweet home!"

Geneva was speechless—again. Tiny yellow rosebuds covered the walls. Sheer curtains edged with lace fluttered in the open windows. No coal dust in sight. Two beds, the same size as her Mama and Daddy's, sat across the room from each other. Both were covered in pale green bedspreads. "I've never seen anything so pretty before."

"I was eight when we came here and felt the same way." Faith put her suitcase down next to the dresser. "This one's yours."

"*All* the drawers?" Geneva was used to storing her clothes under her bed in an old trunk.

"We each have a nightstand too. The bathroom is across the hall." Faith flopped across her bed. "By the way, don't let Mama bother you. She's still cranky because I didn't want the mother's helper position. She even tried to get Brother Vinter from back home to talk me into it." She chuckled. "Backfired on her when he recommended you instead."

"Is there somethin' wrong with the job?"

"Nothing like that. The children are sweet, but that's not what I want to do with my life. I want to attend the CIA."

"The CIA?" Geneva's eyes widened. "You wanna be a spy?"

"Me?" Faith laughed. "No, the Culinary Institute of America, where all the famous chefs get their start."

"Oh. Is that in Bethel?"

"Nope. New York City—and that's the main reason Mama doesn't want me to go."

"When are you leaving?" Geneva was hopin' not too soon.

"After I graduate high school."

Phew.

Faith gave her a lively tour of the house and grounds, chattering all the while.

Maybe this won't be too bad—now that I might have a friend.

Both Mr. and Mrs. Emerson extended their hands and smiled like normal enough folk. "We're pleased you decided to accept the position," Mrs. Emerson said. "Mrs. Lankford tells us Faith helped you get settled. Is the room to your satisfaction?"

To my satisfaction? Geneva had never been asked that before. "Yes, sir. Yes, ma'am."

"Very good." Mr. Emerson said. "Then let's adjourn to the living room."

Mrs. Emerson followed him. "The children are anxious to meet you."

Geneva waited until everyone else was seated before she sat on the one remaining chair. She tried to smooth out the wrinkles in her dress but failed.

Mrs. Emerson did most of the talking. "These are our children. Eliza, Noah, and Daniel. Children, this is Miss Geneva."

They were as tongue-tied as she was.

"Children, please remember Miss Geneva is not here to do your chores or your homework for you. As a *mother*'s helper, she is here to help *me* make sure you do those things yourself. Understand?"

The children nodded and uttered a few, "Yes, ma'ams."

"Miss Geneva, Eliza would spend all her time in her reading nook if we let her. Please encourage her to come out and spend time in the real world too."

Eliza closed the book on her lap.

Mr. Emerson ruffled his youngest son's hair. "Our Daniel here would sleep in the barn with the horses if he had his way."

The little boy protested, "But, Father, they *need* me."

"You're right, son, and Miss Geneva will see that you have time to help the groomsman. She'll even post your after-school chores in the barn on the bulletin board."

34

He squiggled in his seat. "Miss G'neva, you're always s'pose to use blue marker for my chores. 'Liza is pink, and Noah is green."

"Thanks for tellin' me, Daniel." Geneva folded her hands in her lap. "That'll make my duties easier."

Mrs. Emerson said, "As for our Noah, he'll try his best to earn extra allowance by taking longer on his chores." She gave her son a mother's stare. "Miss Geneva will be watching you."

Noah slunk in his seat. "Moth-er!"

Faith entered the room. "Mama says dinner will be served in the dining room in fifteen minutes."

"Wonderful." Mr. Emerson stood. "Then our meeting is complete. If you have any questions, Geneva, don't hesitate to ask one of us."

"I will, sir. Thank you, sir."

Faith helped Mrs. Lankford serve the family's meal, while Geneva set a table for four in the kitchen. She was pleased when Mr. Upton joined them since she knew him best so far.

When the food was set down, Faith elbowed her. "Any of this familiar to you?"

She brightened. "Kilt greens, vegetable pie, and hoe cake?"

Faith whispered, "Yes, that's what we call these dishes in the kitchen. But in the dining room *kilt greens* is 'organic leaf lettuce sautéed with onions and sprinkled with bacon crumbles.' *Hoe cake* is 'homemade cornbread sweetened with all-natural honey.' The curried winter vegetable pie sounds fancy enough already."

No matter what anyone called the food, this meal tasted like home. "Thank you, Mrs. Lankford. This was delicious."

A small smile broke out on Mrs. Lankford's stern face. "I may have cooked it, but you can thank my girl for the menu."

Chapter Four

Geneva: Present Day

Geneva walked through T-bone's garage bay on her way to his office in the back. "Hidey-ho!"

He stepped out, holding a bottle of root beer. "Same to you, Miss Neva. Come for your truck?"

"Yes. I hear I get to keep her on the road for another year. That'll make sixteen. Not bad for American, wouldn't you say?"

He set his drink on his desk. "Chevy's a fine make. Of course, your taking good care of her helps." He reached for her keys and invoice but stopped when Carley came alongside them. "Hi, there. You must be Miss Neva's niece." He peeled off a latex glove and extended his hand. "Adam Stakes. Most folks around here call me T-bone."

Geneva hoped Carley wouldn't go on about his nickname. The ribbing got old real fast—mostly to him. His nickname could've been worse though. He had a cousin called Rib-eye and a sister who answered to Flank.

Her niece accepted his hand and smiled. "Carley Merrill. Nice to meet you, T-bone."

"Likewise." He tried to smooth his hair. "Merrill, huh? Any relation to the Merrills in Rumford?"

"I don't think so, but you never know." Carley glanced around the room. "Wow. This is the cleanest auto mechanic's office I've ever seen."

He raised his gloved hand. "My secret is latex. Keeps the grease and oil off me. Nobody wants grimy paperwork."

Geneva shook her head. "With a secret like that, it's a wonder you're still single." *Oh, that was subtle. Well, too late now.*

"Sorry, I'm not full of witty repartee this morning." He rubbed the bridge of his nose. "I had the nightshift watching Doc Quimby's post-op patients. Faith's Siberian Husky kept me awake most of the night."

"What was Houdini in for this time?" Geneva asked.

"An intestinal obstruction, but the operation isn't what bothered him."

"And you believed that dog?" She loved the expression on his face.

He cleared his throat. "As I was saying, with limited space in my converted garage, I had to cage him between Leo Camire's newly-spayed cat and Martha O'Leary's depressed ferret."

"I'd be depressed too if my name was Piddles." Geneva got her credit card out of her wallet.

"Answering to T-bone, I can hardly talk." He ran her card through. "Anyway, even though the cat was sedated and the ferret lethargic, that dog went nuts. Long about three in the morning, I gave up and moved him to my guest bedroom. The whimpering that followed was even worse."

She signed her charge slip. "Yours or the dog's?"

His lower lip turned into a pout. "Man, I get no respect."

Carley interrupted, "Is there a reason you didn't move the cat and the ferret in the house instead?"

He did an open-mouthed double take. "Two reasons, actually. One, I was sleep deprived, and two, my bulb's not too bright."

Carley grinned. "Sorry."

"There, there, don't be too hard on yourself." Geneva stared at his clean but unruly sandy-colored hair. "You've got a lot going on ... like those cowlicks."

He tried to pat his hair into place. "Tossing and turning after taking a shower can do that."

Geneva lifted his chin with her fingertips. "With those big brown eyes, you're still as handsome as ever." Arm in arm, the two of them walked toward the open door. "Okay if I take my truck and we come back later for Carley's car?"

"Sure. Pull in behind that motor home to the left of the post-op garage. Doc Quimby's coming by around noon. I'm praying all three patients will be discharged so I can get a good night's sleep."

"With all your whimpering, I bet they're praying the same." She chuckled. "Well, we're off. I'm showing Carley around town, introducing her to some of our more interesting residents."

"And you began with *me*?" He faced Carley. "Don't worry, your tour can only improve from here."

Geneva wagged a finger at him. "T-bone Stakes, if you expect us to fall for that pathetic cry for a compliment, you're sadly mistaken."

He mimicked a stab in the heart. "You sure know how to keep a guy humble."

"Exactly the way we like our men." She softened her expression. "Once my niece gets settled, we'll have you over for a special dinner."

He hung his thumbs on his front pockets and perked up. "I'd like that."

"Okay, but first, I need to find out what night is better for Dubber and Warren."

He frowned. "You can be mean, Miss Neva, you know that?"

She laughed on her way out.

Ordinarily, this would've been an ideal time for Geneva to tout her favorite bachelor's professional skills. Then, if she sensed the female was interested, she'd go on about his fine character, immaculate house, and the award-worthy poems he entered every year at Andover's Olde Home Days.

This was different. Even though Carley was family, she knew little about this young woman's personal life—or what she was hiding. And for certain, this girl was hiding something. No one would leave their hometown and a successful career unless there was trouble. If experience were as fine a teacher as it claimed to be, she would bet a man was involved.

Carley climbed up into the truck. "You don't cut him any slack, do you?"

"T-bone gives as good as he gets. He was on his best behavior today because of you."

"Well, he obviously has a soft spot for you." Carley buckled her seatbelt.

"Feeling's mutual. That's why I keep a close watch on him. Pride is always waiting around the corner, looking to pounce on a good man."

Her niece muttered, more to herself. "Isn't that the truth?"

Yup, there's a man involved, all right.

"How long has he been a mechanic?" Carley asked.

"About five years now, only one in town. The townsfolk are pushing him to go to veterinary school so he can take over when Doc Quimby retires." She pulled out after letting traffic pass—one motorcycle, two RVs, four pickups, and sixteen-year-old Rylee Cooper speeding by on her ATV just looking for a place to crash. "Otto and I weren't able to have children. T-bone softened the blow, so to speak. As a young boy—barely ten, he was—he began helping Otto in the garden. Over the years, he spent many a weekend and then summers with us, so he's no stranger to our supper table or sleeping quarters."

"What about his parents?"

She shifted into second gear, wondering how much to reveal. "Like you, he only had a father. Unlike you, his had some issues." She kept her speed at twenty. "Now, to get a feel for the real Andover, you have to pay close attention on my nickel tour."

Carley looked up and down Main Street. "There's more than this?"

"Plenty more, but you have to use more than your eyes to see it. Now, let's pop into the Red Rooster and drop off those peas." Before she could shift into third, they had arrived.

The restaurant was on the ground floor of a creamy-yellow three-story house. The large front porch held hanging plants and chalkboard easels with the daily specials. The only thing red about the place was the rooster on the sign.

"Prior to buying this place a few years ago, Faith was the chef at a four-star restaurant in Augusta for thirty years. Now she provides four-star meals on a budget."

"Want me to run the peas in?" Carley asked.

"No, I want to say hello to Faith." Geneva tilted her head. "You may be surprised how long one hello can last around here."

The minute they entered, heads turned, and shout-outs began.

"Mornin', Miss Geneva!"

"Who you got with you?"

"Nice to see you'll have help in your garden."

"Bring that niece of yours over here!"

Carley whispered, "I've been here less than twenty-four hours. Does everyone know about me?"

"Family coming to visit is news worth spreading in a town this size. And we have a few who are expert at doing the spreading." Geneva turned to her neighbors. "If we have time after we see Faith, we'll come back around."

The kitchen was the same cramped space it'd always been. She still couldn't fathom how a cook, a dishwasher, and two servers could work around each other in a room not much bigger than a horse stall, especially in this heat. "Carley, meet Faith Eversall, the first girlfriend I had in Maine and the maid of honor at my wedding. Faith, this is my niece, Carley Merrill. She has a *peas* offering for you."

Carley held out the bag. "Fresh from the garden."

Faith, a sixty-ish woman with a faded brown bob and fixed smile, wiped her hands on her apron before she accepted the gift. "These will go perfectly with tonight's pork pie and mashed potatoes special. I'd give you both a hug if I didn't smell like onions."

Geneva moved toward the doorway. "I know you're busy now. We'll come for early supper next week when you have time to chat."

"Oh, please do, but not Tuesday. I've got appointments in Rumford that day."

"Oh?" Had she heard something in her friend's tone?

Faith scowled. "Neva, don't you start fussing. They're regularly scheduled follow-ups, nothing more. I didn't get the Red Rooster back up and running to let the Big C stop me."

"If you need any help here, you call me." Geneva hugged Faith despite the onions. "Remember, you've got a bunch of stubborn people praying."

Was that a flicker of doubt she'd seen in her niece's eyes at the mention of prayer? Seemed like medical professionals, even those who were believers, had a harder time praying for miracles. Maybe because they'd seen too much disease and death.

Geneva put her arm through Carley's. "As long as we're here, you might as well take the moose by the antler."

Carley seemed confused. "Excuse me?"

She motioned to the locals seated in the corner. "You're new in town, and they're curious. You also have a fresh set of ears for their stale old stories."

Carley smiled. "I can handle it."

Geneva led her to a full table. "Everyone, this is my niece, Carley Merrill, my brother Waylon's granddaughter—all the way from Pennsylvania."

A chorus of hellos and welcomes sang out.

Geneva started at one end of the table. "Carley, these two civic-minded women are Mary Salatino and Martha O'Leary, on their lunch break from their jobs at the town hall next door. They also live on South Arm, almost across the street from each other. Next is former Andover resident, Cynthia Giroux, who comes by often from neighboring Dixfield to check up on us.

"See the guy on the end? Frank Gregoire. Watch him, he's a charmer. That's his wife Linda—the one clearing dirty dishes and refilling everyone's coffee cups. They live on Cape Cod but have a vacation home a half mile down from my place. Although, most of us agree Linda doesn't know the meaning of the word *vacation*."

Linda smiled at them but didn't stop working.

When Geneva realized who was next at the table, she sent up a silent prayer. "And this is Miss Wilda Weikert, a woman duty bound to stay abreast of all the happenings around town."

Wilda's saccharine voice chanted, "Glory be, if it isn't the so-called niece from away, the one Geneva's been going on about."

Lord, help me. She hid her irritation with a chuckle. "I call Carley my niece because she *is* my niece." She touched

Carley's arm. "And I haven't even begun to go on about this girl."

Wilda's brow arched as she adjusted the collar on her flower-print blouse. "Must be a miracle ... or something ... when a family member no one has ever heard of shows up out of the blue."

Geneva could almost smell the sour odor Wilda's words left in the air.

"Hard to believe, isn't it, Miss Wilda?" Carley almost bubbled. "God is so good, don't you agree?"

Geneva held in a laugh when Wilda's mouth came up empty.

The rest of the group filled the momentary silence and threw a barrage of information and questions Carley's way.

"Are you any relation to the Merrills over in Gilead?" Mary asked.

Carley answered the same way she had T-bone. "I don't think so, but you never know."

"I take it you're not married," Mary said. "My nephew was promoted to head stock clerk over at Deke's Hardware. He's single again too."

Wilda huffed. "Pfft. Mary, everyone knows, besides Deke himself, the store only has one stock clerk."

Carley snuck in, "You must be very proud of his work ethic."

Linda finished straightening the chairs around the tables nearby. "Carley, if you're going to be here a while, I hear the library needs a volunteer a few afternoons a week. Our librarian's sciatica is acting up again."

Wilda, again, "*Our* librarian? Don't you think you should leave town business up to year-round residents before you offer the position to any old body?" She turned to Carley. "No offense."

Carley smiled. "None taken."

44

Frank winked at Carley before he turned to Wilda. "Have you done something different with your hair, Wilda? The exotic flair suits you."

Her pale, lined face blushed as she patted her pin-straight, salt and pepper pageboy, sans bangs on her six-inch-high forehead. Still patting, Wilda said, "Well, my girl was out, and the new one might have used a different conditioner."

"Yes, yes." Frank framed her face with his hands like a photographer would a model. "Maybe you could give Linda your girl's number. She's been looking for a hairstylist up here, haven't you?"

"Hm-hm." Linda gave her husband an I'll-get-you-later grin.

"Could I have her name and number too?" Carley asked.

If her niece were serious, Geneva couldn't tell.

Cynthia changed the subject. "Carley, did Miss Neva happen to mention I'm a direct descendant of Molly Ockett of the Pigwacket Tribe? She was a healer and herbalist back in the 1700s. Probably why I was drawn to the curative properties in herbs and essential oils."

Wilda made an ugly face. "A lot of quackery, if you ask me."

Martha shot back, "No one asked you."

Wilda countered. "I was talking to *Cynthia*."

"Cynthia, funny you should mention your forebearers," Carley said, "because my aunt found me searching our family's ancestry."

Wilda's face pinched. "Yes, a real miracle that was."

Though impressed with the grace and ease at which her niece was handling the townspeople—especially Wilda—Geneva put an end to their interrogation. "Sorry, folks, we've gotta go. The sisters are waiting."

"Thanks for the friendly welcome," Carley said. "Oh, and Miss Wilda, maybe next time we can talk more about those miracles."

Oh, my niece is good, exceptionally good.

Chapter Five

Carley: Present Day

After her grilling at the diner, Carley figured the people in Andover knew almost more about her after twenty minutes than her Philadelphia neighbors did after her ten years there. Another thing, she was wrong about the people in Maine minding their own business.

"So, what kind of cancer does Faith have?" Her conscience nagged, *Oh sure, it's okay for you to ask nosey questions.*

That's different. I'm a medical professional.

"She *had* breast cancer almost seven years back. All her check-ups have been clean since then."

"Mastectomy?"

"Yes, as a precaution."

Carley didn't follow-up, knowing all the statistics floating around her head might not be encouraging. "So, what's the story with Wilda Weikert?"

"The story? None of us are sure if she was born miserable or took it on as a passion later in life."

Carley chuckled. "An ideal candidate for anti-stalking?"

"What?"

"You know, you get to know a person's routine, so you know when and how to avoid them."

Her aunt laughed, "You catch on quickly."

Northeast of the village center, her aunt pointed out a sprawling yellow house with a red shingled roof. "That is the Merrill-Poor House, which is on the US National Register of Historic Places. Probably the reason people keep asking if you have relatives in the area."

"Merrill-Poor?"

"Yes. The original structure was built in the late 1780s by Ezekiel Merrill. Old Zeke was granted the land for his service in the Revolutionary War. His daughter married Henry Poor who started a little firm you may have heard of—Standard & Poor's?"

"S&P?" Carley stared at the house. "I would have guessed Poor was from New York."

Geneva chuckled. "We're not all hicks, you know."

Carley ignored her comment. "Do their descendants still live there?"

"There and all over Oxford County. They rent this place out for weddings and reunions and such. The family I worked for when I moved to Maine were descendants of the Merrill and Poor dynasty. Good people—and smart. Much of what I know about business and finance, I learned through osmosis living with them."

A few miles later, they arrived at a small cottage with a lavender door and shutters to match. Carley marveled at the English ivy crawling up the front of the house.

"We're a little early," Geneva said. "I don't think the sisters will mind."

"Who are these sisters anyway?"

The front door opened before her aunt could answer. Two elderly women greeted them with happy hellos. One was tall and straight, the other bowed, yet they had the same face and up-do.

The tall one called out, "Miss Geneva! How wonderful you came, even with your niece's recent arrival."

After a round of introductions, twins Josette and Lorette Antoine ushered them in.

The foyer was covered with faded wallpaper, the kind that had made a comeback and gone out of style again. The formal living room, which the ladies referred to as the *parlor,* was decorated in deep shades of red and gold. From the thick dust on the ornate mahogany furniture, Carley suspected one whack on an overstuffed chair would result in a few cumulus clouds.

The scent of cedar and jasmine swirled with the aroma of fresh-baked goods. Tolerable, if all three scents hadn't been infiltrated by the hint of mildew.

"Come along!" Josette said. "Sister and I have everything ready in the dining room."

What everything? If Carley had ventured a guess, she would have been wrong.

A large Queen Anne style dining table nearly filled the room. Stacks of leather albums sat at the far end of the table. A similar album lay open nearby, revealing a variety of postage stamps.

"As your aunt may have told you," Josette said, "we're lifelong philatelists. For years now, Miss Geneva has been helping us organize our collection."

Lorette, the bow-backed twin, turned to a page in one of the albums. "Back home in Quebec, sister and I began collecting on our fifth birthday." She pointed to a stamp. "That's when Papa gave us this Princess Elizabeth stamp. Wasn't she adorable?" A yellowed newspaper clipping about the British monarchy was tucked in a plastic sleeve on the opposite page.

Josette added, "Papa loved history. He made sure we knew the story behind each stamp." She reached for a bright red album. "Later, to his utter dismay, we began collecting commemorative stamps of movie stars. John Wayne, James Cagney, Edward G. Robinson." She turned a page. "Oh, see how handsome Tyrone Power was in his uniform? He was a lieutenant in the Marine Corps, you know?"

Lorette tittered. "Sister had a crush on all the bad boys."

Josette swatted her. "You're the one who's bad, sister."

Carley was charmed by their French-Canadian accent, where *everything* became *everyt'ing*, *three* became *t'ree*, and *handsome* Tyrone was *'andsome*.

Lorette sobered. "Since we have no heirs, finding the perfect person to bequeath our legacy to has been a challenge."

Geneva shifted in her seat. "Before Miss Lorette and Miss Josette make this weighty decision, they feel obligated to catalog and organize the entire collection."

Carley noticed sticky notes with the word "Complete" stuck to the top of two album stacks. "Seems like you've made some progress."

"We have indeed," Josette said. "When we finish with these, we'll move on to the contents of our four remaining closets."

Four remaining closets? Carley had no words.

Geneva turned to the sisters. "Ladies, shall we start with our usual tasse de thé?"

Lorette clapped her hands. "Let's! Sister even baked the maple crème cookies you like."

They spent most of the afternoon chatting over refreshments, only managing to get through one album. With the ninety-year-olds' leases on earth nearing an end, finishing this monumental task at this geologic pace seemed doubtful to Carley.

Carley observed the three women for a few more moments. *Finishing* wasn't really the goal here, was it?

Back at the house, Carley helped Geneva in the greenhouse until early evening, planting, picking, and weeding. By the time she got in the shower, the spinach and chard she'd picked weren't the only ripe things.

The hot water pummeled her aching muscles—muscles she had never used, apparently, in her capacity as an NP. Even lifting her arms to wash her hair hurt. *What a wimp. Sheesh. Your aunt is probably out chopping trees and splitting logs now.*

She dressed, unpacked her suitcases, and stretched out on the bed.

Had she only arrived yesterday? The hours since had been chock-full. On the upside, keeping busy hadn't given her much time to worry about her situation—until now.

Six weeks had gone by since her initial call to the Medicare and Medicaid fraud hotline. Being a whistleblower wasn't as glamorous as it sounded. You don't really get a whistle. Instead, you get an intimidating False Claims Act Form to fill out. You get put on hold more times than not, and then you get brusque answers to all your questions. You get no praise for doing the honorable thing, only suspicion and doubt until you even second-guess yourself.

Finally, you get a lawyer ... who gives you a Confidential Federal and State Fraud Form to fill out.

Then you wait.

Carley had been told investigating her claim might take months. Even though the wheels of justice turned slower than Fred Flintstone's foot-mobile, once she had reported Dr. Nichols's offenses, her biggest challenge was looking him in his sea-green eyes. Her heart still skipped a beat but now for a different reason. No, she'd had to get out before Dr. Show-Me-the-Money suspected she was onto him.

"Carley!" Geneva called up the stairs. "Your phone is ringing."

Carley froze. *What? Where did I leave my phone?*

"Do you want me to answer it for you?"

She hotfooted down the steps. "No, I'll get it." She trembled as she snagged her cell off the counter and checked the caller ID. *Unavailable.*

She tapped to answer. "Hello."

"We've been trying to reach you about your car's extended warranty."

She tapped to disconnect. "Telemarketer."

"They are a nuisance, aren't they?" Geneva turned back to the counter. "You must be starving. All we've eaten since breakfast is a few cookies. How about a sliced chicken sandwich with a side of coleslaw?"

"Sounds great. I'll get the drinks."

Why had that call spooked her so? Dr. Nichols wasn't due back from Los Angeles until the middle of the following week. He was probably too busy fending off all the accolades to check his phone messages. Anyway, her new number was unlisted—to everyone except telemarketers.

I did ask for an unlisted number, right?

CHAPTER SIX

CARLEY: TWO YEARS EARLIER

PHILADELPHIA, PENNSYLVANIA

Carley knocked on the door stenciled with Harrison D. Nichols, MD in large gold letters.

She expected to hear "Come in," but the doctor opened the door himself. "A pleasure to meet you, Ms. Jantzen. I'm Dr. Nichols, the physician you'll be assisting most of your time."

"Nice to meet you, sir." *Hmm. Firm handshake ... more handsome than his website photo.*

"I apologize for not being here for your initial interview. A number of unavoidable speaking engagements kept me out of town." He motioned for her to sit, then walked around the desk to his chair. "Accepting a position without meeting the person you'll be working with closely is uncommon, but I'm glad you did."

"I'm pleased for the opportunity." *Nice eyes. Kind, too.*

"I've heard stellar reports from the others. We believe you'll be an excellent fit for our team. As you know, Dr. Reinhart's specialty is pediatrics, while Dr. Stryker and I handle the balance of our family practice patients. Your curriculum vitae states you've had experience with patients of all ages."

"Yes, the hospital where I worked the last few years had a policy against patient age discrimination." *What a stupid comeback. If only those green eyes weren't staring at me.* She cleared her throat. "I'm anxious to get to know our patients." *Our patients? Now you sound presumptuous.*

He crossed his arms and smiled. "I'm glad you think of the patients as *yours* already. After all, they're the reason we're all here."

"Yes, they are." She noticed his left-hand ring finger was bare. *You're pathetic.*

Their brief meeting ended when the front desk buzzed to say the office administrator was there to show her around and go over the policies and procedure manual.

Dr. Nichols escorted her out. "So then, we'll see each other tomorrow morning at seven-thirty."

"I'll be here." *I'll be here. Could I have said anything any lamer? Is lamer even a word?*

"Remember me?" Roxanne Ingram introduced herself again. "I'm so glad they heeded my advice and hired you. What do you think of our Dr. Nichols? Kinda cute, huh? Single, too, in case you're wondering."

"Uh, well ..." *Sheesh. Way to be transparent, Jantzen.*

"I'm joking—not." Roxanne chuckled. "Not only does this practice need another NP, but we also need one savvy with medical software. Your CV mentioned you have a lot of experience with medical applications."

"I do, but I hear you're switching systems."

"Yes, the new software is supposed to be more comprehensive."

"For better or worse, I've been blessed with a quick learning curve in computers."

"Perfect. You may be drafted to do some tutoring—maybe even a few one-on-one sessions with Dr. Nichols." She winked. "Any problem with that?"

"Not at all ... I mean, I would ..." Her face warmed.

Roxanne laughed again. "So, you *do* think he's attractive."

Carley faked a frown, "It's gonna be like this, is it, Roxanne?"

"Worse. And call me Roxy, please. All my friends do."

She smiled. *I think I'm gonna like working here.*

In Carley's first six months at Key State Family Medical, her affinity for the technical was an asset. She found the new medical management software intuitive and became the go-to tutor, training the staff in aspects of coding, billing, referrals, and file management. Roxy, having worked with this system at a previous position, was the only other one who caught on quickly.

Drs. Reinhart and Stryker sat in on a few of the initial training sessions. She suspected they'd handed off the task to an underling soon after. Wouldn't be the last time physicians delegated their administrative duties to staff.

Dr. Nichols was the only partner in compliance. If he minded that, he never let on to her. He called on her repeatedly when he believed he'd "passed the technical point of no return." His words, not hers.

So, when he approached her one day, Carley assumed he needed to be rescued again.

"Carley, may I speak with you in private for a moment?"

"Sure." She hated that her stomach still did flipflops whenever he asked to see her alone. She followed him into his office, wiping her sweaty palms on her scrubs.

He closed the door. "Our patient, Mr. Kumar, will be in early tomorrow. He's a bit reticent." He inhaled deeply and then emptied his lungs in a rush. "That's not true. He can be downright intractable."

She chuckled. "You want me to know because ...?"

"So far he's ignored my instructions and refused to go for further tests. I suspect the only reason he comes in at all is to pacify his daughter. I've seen how good you are with the patients and, well, I was hoping you might give me some suggestions on how to reach him."

"Maybe if you told me a little about him."

He handed her a file, labeled, *Kumar, Abel.* "Here's his medical history."

"That's a start." She took the folder. "I was thinking more along the lines of personal information."

"Um, well, I'm not sure." He raked a hand through his hair. "He's from India, I believe ... or maybe Nepal? I don't know how long he's been in the US, but he has a strong accent. Oh, and he must be married because his daughter brings him in."

She'd figured out early on Dr. Nichols wasn't used to getting personal with his patients. In her experience, most doctors weren't. Nature of their position or of their makeup? She wasn't sure. Maybe both.

"If his daughter is aware of her father being 'downright intractable,' maybe I should call her to get some insight?" She could almost hear Roxy. *Is this something you would offer to do for any other doctor?*

"Would you?' His hand touched hers as he reached for the file. "I'd appreciate that."

She let go of the file and backed away before he could feel her pulse quicken. "I'll see what I can do." *What is wrong with me?*

That night, after a quick supper, Carley called Mr. Kumar's daughter, Asha. She learned Mr. Kumar was a widower of Indian descent who had recently moved to the US to live with his daughter.

Asha explained, "After I graduated from Columbia, I was offered a position as an editor with a New York publisher, working from their offices in Philadelphia. When my mother died, my father came to live with me."

"That must have been tough on both of you."

"In some ways, tougher on my father." Asha sighed. "He'd always lived and worked in the agrarian society of Mizoram, so city life has been a difficult transition for him."

Following the call, Carley researched Mizoram, India, a northeastern state, which bordered Bangladesh and Myanmar. Known for its high literacy rate, Mizoram is also one of the three states in India with a Christian majority.

At least she had a place to start.

She printed out an aerial shot of Mizoram, depicting its rolling hills, valleys, rivers, and lakes. The next morning, she tacked the photo up on the wall directly across from the table in the exam room.

After Carley led Mr. Kumar into the exam room, she invited him to sit so she could take his vitals.

His eyes landed on the photo behind her. He squinted, then smiled. "That place, in the picture, I know it."

Carley put the blood pressure cuff on him. "You know Mizoram?"

"Yes, yes, that is ... *was* my home."

"Is that so? I read people grow most of their own food there."

"That is correct." Mr. Kumar's chest seemed to swell. "We share our harvests with one another too."

"Like in the book of Acts?"

His face brightened. "You know the Bible?"

"I do." She put the thermometer in his mouth. "After having lived in such a lush land, moving to Philadelphia must have been quite a challenge."

He nodded.

Carley surmised by the moisture in his eyes that if he had tried to speak at that moment, the words would have lumped up in his throat. She finished with the preliminary portion of the exam. "Dr. Nichols will be in soon. Please be kind to him, Mr. Kumar. He's never known a land like Mizoram."

By the time the doctor joined them, Mr. Kumar's tongue had been loosed.

And the doctor took time to listen. "Thank you for telling me about your previous bout with malaria. I'm referring you to a neurologist to make sure there are no underlying symptoms." Dr Nichols made eye contact with his patient. "Do you promise to keep the appointment?"

"Of course," Mr. Kumar answered as if he hadn't ignored the doctor's advice before.

Carley smiled at the personal growth in both men.

Later that afternoon, Carley received a call from Mr. Kumar's daughter Asha. "I don't know what you did to turn my father's attitude around, but I owe you a debt of gratitude. If you ever need editorial services, call me."

During the ensuing months, Dr. Nichols sought her opinion on other patients too. The mother of six who thought she was losing her mind. The retired executive suffering from depression. The teenage girl with severe acne who was threatening to hurt herself.

At the end of one long day, the two of them conferred in his office.

"Thanks again, Carley. Together, we made a difference."

Together? I wish. She caught herself before her emotions bounced too far afield. "My pleasure."

He folded his hands. "I'm afraid my people skills could still use some sharpening."

Without agreeing outright, she asked, "Why do you think that is?"

He shrugged. "Could be because I was the only child of introverts, born when they were in their early forties. They approached their parental duties soberly, believing schoolwork was more important than social events or friendships."

"I'm so sorry."

"Nothing to be sorry about. I didn't have a bad life, just not as active as other children. Of course, having a tendency toward introversion didn't help." He removed his reading glasses. "How about you?"

"My mom died within days of my being born, so Dad raised me alone. I had a happy childhood. We always had a houseful, whether friends, neighbors, or people from church."

He chuckled. "I was brought up in church too, but *without* the fellowship. That's not to say my parents weren't happy. They preferred each other's company, that's all."

"And that was enough for them but not for you?"

He smiled wanly. "Your intuition is showing." He leaned back with his hands folded behind his head. "Growing up, the world seemed big and colorful to me, while home was small and sepia-toned."

"Did you always want to be a doctor?" She couldn't believe their personal conversation had gone on for this long.

"Not early on, but I was one of those weird kids who looked forward to their yearly school physical. My pediatrician used to let me listen to my own heart and take my temp and blood pressure. I always had a thousand questions for him. He was the one who first suggested I consider medicine."

"What did your parents think?"

"They couldn't see past the prohibitive costs. My family GP was the one who helped me find scholarships and grants." He leaned forward. "Enough about me. You're an excellent NP. Ever thought about going for your MD?"

Of course, she'd thought about it, but lacked the desire. "I have, but I like my current job of aiding and abetting physicians."

His brow furrowed. "*Aiding and abetting*? That's a curious choice of words."

She chuckled. "A phrase my dad loved to use."

"I see." After a semi-awkward break in their conversation, he stood. "Well, until tomorrow then."

And just like that "their moment" was over.

CHAPTER SEVEN

GENEVA: PRESENT DAY

My niece sure is skittish! When her cell phone rang, she stared at the nuisance as if it would explode. Suspecting Vern might know more about Carley than he'd let on, Geneva planned to corner him soon.

Carley took a bite of coleslaw. "Yum. This is the best I've ever had."

"Fresh from the garden makes all the difference. You'll find gardening does wonders for the appetite too."

Carley chuckled. "'A worker's appetite works for him, for his hunger urges him on.'"

"Exactly! Proverbs 16:26." Somehow, she sensed she wasn't to ask her niece any personal questions tonight. "So, about our little tour today, what did you think? I mean, outside of Wilda Weikert?"

"Small towns are a lot different than cities." Carley seemed to falter. "I mean, not that I always lived in a city. Uh, I didn't. I had neighbors in Philly, but I didn't know them as well as you know yours."

"We do get in each other's business. I believe when we know others well, we know better how to serve them." *Don't push, Neva.*

"I guess." Carley downed a half glass of iced tea. "Speaking of getting in people's business, do you think T-bone will actually become a veterinarian one day?"

"Why?"

"Well, he's a small-town mechanic. How will he find the time to study or the money to pay for veterinary school?"

"I can't say. T-bone's only in charge of submitting his gifts and talents to God. The Lord takes over from there."

"Thanks, Miss Neva. I needed that reminder."

"We all do from time to time, dear."

Carley put her plate in the sink. "All I know is, between my arrival and your fresh air, I'm about to drop. I hope you don't mind if I head up to bed."

"Not at all. I won't be long myself."

Once the few dishes were washed and put away, Geneva sat on the small screened-in back porch, waiting for the sun to set. Sounds of her sanctuary serenaded her—owls screeching, red squirrels whirring, their gray counterparts squealing, and breezes rustling the leaves, all to the squeak-squeak of her old wicker rocker.

Now that her niece was here, she wondered if her invitation had been premature. Then again, she'd been questioning her every decision in the years since Otto had passed. After decades of mulling things over together, making decisions alone didn't come easily.

Yes, she could depend on Vern—but only so much. No need to be more of a burden than she was already.

"Lord, please, I need your leading." After her simple prayer, God quickened to her spirit. *I'm with you always. You're not alone.*

Filled with his peace, Geneva headed back inside.

Humming her favorite hymn—"It Is Well with My Soul"—she readied the coffee machine and set the table for breakfast. Since she'd used up the last of the preserves that morning, she made a beeline to her stockpile in the basement. She chose a jar of each: raspberry, strawberry, and blackberry.

Admit it, you're enjoying the girl's company.

She smiled.

On her way back upstairs, Geneva was startled when the overhead light blew. A jar slipped out of her hand and crashed to the floor. "Oh, terrific. Just what I need." Hurrying to secure the other jars, she lost her balance and tumbled down the half flight of stairs. She landed hard on her side in a mess of glass and preserves.

The fall knocked the wind out of her. Afraid she would pass out, she lay still to catch her breath. Her arm hurt like never before. When she tried to raise herself up, shards of glass pierced her palm. She gasped in pain.

Though her voice was weak, she called out, "Car-ley! Car-ley!" Nothing. She called again. Still nothing.

After resting a bit to replenish her strength, she fumbled around in the dark. Her fingers landed on the tines of a rake leaning against the railing. She toppled the rake to get a hold of the handle. Again and again, with as much power as she could muster, she beat on the steel column adjacent to the steps.

Spent, she laid back on the concrete floor and prayed. Moments slipped by before she heard a soft voice.

"Miss Neva? Are you awake? Did you hear that?"

She shouted as loud as she could. "Carley! Down ... here. My arm ... Call 911."

The basement door flew open wide, the hall light illuminating Carley.

"Miss Neva, no!" She flipped the wall switch up and down. "Where's the light?"

"Bulb blew." She took a deep breath. "Flashlight ... on shelf ... mud room."

A minute later, Carley came down the steps with the flashlight. "Rescue's on the way."

"Switch ... near workbench."

Carley found the light switch, then stooped down beside her.

"Watch out ... the glass."

"I will. Now please stay still until the EMTs arrive."

"So sorry, dear. I can't believe I could be so—"

"Shh. I'm only glad I was here. Now, I need to get a wet cloth, but I'll be back in a minute."

Geneva prayed, *Lord, is this truly how you want my niece and me to begin our relationship?*

CHAPTER EIGHT

CARLEY: PRESENT DAY

Carley dabbed Geneva's forehead and the cuts on her hands with a cool, wet cloth. She knew better than to move her. Her aunt was likely in shock.

Where is that ambulance?

A man's voice came from upstairs. "Miss Neva. Carley. T-bone and Leo here!"

T-bone? From the gas station? Could there be more than one in town? She called out, "We're down here!"

His footsteps to the basement sounded deliberate but calm. Another man followed behind him. Both were dressed in uniforms.

T-bone knelt at her side. "Miss Neva, why don't you tell us what happened?"

Her aunt rolled her eyes. "I'm in trouble if you two geniuses can't figure it out for yourselves."

"Looks like you've aced your cognitive exam." T-bone did a terrible job hiding a grin.

"My aunt believes her arm is broken. She also fell on broken glass. Some of what you see here is homemade preserves. I didn't move her."

"Good." His voice was slow and steady. "Leo, I need you to remove the debris from around Miss Neva."

"Right." Leo grabbed a broom and pushed the shards and preserves away.

After checking her heart and pulse, T-bone immobilized her head and neck before securing her injured arm.

Her aunt yelped and winced and called out to God.

"Sorry," he said. "Med-Care's on the way."

Carley stared at him. "Med-Care?"

"Med-Care's the primary emergency team who'll transport your aunt to Rumford Hospital." He turned to his patient. "In the meantime, we're going to get you out of here. We'll be as gentle as possible."

Once Leo slid the backboard over, both men lifted her aunt onto the board and strapped her in.

Helplessness and guilt taunted Carley. *If only I hadn't gone up to bed so early.*

Leo looked over his shoulder. "Might be easier to go through the bulkhead, eh?"

"I agree." T-bone turned to her. "Carley, can you get the bulkhead doors for us?"

"Bulkhead?" Clueless, she searched the basement. "Sorry, what's a bulkhead?"

Leo snorted. "City mouse, eh?"

T-bone pointed. "Behind that door. Push up and out on both metal doors."

She did as he instructed.

They carried her aunt out of the basement. Med-Care arrived minutes later and loaded her into their vehicle.

Once they were off, T-bone said, "I've got to get back to the stationhouse. The hospital is located at 420 Franklin Street in Rumford, about a half hour away."

"Thanks. I'll find my way."

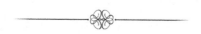

Carley hadn't been at the ER five minutes when Vern burst in. Running a hand through his disheveled hair, he sputtered, "What happened? Where is she? What did they say?"

To calm him, Carley flipped from concerned niece to competent nurse. "She's been here less than forty-five minutes. The ER team needs more time for a thorough evaluation. All I can say is she was conscious and complaining—two good signs."

He rubbed the back of his neck. "What happened? Dubber said she fell down the cellar stairs."

"Yes, halfway down. She may have broken her arm and sustained some cuts. She'll have some bruises."

He paced back and forth. "How in heaven's name did that happen? Neva's always so careful."

Carley repeated everything her aunt had said about the accident. "How did Dubber find out anyway?"

"He was over helping Leo wash the firetruck when the call came in. He knew I'd want to know." He sat, his knees bouncing up and down.

She kept him talking. "I was surprised *and* impressed when T-bone showed up. I thought his specialty was animals and automobiles."

"When you live in a town the size of Andover, most people have to hold down two or three part-time positions to make ends meet. He and Leo are certified EMTs *and* volunteer firefighters."

For a reason she couldn't fully explain, she wasn't surprised there was a lot more to T-bone than she'd originally learned.

After another twenty minutes of small talk, the doctor came out. "Mrs. Kellerman's right arm has a single oblique fracture. A few days in a splint, then five to six weeks in a cast, and she'll be as good as new. She also sustained multiple cuts on her hands, side, and back, some requiring stitches."

Vern sighed long and loud. "When can we see her?"

"I prescribed something for the pain and a mild sedative," he said. "The nurse said she fell asleep soon after."

Carley asked, "Will she be released tomorrow?"

"The day after, most likely," the doctor said. "That fall was quite a jolt to her system. No sign of a concussion, but we want to keep her for observation. Of course, once she's home, she'll need full-time assistance."

"I'll be there," Carley said.

Vern nodded. "So will I."

Carley didn't get back to the house until eleven. Unlike Philly, the streets and yard were not lit. She quickly put on some outside lights. Being there alone felt weird, like she was trespassing.

A loud knock scared her witless. She peeked through a side window, then opened the door to T-bone standing on the porch.

"Sorry. I saw the lights when I drove by."

She squinted. "'Drove by?' I thought you lived behind the gas station not far from the fire house?"

He dropped his head. "You found me out. I want to know how Miss Neva's doing."

"She's doing okay." She joined him outside and told him what the ER doctor had said. "You know, I saw plenty of EMTs in action during my stints working in the ER. You and your partner did an admirable job keeping your patient calm."

He smiled. "Helps that your aunt doesn't rattle that easily."

"Then, you helped keep *me* calm." She smiled back at his friendly face. "The doctor said she'll probably be discharged day after tomorrow."

"Looks like your visit couldn't have been timed any better."

She nodded. "Sure seems that way."

"I better let you get some sleep."

She hesitated a second. "Mind if I ask you something before you go?"

"Well, probably best to ask me now rather than wait until after I'm gone."

She grinned, then crossed her arms. "So ... you own a gas station, you work part-time for a vet, *and* you're an EMT?"

He shrugged. "That's what folks do around Andover. But before you think I'm rolling in dough, the EMT position is strictly volunteer."

"I see." She was even more impressed.

T-bone reached into his pocket and gave her a card. "Call if you need anything, day or night."

"Thanks."

He got in his truck and took off.

Carley was beginning to see the advantage of knowing her aunt's neighbors, especially ones as caring and capable as T-bone Stakes.

Wide awake from the night's excitement, Carley did a quick assessment of her aunt's bedroom. The height of the bed was low enough for her new patient to maneuver. The room was large enough to accommodate a chair for Carley. The walk-in closet had clothes hanging neatly on either side of a clear path. Nothing to trip over.

Next, she took inventory of the contents of the medicine cabinet: gauze, tape, salve, a thermometer, and NSAID tablets.

The sticky mess in the basement would have to wait until she had better light. She didn't need to fall down the stairs herself trying to change the lightbulb.

She turned in around twelve thirty, but her mind kept running for another hour.

And you thought Maine would bring you respite.

The next morning, Carley had just finished moving all her things from the upstairs bedroom into the room across from her aunt's when Vern phoned.

"Seems Neva had a restless night," he said. "The nurse suggested I wait until late morning to visit. If you want to tag along, I can pick you up around ten." He sounded a bit calmer than he had the night before.

"Thanks, I'll be ready." She'd have to put off tackling the basement again. Carley shuddered at the thought of what insects and rodents those sweet preserves would attract. Then she shuddered again.

After packing a few toiletries and a change of clothes for her aunt, she waited on the porch for Vern.

Chapter Nine

Geneva: Present Day

Less than two days into her niece's arrival and here she sat—an invalid, after all. One useless hand at the end of a broken arm, the other covered with stitches and a bulky bandage. What could she do without hands? Who'd tend her garden and cook? Who'd visit the sisters? How could she entertain her niece while they were stuck in the house?

Geneva's jaw clenched as she muttered, "Lord, I should be grateful I didn't do more harm to myself than I did—but this is not going according to plan."

Whose plan?

She cringed. Having lived most of her years under the Lord's sovereignty, she should know better. Slumping, she expelled her frustration. No matter how much she fumed, she had no choice but to make the best of the situation. "Better get used to being on the receiving end of help for a while, ol' girl."

A voice at the open door. "Who're you calling 'ol' girl'? Not Neva Kellerman, I hope." Vern walked over and brushed her temple with a kiss.

He must really be worried because he's never done that before.

Carley wasn't far behind. "How was your night?"

"Let's say being hogtied and in pain, followed by a lousy night's sleep, can make anyone feel old."

Her niece put a small tote at the foot of the bed. "Maybe a change of clothes and your personal toiletries will help a little."

Geneva noted how Carley straightened her covers and plumped her pillows with the ease born of experience. "Thank you, dear." Her niece may have been a novice in the garden, but she slipped effortlessly into her role as a nurse—ironically, the role she had expected to play from the start.

"I brought you a little gift too." Vern reached in his jacket pocket and pulled out a box of Raisinets. "Ta-da!"

"You remembered my favorites. Thanks. Now, Carley, help me get dressed and out of here."

"Not so fast," her niece answered. "The doctor wants to keep you another night to make sure nothing new pops up—besides the normal swelling."

She groaned. "Can't you watch for that at home?"

"You know the doctor wouldn't keep you any longer than he thought necessary." Vern tore the flap on the box of Raisinets. "Open up." He popped one in her mouth.

Carley added, "Besides, I need to do a few things around the house before you come home."

Geneva remembered the basement. "I am so sorry for the mess I left you."

"No need to apologize," Carley shook her head. "I'm thankful you weren't alone when it happened."

Soon after, a member of the kitchen staff brought a meal tray in. She tried her best to sit up straight and be less whiney. "Mmm. Chicken pot pie. Smells delicious."

Carley unfolded a napkin for her, laid it across her chest, and tucked it under her chin. Her niece was steady as she fed her, the napkin spotless when they were through.

Though she herself had expended no real effort, finishing the meal had exhausted her.

Vern moved the tray aside. "Anything else you need us to attend to in the next few days or so?"

She hesitated. "I'll need help with the garden. Never did plant those beets and pick all the asparagus. After weeks of work, nothing worse than having your crops spoil on the vine."

He chuckled. "Now you sound like Otto." He straightened her blanket. "Don't worry, we'll figure things out."

Being stuck in bed and unable to move for another night gave Geneva plenty of time to pace mentally. How would she and her niece get along once Carley had to feed her, dress her, wash her, and help her with her most personal needs? No bargain for either of them.

And what about Vern? They'd been good friends since the day she'd arrived in Andover forty-seven years ago this September. He and Otto had been best buddies. As the years passed, they'd become more like brothers. She'd even begun to think of him in that way too.

But something had changed between them since Otto passed. Although not obvious, that "something" was unsettling. Awkward pauses and silences showed up in places they'd never been before. Did being around her remind him of how much he missed his old friend? She didn't want to lose him, but could their relationship ever be the same without Otto?

Mercy, not something you can solve today.

CHAPTER TEN

HARRISON: PRESENT DAY

LOS ANGELES, CALIFORNIA

Dr. Harrison Nichol's celebrity status was an enigma to him—and annoying. The concepts he'd presented at this latest conference weren't any more innovative than what his peers were touting. A quick online search on "integrating global health in family practice" could tell them most everything they needed to know. Sad that even medical professionals seemed to crave their symposiums, celebrities, and awards.

To escape the room full of sycophantic devotees, Harrison snuck out the side exit and returned to his fifth-floor hotel room via the emergency stairway. His head pounding, he flopped across the bed and closed his eyes.

I could use some fresh air, but I'm not sure Los Angeles has any.

Bryce Reinhart and Peter Stryker, his partners at Key State Medical, had pushed him to accept these out-of-town speaking invitations by citing his debate skills at their alma mater, the University of North Carolina, Chapel Hill.

"You ooze integrity," Bryce had claimed. "That gives you an edge."

Peter had confronted him. "What are you whining about? Audiences love you."

Their looks, charm, and connections had earned these two the unofficial most-likely-to-succeed awards at med school. He'd envied them back then and was honored when they recruited him to join their practice.

Now, he could no longer fake his admiration for this medical merry-go-round ride. The sooner he was free from his partners the better. Until then, he preferred not to leave them alone for too long. Never knew what they'd do or what they'd find.

In a breath, his plan could go south.

Harrison rolled over and checked his messages, replaying the one from his nurse practitioner, Carley Jantzen. Her voice sounded strained and stilted. With loyalty at her core, he knew the only way she'd take unplanned leave was if her father's health was in jeopardy.

Carley's wizardry with medical software had been a boon, but what he valued most about her was her proficiency and empathy with patients. She'd taken on more than her share, which gave him time to do what he needed to do. For selfish reasons, he hoped her father would recover soon so she could get back to work.

Truth is, he liked Carley—a lot. There'd been a few moments between them when he'd sensed she might feel the same way about him. Sadly, once she found out what he had done, their relationship would die a quick and painful death.

Chapter Eleven

Carley: Present Day

Vern led Carley to the Liar's Table—one of two communal tables in the rear of Sawmill Market. At three in the afternoon, the lunch crowd had gone back to work, and the supper regulars hadn't arrived yet.

"Mmm. Smells good in here," she said. "I'm starving."

He pointed to a whiteboard. "Daily specials are listed there."

They gave their order at the counter, then retrieved their cold drinks from the glass-front cooler. Carley grabbed some napkins and plastic flatware.

Vern twisted the cover off his bottled water. "A lot has happened since your arrival. What's it been now? Three days, four?"

She chuckled. "Try two."

He shot her a look. "Wow. Rethinking your decision, are you?"

Carley mulled over his question for about three seconds. "No, now that you mention it." She grinned at the realization.

"I'm glad. I can tell Neva likes having you around. And now that you're needed in your capacity as a nurse, I'm even more grateful you're here."

"I have a feeling getting my aunt to rest will be a challenge. She'll worry about all the chores to be done and the people who need to be seen."

"That she will, but you'll have help. I'll come by, and so will others. She'll have no choice but to be patient."

"Has she always been, well, so strong and capable?"

"Not always. When Neva started working for the Emerson family, she was only fifteen. Tall and skinny, with a face as pale as her hair was dark. She tried not to let on she was afraid, but those big blue eyes couldn't lie."

"She made moving here from Kentucky sound like no big deal."

"That's Neva." He repositioned himself in the chair. "Back in the 1970s, families in that part of coal country didn't have much choice if they wanted to survive. Things aren't much better there today, mind you. Nevertheless, leaving your family and everything you've ever known takes courage."

Carley was twenty-eight. Was *her* fear greater than her courage? "How did you and Otto meet her?"

"As teens, Otto and I did odd jobs wherever we could find them. When we heard there was a new girl in Bethel, we made sure to offer our services to the Emerson family whether they wanted them or not." He winked. "Even then Otto was the brawn, and I was the mouthpiece, saying things like, 'Want us to touch up the paint on your shutters before more rot sets in?' Or, 'In just a few hours, we can stop those weeds from choking your flowers to death.' And, 'Want us to remove that snow off your roof before it caves in?'"

"And you've been friends ever since?"

"That we have, though Faith only chummed around with us when she didn't have some recipe to make or some cooking contest to enter." He sipped his drink again. "I was best man at Otto and Neva's wedding."

She waited until the waitress dropped off their food. "How about you? Ever marry?"

"Nope. Still an eligible bachelor." He bit into his sub.

She dribbled bleu cheese dressing on her salad. "Eligible, huh?" She grinned. "Then there's still a chance?"

He laughed. "Confidentially, I like to think there is."

His response surprised her. How many men would be willing to give up the life of a bachelor once they'd passed sixty?

Vern rested his elbow on the table. "Turnabout's fair play. How has an intelligent, attractive girl like you remained single all these years?"

"All these years?" Carley pretend-pouted. "How old do you think I am anyway?"

"Old enough to be noticed by a number of young men, I'm sure. Seems to me people are waiting longer these days, that's all. My advice? Don't wait too long."

"Ha! Look who's talking."

He raised his arms in surrender. "Point taken."

On their way out, Vern asked, "Mind taking a little detour with me? I need to take care of something."

"Not at all."

About a mile out of town on South Main, Vern turned right at the sign for the town transfer station. He'd passed the entrance when he came to a quick stop. "Whoops. Almost missed them."

"Missed who?"

"Dubber and Warren. This is one of their hot spots."

They exited the car. Carley followed him to where two men were grubbing their way through a dusty pile of junk.

Dubber waved them over. "Hey, Vern! Carley! How's Miss G doin'?"

"Other than a broken arm and some cuts and bruises, she's fine," Vern said. "Coming home tomorrow."

He nodded. "So glad to hear."

A tall, skinny man with wiry, copper-red curls joined them. A black trash bag was slung over his shoulder. He tipped his ballcap to Carley. "Howdy. You must be Miss G's niece. Warren Churner, here. Dubber's younger brother."

The two brothers couldn't have looked more different from each other. "Nice to meet you, Warren ... uh ... Churner, did you say? I must have misunderstood. I thought Dubber's last name was Polaski?"

"You'd be right 'bout that. We was adopted by different folks," Warren said. "I grew up in the mid-west part of the state, my brother Down East. That's why he talks funny."

After a few mock jabs at one another, accompanied by good-natured guffaws, Warren went back to picking through the construction debris site and grumbling, "We been through this stuff before."

"Calm your livah, boy. Word is contractors dumped yesterday." As if on cue, he dug out a quarter sheet of plywood and a nearly half-full pack of asphalt roof shingles. "See? Wha'd I tell ya?"

Warren raked his hand through his thick, coarse curls until his fingers got stuck. He cursed, apologized, and then struggled to get his hand loose. Looking like he would explode, he spat out, "What are we s'pose to do with that?"

Dubber ducked to avoid Warren's spray. "Sorry, Vern, Carley. Excuse me while I edumacate my younger brother on our business model again."

Captured by the odd drama, Carley sidled up to eavesdrop.

Holding up the plywood and shingles, Dubber said, "Warren, first we add our finds to our stockpile. What do stockpiles do? They builds a business."

"I know." Warren rubbed his jaw all the way around to the back of his neck. "Truth is I'm cranky about us missin' that ad in *Uncle Henry's*. If we'd been quicker, we coulda got that rowboat. Only had one hole in the bottom. Coulda patched it easy enough, then traded it for the used cement mixer."

Dubber scratched his week-old beard. "Why do we need a cement mixer?"

"*We* don't." Warren smirked. "But Miss G'll need one if she wants us to fix the big crack in the floor of that barn of hers. Ain't that right, Vern?"

Vern shrugged. "Could be."

Dubber's eyebrows almost reached his hairline. "You thinkin' the mixer'll be a down payment on an ol' John Deere?"

"You betcha!" Warren's grin spread pride all over his face.

Dubber turned to Vern. "We don't mean no disrespect to Miss G, but it's been four and a half years since Mr. Otto passed. We waited a full twelve months before startin' on Miss G to let one of those tractors go in trade."

Vern explained to Carley. "Otto collected John Deeres like some people collect coins. Their barn is full of them."

"An' tractors ain't like coins," Dubber protested. "They need to be used to fulfill their callin'."

Warren added, "For years, we've been tellin' Miss G that—only 'cuz it's true."

Dubber slapped his brother on the back. "You know, a cement mixer might tip the scales in our favor. All we need to do is find us something as good as that ol' rowboat to trade for it."

Vern leaned in and whispered to her. "Everyone around these parts barters and dickers, but these two have turned haggling into an art form. They'd have their own TV show if those Down Easters hadn't beat them to the punch."

Carley was struck mute. How could they keep track of their so-called business transactions?

Vern tapped his upper lip with a finger. "As Neva's legal advisor, I might be able to help you boys out. My client will need some work done around the house now that she's laid up. Maybe you could trade labor for the down payment on a tractor?"

The brothers eyed one another.

"We might could do that," Dubber said. "You know how we are once we put our minds to somethin'."

"I sure do." He stuck out his hand. "Labor for down payment? Do we have a deal?"

All three men shook to seal the deal.

"I may already have a job for you," Vern said. "Kind of a sticky situation."

Carley studied the grubby twosome. What did this lawyer have in mind?

Dubber raised his chin. "Might you be talkin' about Miss G's cellar?"

Vern's brows shot up. "You catch on quick."

"Quicker than ya know." Dubber chuckled. "T-bone let us in the house this morning so's we could take care o' that mess of glass and jam. Couldn't have no mice and ants getting all in it, now could we?"

Vern shook his head. "I should've known you two would be way ahead of me."

"We put a 100 watter in so's we could see better." Warren threw a full trash bag into the back of their stake body truck. "Gave that floor a thorough bleachin' too."

"Me and Warren even rigged up a pulley clothesline and basket so Miss G doesn't have to carry all those jars upstairs in her hands anymore."

Vern pulled out a pencil and small notebook. "So how much should I apply to your account?"

Dubber waved him off. "You put that away. Helpin' out a neighbor in *need* is somethin' altogether different."

Warren explained, "Yup, we don't charge for emergency needs—only everyday ones."

Under the sting of conviction for her prejudgment of these men, Carley stared at them.

Dubber tilted his head. "Is there somethin' wrong, Carley?"

"Not at all." She grinned. "I just never thought fairy godfathers were real."

Chapter Twelve

Geneva: Present Day

Another fitful night of sleep. Geneva grumbled as she kicked off the hospital bed covers.

Her goal was to be dressed and packed when Vern and Carley arrived. Without the use of her hands, her efforts at dressing herself proved futile. If the sweet-natured nursing assistant hadn't been so competent and insistent, she might have gone home wrapped in a sheet.

She sat in the bedside chair, allowing questions to play havoc with her usual positive outlook. *How many days before the cuts on my 'good' hand heal? When will I be able to drive? How will I feed myself? Take a shower? Use the bathroom? Agh! Will my niece put up with me once we're home? Or will she hightail it back to civilization the first chance she gets?*

"Morning, sunshine!" Vern walked in, pushing a wheelchair.

Carley was behind him, humming.

Glad their cheery faces can't read my mind.

"Since the doctor has officially discharged you, I'll gather your things." Carley unzipped a tote. "We'll be out of here *tout de suite*."

Geneva scolded her cranky self for doubting. After all, when Carley accepted Vern's invitation, she'd initially thought she would be caring for an invalid. Prophetic or what? Yes, her niece would stay. If not out of duty, then out of fear—a fear Geneva was determined to uncover.

Her personal support team wheeled her out and helped her into Vern's car.

After a few attempts at finding comfort in the backseat under the rigged seatbelt, she prayed silently. *Lord, you know I stink at being a patient. Help me to have a better attitude. For all our sakes.*

When Vern pulled out into traffic, Geneva said, "I know you two probably want to take me to a carnival or something, but if you don't mind, I think I'd rather go straight home."

His laugh was deep and warm. "Yes, I figured as much. Carley can get you settled while I pick up your prescriptions."

"No need to bother about that," she said. "One broken arm and a few stitches doesn't mean I have to turn to a life of drugs."

Her niece chuckled. "The prescriptions aren't only for the pain. One reduces inflammation, the other wards off infection. As your medical professional, I recommend we stock them."

Bossy little thing, isn't she? She tried to disguise her smile with a yawn. "I'll defer to you, dear." *This time.*

Vern eyed her through the rearview mirror. "By the way, Dubber and Warren cleaned up the mess in the basement. They promised to help out with the chores too."

Geneva nodded. "Hard workers, those two."

"I agree." He took the ramp to Route 120. "So how long before you let them have one of Otto's tractors? Not like you can use them all."

"Soon." She repositioned herself. "But don't tell them. I'll lose all my bargaining power."

He shook his head. "You're a pip, you know that?"

86

"Ha! The last time you called me a pip I looked up the definition. *Pip*, or the more formal *pipperoo*, means 'something or someone wonderful.' Now, just so you both know, I'm mentally crossing my arms to punctuate my point."

Vern's and Carley's laughter tickled her. She was glad they got along.

As they pulled into her yard, she called out, "Home at last!" *My own bed, my own books, my own peace and quiet.* Once they entered the house, "I feel better already."

Vern reached into the canvas bag he was carrying. "Thought you could use these." He pulled out an array of faded tee shirts.

She was confused. "Um ... thanks?"

"You don't want to cut up your clothes, do you? Because that's the only way you'll be able to wear something with that getup."

"Smart idea." Carley held up one of the tees for her aunt to see. Below the image of a man with a fishing rod, the text read, *Can't work today. My arm's in a cast.*

Geneva chuckled. "I like it."

"So, you ladies need me to fix lunch or anything?"

"No, thanks," Carley said. "I've got that covered."

"I guess I'll head out to the pharmacy. I shouldn't be long."

"Miss Neva isn't due to take anything until this evening, so there's no rush on the prescriptions."

"Oh." His eyes fastened on the kitchen. "If you like, how about I go to the market for you?"

"Unless my niece went hog wild while I was away, my cabinets and freezer are full."

"I guess I'll see you later. Try to be a good patient, Neva." He glanced over at Carley. "You've got my phone number, right?"

Once he was out of earshot, Geneva mumbled, "Worry much, Vern?"

"Your fall scared him." Her niece examined the seam on one of the shirts.

"My fall scared *me*!"

Carley chuckled. "I for one am glad he'll be around more." She pointed two fingers at her own eyes, then aimed them at Geneva. "Because I need a second set of eyes watching you."

Geneva was too exhausted to finish the light lunch Carley fed her. "I hate to do this to you, dear, but could you help me in the bathroom and get me settled in bed? I feel like I could sleep for a week."

"Normal after all you've been through. The stress alone can wipe you out." Carley escorted her to the master bath.

Before she could concern herself with modesty, her niece said, "Mind my asking how old you were when you got married?"

"I was a mature twenty-two." She chuckled. "At least I thought so."

"Was Otto older than you?"

"By a few years."

"Did he attend college?"

"No. After high school, Otto entered a two-year agricultural program. Having come from generations of farmers, he could've taught the classes."

"How about you?"

"I graduated high school but didn't attend college. You might say I majored in finance during my years with the Emersons. They fostered my passion for the subject. As long as we're on the topic, I'll start paying you a stipend this week. As for food and other household expenses, you'll find cash in the tin in the cabinet above the stove."

Their casual chatter continued until she was tucked into bed in clean pajama bottoms and Vern's fishing tee shirt, cut and pinned at the side.

She closed her eyes, a smile on her lips. *I see what that girl did. Left me no time to feel self-conscious ... or sorry for myself.*

Chapter Thirteen

Carley: Present Day

Over the next few weeks, Carley and her aunt eased into a semi-flexible routine. Per Miss Neva, the alarm was set for six. Morning ablutions came first, sometimes accompanied by music, other times chitchat, whichever worked best to lessen her patient's self-consciousness.

Next, they took turns reading a few chapters in the Bible kept on her aunt's bedside table. Often, their readings turned into discussions which continued through breakfast.

About midmorning, the two of them headed out to the greenhouse. Under her aunt's supervision from her perch on the golf cart, Carley weeded and picked whatever was ripe. When her patient napped after lunch, she showered and revived herself. When Vern showed up to relieve her, she ran errands. He usually stayed for supper. Before Vern left, their evenings included a reading from Psalms.

Though Miss Neva's sling had been replaced by a cast, her limited mobility was still the main source of her pain and aggravation. Her minor scratches were healing and her bruises fading. Carley had even removed some of the stitches on her leg and arm, but the deeper cuts on her hip and left hand would need another week or so.

Dubber and Warren had been by three times to mow, both the expansive lawn and the field behind the house. They looked more like a couple of kids on ponies riding Otto's John Deere mowers. When Geneva asked them to switch off so all the tractors could get a workout, they could barely contain their excitement. After each mowing, they wiped down the tractors, put them back in the barn, and refilled each tank.

When Grace Bible Church and Andover Congregational both called early on to set up meal deliveries, Miss Neva had been firm. "You folks are so kind to think of me, but there are so many foods I can't eat, I must decline."

Shocked, Carley asked, "Why didn't you tell me you had food allergies?"

"Never said I had allergies. What I said was, 'there are so many foods I can't eat'—which includes those curious casseroles from church ladies—no matter what the denomination."

However, the offerings from her neighbors were more than welcomed. Grilled chicken and potato salad from Mary. A cheese and cold cut platter from Martha. Two quarts of homemade ice cream from Leo.

In between, Carley herself managed to feed the three of them some delicious meals before the truth came out.

Her aunt swallowed the last bite of lasagna Carley had fork-fed her. "This is wonderful! I don't think Faith's could have been any better, don't you agree, Vern?"

"I do. Carley, did you use both sweet and hot sausage?" He took another mouthful, then nodded. "Mmm, mmm."

"You must have found my pasta maker." Miss Neva licked her lips. "Nothing tastes quite like homemade pasta, though I admit I haven't used that machine in years."

Vern added, "I didn't think anyone's cooking could compete with Faith's and Neva's, but that parmesan crusted haddock you made last night proved me wrong."

Carley scrutinized their faces and caught his wink at her aunt. "Okay, you two, who told you?"

"Told us what?" Miss Neva's face did not read innocent. "That you make the best chili and cornbread around?"

Carley pulled Vern's plate away. "Spill. Unless you don't want the rest."

He held up his hands. "No! I surrender."

Her aunt chuckled. "Who *didn't* tell us, Vern?"

He nodded. "Wilda was the first to call, of course. She made a point of telling us you bought the last of the chili and cornbread at the Sawmill Market before she could place her order. I believe her exact words were, 'She cut in line right in front of me!'"

"That is not true! I called ahead to place my order."

Miss Neva added, "Then, when Dubber and Warren came by to change the oil in the tractors, they asked how we liked how the Country Store had fixed the fresh haddock they'd gotten by bartering with one of the fishermen Down East."

Carley crossed her arms. "Big mouths."

"And this morning when I stopped for coffee at the Red Rooster, Faith told me she'd set aside the lasagna as you'd ask her to."

She plopped down in her chair. "Is anything sacred in this town? Truth is, I can't cook. Not one bit. I wasn't trying to hide that fact, but I didn't want you to worry or starve or be poisoned."

Her aunt extended her bandaged hand. "If you want to learn how to cook, I can teach you as much as I know. If you don't, that's okay too. Each person has their own gifts. You've blessed me abundantly by putting yours to work helping me."

"Thanks." Carley blushed.

"Neva, speaking of using one's gifts," Vern stretched. "When's Norm Fournier due to come by next?"

"Oh, my, with all the fuss, I almost forgot. His standing appointment is for the second Tuesday of the month."

He opened his pocket calendar. "That's next week."

Carley checked the date on her phone. "Who's Norm Fournier again?"

"He runs the tree farm over in Rumford. After Otto passed, I made him a rent-to-own offer he couldn't refuse. He likes to make his monthly payments in person so he can give me a full accounting."

Vern mumbled. "At least that's what the widower claims."

Her aunt looked at him over the top of her glasses. "What are you trying to say?"

He brought his plate to the sink. "Nothing, but maybe I should stick around that night."

"As long as Carley's here, I'll be fine."

Carley caught the disappointment on Vern's face. She joined him at the sink to start on the dishes.

Miss Neva turned around in her chair. "There's one other thing, Carley. Any chance you could visit the Antoine sisters for me tomorrow?"

"Uh, I guess, but I don't know much about stamps."

Her aunt mugged. "Neither do I, dear."

As she'd done almost every night since her arrival in Andover, Carley thought about the people she'd left behind in Philly—including Roxy Ingram. Having worked together for over two years, they'd become close. Even though Carley's intention had been to protect her friend, she felt guilty about keeping secrets from her.

Doubt nagged her now. *What if she unknowingly gets caught up in the whole fraud thing? Who'll protect her?*

Then there was Dr. Harrison Nichols ... Dr. Punch-in-the-Solar-Plexus. The man she'd been wrestling with her feelings over since her first day at work. His tender manner with the patients, especially the elderly ones, had impressed her. She hadn't worked as closely with his partners, Drs. Reinhart and Stryker, but they'd come off as aloof, while Nichols had been nothing but kind and respectful. A certain noble quality ...

Tender? Kind? Noble? He's the reason you're hiding in Maine in the middle of a whistleblowing investigation. Get real and get over him!

The lack of news from her attorney didn't help. All the man ever said was, "These things take time. We'll let you know."

Midafternoon Friday, Linda Gregoire dropped off a homemade shepherd's pie and all the makings for fresh strawberry shortcake. "Directions for the pie are on the sticky note. We're not going back to the Cape until Sunday night, so call if you need us."

When Vern arrived, Carley was ready to leave for her visit with the sisters.

"Vern, if I'm not home by five, could you please put the shepherd's pie in the oven at three hundred fifty degrees?"

"No problem."

Miss Neva arched a brow. "Don't worry, if he nods off in the rocker, I'll wake him."

Lorette and Josette had not expected anyone to come by that week, so Carley's knock surprised them. She spent almost two hours there, chatting about stamps and golden age movie stars while sharing tea and maple crème cookies.

These nonagenarian twins had never been married or had any sort of career. Their sole purpose and passion in life had been stamp collecting. Carley found that sad.

Why? You haven't been married either. And you're a certified nurse practitioner serving as a nurse's aide. Now that's sad.

As her visit with them wound down, both sisters began to fidget and fuss.

"You seem upset," Carley said. "Is something bothering you?"

"Papa died twenty years ago today. He was ninety-three." Josette squeezed her sister's hand. "We have no reason to believe we will live much longer than he did, yet we still have no solution to our dilemma."

Lorette sighed. "Securing a proper curator for our collection is imperative—before it's too late."

By the time Carley bid the sweet women good-bye, she had promised to do all she could to help them ... even if she had no idea how.

On her way home, she pulled into T-bone's service station. He was pumping fuel into the tank of a large camper. Though he'd been checking in with her aunt by phone—had even stopped by a few times—Carley herself hadn't seen him since the night of her aunt's fall.

When he finished with the camper, he came around to her. "Hey! I was starting to think you were avoiding me. How've you been?"

"Fine, but busy." She turned off her engine. "Fill her up, please." She held out a twenty and chuckled when he reached for the bill. "I see you're still sporting the latest in latex."

He looked down at his gloved hands. "I do believe you're mocking me, Ms. Merrill."

"Maybe a little."

He frowned. "You do know this is the only gas station in town, don't you?"

"Any chance I can salvage our strained relationship by inviting you for supper? We're having homemade shepherd's pie and fresh strawberry shortcake."

"I'd be a fool to say no to Linda's cooking."

"Why am I not surprised you know about that?"

He shrugged. "Is six too late?"

"Not at all. Vern will be there too. He's been a bit overprotective since the accident."

"He's always fussed over Geneva, but more so since Otto passed. Loyal as an old hound dog." He screwed her gas cap back on and gave her a few dollars change. "By the way, did the deputy sheriff find Miss Neva's place?"

She froze. "What do you mean?"

"He came through a bit ago, making sure he was headed in the right direction."

"Uh, I've been visiting the sisters for the past few hours." She tried to keep her grip loose on the wheel. "Guess I'll find out when I get home."

He smirked. "I like the way you say that."

"Say what?"

"*Home.*"

She grinned and started her car. "See you at six."

Chapter Fourteen

Carley: Present Day

Carley idled slower than the speed limit, which wasn't easy since it was posted at twenty-five. When she rolled up to the house, a county sheriff's Dodge pickup was parked alongside her aunt's Chevy and Vern's Buick, their owners all seated on the porch.

Why was she nervous? She'd done nothing wrong. No one knew a thing. She pulled her shoulders back and sprinted up the steps. "How did you two manage to get in trouble with the law in the few hours since I've been gone?"

The deputy stood and tipped his hat. "Deputy Sturgis, Miss ...?"

"Carley Merrill. Nice to meet you." She leaned against the railing.

"Merrill, huh? Any relation to the Merrills over in Newry?"

Eesh! Could I have picked a more common name?

"I don't think so, but you never know." She remembered to add a shrug.

"Deputy Sturgis is here about a missing person," Vern said.

She crossed her arms loosely. "A missing person?"

"A woman at the Red Rooster Diner told me the only new, full-time resident in town was Miss Geneva's 'so-called niece', to quote her directly." The deputy checked his notebook. "Wilda Weikert was her name."

Vern sighed. "Why would Wilda say that?"

Miss Neva waved his concern away. "Who knows why Wilda says anything?"

"Local tongue-wagger?" Sturgis smirked. "Every town has one. My mother-in-law holds the title in Fryeburg."

Carley was scared to hear the deputy's answer, but she asked anyway. "What did you say the missing woman's name was?"

"I didn't." He thumbed back a few pages in his notebook. "Roxanne Ingram."

Why would anyone be searching for Roxy? In Andover, no less?

Before she could ask, he continued reading. "Age, thirty-four, medium-length, dark brown hair, brown eyes, about one hundred sixty pounds, all muscle."

Carley tried to keep her face blank. He'd described her friend to a tee. In fact, the 'one hundred sixty pounds, all muscle' comment was how Roxy always joked about her curves. What was going on?

Her aunt broke in. "Was the woman a hiker? Despite all the white trail blazes, the Appalachian can be ruthless on the skilled and unskilled alike."

He checked his notes again. "No mention of hiking. Says here the female caller wasn't even sure if Andover was in Maine or Massachusetts."

Miss Neva shook her head. "There's another fine waste of our sheriff department's valuable time."

"No harm in asking around." Sturgis gave Miss Neva a card. "Please call me if you hear anything."

The three of them waved as the deputy pulled out of the driveway.

Before her trembling legs gave out, Carley lowered herself in a chair.

Her aunt stopped rocking. "Carley, what's wrong?"

She was about to say "nothing" when Vern interrupted. "Carley, ever hear this quote by Albert Schweitzer, 'Truth has no special time of its own. Its hour is now—always'?"

She couldn't argue. "I've got something to tell you. Sorry I've taken so long. Vern was right. I should have trusted you." She breathed in deep, then faced her aunt. "My name is Carley *Jantzen*, not Merrill."

"Jantzen, huh?" Her aunt resumed rocking "Truth is when you've been around as long as I have, you sense when something's a little off."

Carley was relieved but not surprised by her aunt's reaction to her lies of omission. Not much got by that woman, a woman she'd become close to in such a short time. Before Carley could continue, T-bone pulled up. She groaned. "I forgot to tell you I invited him for dinner."

"Perfect," Miss Neva said. "You'll save yourself some time repeating. Anything you can say to us, you can say to T-bone."

Vern stood. "How about we have this talk over supper. That shepherd's pie is hot and smelling mighty good."

After Carley told her whistleblowing tale, everyone had questions. She addressed theirs but had a concern of her own. "Roxanne Ingram is the name of my friend and coworker. The words the deputy used to describe her match Roxy's own description of herself to the letter. None of this makes any sense."

T-bone asked, "And how would they know to look here in Andover?"

Vern scratched his chin. "You know, when I was a boy, we'd visit my grandparents in Bangor. Long trip, even longer fifty years ago. When we got back home, my mother would call my grandmother *collect* and ask for herself. My grandmother would know we got home safely, and my mother wouldn't have to pay for a long-distance call."

"And?" Miss Neva prompted.

"I believe Carley's friend might be putting a new twist on that old ruse. By using her name and describing herself, she's letting you know she's onto something. I'd call her."

T-bone raised a brow. "Wait. Do you trust this person, Carley?"

"Yes. The only reason I didn't confide in Roxy was because I didn't want her to get sucked into the maelstrom."

"There are other considerations." T-bone set his fork on his empty plate. "If the charges stick and this doctor is found guilty of fraud, the ramifications are life changing. He could lose his medical license, his fortune, his freedom. Who knows what length he'd go to if he suspected someone was trying to take all that away from him?"

"He's right," Vern said. "We need to take precautions before you talk to your friend."

Carley pulled her phone out of her pocket. "Does this count? Before I left Philadelphia, I got one of these burner phones like you see on TV crime shows."

"That's a start." T-bone added, "Do you keep it on?"

"Yes, but I've only used it a few times to check in with my attorney."

"Doesn't matter." He drummed the table with his fingers. "Miss Neva, do you still have your cell phone?"

"Yes." She motioned to a kitchen cabinet. "In the top drawer. Never use the thing—too temperamental."

Vern chuckled. "You ... or the phone, Neva?"

She knocked on her cast. "This is hard enough to bruise a person, you know?"

T-bone plugged in the phone to charge it. "I suggest you use your aunt's around town. Keep yours *off* until you call your friend."

Carley didn't see the point. "But my new phone number is unlisted."

"They might not know who's calling, but they can ping your location via the phone's GPS." T-bone smiled. "I watch TV too."

Miss Neva added, "Doesn't the FBI need at least three minutes to trace a call?"

"Way back when they did, but not anymore," T-bone said. "Now tracking is almost instant. Look, we're dealing with a doctor here, not the FBI or the CIA. I think we'll be safe if you use the burner, keep the call brief, and remove the battery after you hang up."

"You're making me nervous." Carley's mouth went dry. "What should I say when I reach her?"

Vern's brow furrowed. "If you control the direction and pace of the conversation, your friend won't have time to ask you questions you don't want to answer."

"The woman already suspects Carley's in Andover," Miss Neva said. "Why and who else knows?"

"Maybe the call will reveal more information." Vern folded and unfolded his hands.

"Okay, remember these things." T-bone counted on his fingers. "One, control the conversation. Two, be brief. Three, tell her your trip to La Paz took an unexpected detour for personal reasons. Four, don't give her any details."

Vern snapped a nod. "Are you ready?"

Carley repositioned herself in her chair. "Ready."

T-bone checked his watch. "I'll signal when to hang up."

She punched in Roxy's number and hit speakerphone.

"Hello."

"Roxy? It's—"

"Carley! So happy to hear your voice! How's your dad? And La Paz?"

Caught off guard, she improvised. "Um, he's showing a few signs of improvement, thanks, but not enough for me to come home yet." She got a thumbs-up from her aunt.

"I'll keep him in my prayers," Roxy said. "Funny, you were on my mind. My apartment's being fumigated now, so I'm spending the next few hours at our favorite gym."

Favorite gym? Her friend never went to the gym.

"You know, the one above that Indian restaurant we love?"

She hated Indian food. "Oh, yeah."

"What did you say?" Roxy sounded far away. "Carley, you're breaking up."

I am? She hadn't noticed.

Roxy's voice faded, "Call me this evening when you have a better connection."

"I'll try, but you know how crazy it gets in La Paz."

T-bone signaled to wrap it up.

Carley doublechecked to see that her phone was off. "I have no idea what just happened."

"I'll get the battery for you." T-bone took the phone from her.

Vern laughed. "Seems like your friend is the one who had control of *that* conversation."

"Obviously, the girl was afraid to talk," Miss Neva said.

Carley settled back against the chair. "What Roxy *did* say about the gym and Indian food were lies. The only times we ever went *near* an Indian restaurant were on Friday nights when Roxy babysat her nephew to give her sister and brother-on-law a break. The little guy has health issues. Their apartment is—"

"Near an Indian restaurant?" T-bone tapped his finger on the table. "Anyone in the family named Jim?"

"Yes, her brother-in-law!"

Vern put his coffee cup down. "And people have their apartments fumigated when they find bugs. Considering her cryptic remarks on the whole, she may have found a listening device."

"Do you really think so?" Carley's head began to ache.

Miss Neva cut a quick glance at her. "Do you know her sister's phone number?"

"Not by memory, but I can find it."

T-bone checked his notes again. "Look, the main message she was trying to get across was that her line wasn't secure, but her sister's line was. How long do you think it'll take her to get to her place?"

Carley thought back on her trips with Roxy. "If she was at her place, no more than a half hour."

Vern stretched. "Then I say we call her back in an hour."

T-bone pushed himself up from the table. "Until then, I'll make a fresh pot of coffee to go with dessert."

Carley chuckled when Roxy answered her sister's phone. "I see those mystery novels you love so much are paying off. Seriously, how on earth did you know where to find me?"

"I didn't. Your father called the office when he got the out-of-service message on your cell. You should be glad I answered, or you might not have a job when you decide to come back. By the way, you should call him. He's wracked with worry."

"I will, but back to how you found me."

"The only clue your dad gave me was that you'd heard from a long-lost relative in New England. All he could remember was the town—Andover. We tried Connecticut first. Did you know five out of the six New England states have a town named Andover? I guess Rhode Island didn't have room."

"Please explain to me how *you* could get a sheriff's department to search for a missing person?"

"I couldn't," she said. "My uncle's a lieutenant with the Penn State Police. He called in a few favors."

"Did you tell anyone where I was?"

"How could I? I still don't know where you are, exactly."

"Then I won't tell you now either."

"Carley, you're scaring me. I thought your weird moods had something to do with Dr. Nichols—who, by the way, has been a tad grumpy since he got back and found you gone."

Carley's sharp tongue was ready, but she held back.

"The weirdness has escalated, and the atmosphere is thick with tension. I feel like the doctors are watching our every move. Even a few of the patients have noticed. Carley, what's going on? You can trust me."

"I *do* trust you, but I'm not at liberty to discuss the matter with anyone. In the meantime, as far as you know, I'm still in La Paz. I'll explain as soon as it's safe."

"On one condition," she said.

"What's that?"

"That you call me at my sister's apartment every Friday night. I want to know you're all right."

"Deal." She didn't feel so alone knowing Roxy was on the inside and on her side. "By the way, was your place really bugged?"

"I'm not sure, but someone found a listening device stuck under the table in the breakroom at work. I was so creeped out I've got a spy-guy going through my place now."

Chapter Fifteen

Harrison: Present Day

That morning, Harrison had been terse with office administrator Roxanne Ingram when she'd tried to set him up with a new nurse. Working with someone other than Carley wasn't easy. From day one, she'd been a perfect fit as his NP. He wasn't in the mood to break in another, especially since his first choice would be back soon ... he hoped.

Carley's diagnostic skills, especially with the geriatric patients, easily matched his and even surpassed those of his partners. Her honest yet easy way with all the patients made up for his own sober bedside manner. *She* made *him* look good.

And, with her tech skills, she'd inadvertently taught him how to get in and out of their software program without leaving a trace. What would she say if she knew? What would she think of him then? For that matter, what did she think of him now?

Harrison contemplated calling her. He had no idea what he'd say when she answered. If she answered at all. Did they even have cell service in that part of La Paz? Where was La Paz anyway? Mexico? Bolivia? Why hadn't he thought to ask?

His ego mocked him. *The information didn't revolve around you, that's why.*

Shut up.

Maybe he'd say he needed assistance with their new software upgrade. She would believe him. Better yet, he could give her an update on Mr. Kumar. She'd connected with the old man when no one else could.

Or, idiot, ask her about her father's health and when she plans to return.

His conscience this time. *Admit it. You sound selfish because you are selfish.*

He punched in Carley's number.

"The number you dialed has been changed, disconnected, or is no longer in service. If you feel you have reached this recording in error, please check the number and try your call again."

He did try again and got the same message. *Weird.* Seemed odd she would change her cell service in the middle of a family emergency. He had seen enough of her efficiency and common sense in action to know she must've had a good reason.

Carley. Carley. Carley! What is wrong with me?

His distraction with this woman was competing with his concentration—and winning. He needed to stay calm and behave ... only a few more months.

The scope of the plan had gotten bigger than he'd originally thought possible. With three physicians, each with a diverse patient base, billing for unwarranted tests and procedures had been easily overlooked—at least until now.

He still worried Bryce and Peter would catch on. Had they been on edge lately, or was he being paranoid? He'd known the wily twosome too long to discount their street smarts. They'd long-ago established a pattern of getting what they wanted when they wanted it.

And who were those suits in sunglasses he'd seen them talking to out back?

While at Chapel Hill, they'd taken advantage of Harrison's close relationship with his anatomy professor and convinced the man to write letters of recommendation for them. They both secured residencies at a prestigious Pennsylvania hospital following their families' timely donations. And when Bryce had wriggled out of a malpractice suit a few years into private practice, Peter had remarked, "Helps when you've got a fraternity brother on the bench."

He was ashamed to admit they'd gotten the better of him more than once. Even more ashamed because of the reason. Young and immature, he'd envied their confidence. Like a couple of snake oil salesmen, they'd convinced him to invest the small inheritance he'd received from his grandfather into the practice. Then, once he stood to lose his investment, they coerced him into co-signing a loan which covered their share.

Yes, he'd learned his lesson. Now it was their turn to learn theirs.

After two light knocks, Roxanne entered his office. "Excuse me, Dr. Nichols, the nurse said you have patients waiting in exam rooms five and six. Should I tell her you need a few more minutes?"

He inhaled deeply, trying not to show his impatience as he had earlier. "No, thanks. I'm on my way."

"One more thing." She handed him an envelope. "From Carley."

He stared at the envelope with his name written in Carley's precise cursive. "She sent the letter through you because ...?" When his pulse quickened, he feigned nonchalance.

"Mail delivery in La Paz is almost as bad as the phone service. Rather than risk losing one piece of mail along the way, she sent all our notes in one express package addressed to me."

"'All our notes'?"

"Yes. Yours, mine, and HR's."

"I see." That Carley had sent something to human resources did not bode well. Dread held him back from tearing open the envelope. He slipped the note in his lab coat pocket. "Thank you, Roxanne."

The letter crinkled in his pocket all afternoon. He found the privacy he wanted once office hours had ended and the staff had gone home.

> Dear Dr. Nichols,
>
> Upon my arrival in La Paz, I realized the situation here demanded my presence far longer than I had expected. I'm not sure when I will be able to return home. I have notified HR. If this is not acceptable to Drs. Reinhart and Stryker and you, I certainly understand if you choose to terminate my employment.
>
> I am sorry and disappointed things have turned out the way they have.
>
> Sincerely,
> Carley Jantzen

Frowning, he reread the note, this time more aware of her formal tone. He turned the sheet of paper over. *Nothing.* What had he expected to find? A personal message expressing her desire to pursue a relationship with him when she returned? Why? He'd purposely been nothing but professional with her. The few compliments he'd given her had been about her manner with their patients. Not once had he even suggested she call him Harrison.

He groaned and rested his head in his hands.

The pathetic truth was he'd often thought about confiding in Carley, believing she'd be the one person who would understand why he was doing what he was doing. Once she knew the whole story, he'd always imagined her to be understanding and forgiving. Besides, considering what Peter and Bryce had put him through already, didn't they deserve what they got?

Now he had no one. He crumpled the letter and tossed it in the trash. Not that he ever had Carley.

Chapter Sixteen

Geneva: Present Day

Sitting at her desk in the library, Geneva perused her daily edition of *The Wall Street Journal*. She pushed the paper aside.

Why am I not upset about Carley withholding part of her story? She chuckled. *Probably because I'm guilty of holding back on a few facts myself—and not only from her.*

From the moment Carley had been drafted into caring for her, that girl had displayed an inordinate amount of skill, gumption, and compassion. Those traits made up for any secrets she wanted to keep.

Carley interrupted her. "I thought I'd dust and run the vacuum in here before your guest arrives." She eyed the bookshelves, which filled one whole wall. Fingering book spines, she read, "*Managing Real Estate Holdings ... Day Trading ... Charting Your Financial Course.* Have you read all the books on these shelves?"

Geneva half-shrugged. "Most twice, some more."

"Really?"

"Why do you seem so surprised?"

Carley flushed. "I guess when you said you were interested in finance, I thought you meant household or business. I didn't think stock market and real estate."

She raised a brow. "A stereotypical assumption, don't you think?"

Carley grimaced. "You're right, I'm sorry. Truth is I've always wanted to learn how to manage or grow my money better, but I never knew where to start."

Geneva walked over to the shelf and pointed a title out. "If you're serious, here's a fun read on the basics."

Carley plucked the book from the shelf. "*Stocks and Bonds: Not Just for the Rich and Famous.* I'm the right demographic, for sure."

Geneva glanced around the room. "Since I've hardly been in here all week, I think we can forgo the vacuuming and dusting for now. We will need another chair from the dining room, however. Mr. Fournier's son Skip is joining us today."

"Sure thing. Would you like me to set out some refreshments? I can make some coffee, and we've got that plate of cookies the sisters sent home with me."

"No, that won't be necessary. Norm doesn't often linger." She returned to her desk. "Though I would like your clear head in the room with me. I don't trust myself with all the drugs you people have me on."

Carley snickered. "Yes, because acetaminophen is such a hallucinogenic."

She mentally waved her niece's wisecrack aside. "Besides, I'll need you to take notes and write out the receipt Mr. Fournier expects."

"Well, before they get here, let's change your dressing," Carley said. "Wouldn't do to get an infection on your palm when all else has gone so well."

"You're the nurse." Geneva followed her to the bathroom.

Her niece unwrapped the gauze, then cleaned the wound. "So, how long has Mr. Fournier been running the tree farm anyway?"

"He was a manager before, but he assumed full charge the day after my husband passed. I made the rent-to-own deal with him about six months later, only because I knew Otto would approve."

"All set." Carley gathered the tape, gauze, and salve. "We might be able to remove those stitches in a few days."

"Sure will be glad to have full use of at least one of my hands—"

A loud knock at the front door interrupted.

Geneva called out, "Door's open, Norm. Come on in."

Norm lumbered in, a grin on his weathered face. His son was on his heels. "Miss Geneva! You're looking so much better than I expected after hearing about your accident. Some scare, eh? How're you feeling?"

"Better each day, thanks to the excellent care I'm getting. Good to see you again, Skip. This is my niece Carley. She'll be sitting in on our meeting today."

Norm extended his hand. "Nice to meet you, Carley, real nice."

"No one said anything about a niece." Skip's expression clouded. "We were hoping this meeting would be private."

"It will be ... with Carley as my assistant." Did his tone sound presumptuous, or was she overreacting? He had the same features and mannerisms as Norm's late wife—thin, pale, and high-strung. "Shall we get started, gentlemen?" She led the way. "Carley, you take my desk chair. I'll sit here with the men." She motioned to the tight semicircle of armchairs facing the desk. "So, Norm, what do you have to report this month?"

"Everything is super, super. Crops are healthy, workers too." He chuckled. "Should be a banner holiday season."

Geneva rested her bandaged hand on her lap. "Good to hear."

"There is one thing though." Norm leaned forward.

"Does that one thing have anything to do with your son being here?" Geneva smiled.

Norm cleared his throat. "Skip and I were just saying how nothing gets by you, Miss—"

Skip interrupted. "All our years of tree farming have taught us we need a larger profit margin to support two households."

"'All our years of tree farming', huh?" She tilted her head. *What was this kid, all of twenty-three?* "How long have you been working with your dad now?"

Skip bristled. "Long enough to know we need more land."

Norm's face reddened a bit before he nudged his son's knee. If he was trying to send him a message, the kid didn't receive it.

The young man's chest puffed up. "We've got a twenty-acre parcel in mind, Geneva. At a low-ball price too."

She motioned to a legal pad on her desk. "Carley, would you mind taking notes? I want to make sure I get all Skip's ideas down."

Carley picked up the pen.

"Go on, son," she said. "Where is this land?"

He folded his hands across his middle, a smirk on his face. "The land abuts the creek which runs along the rear property line of the tree farm." He chin-nodded to Carley. "Don't forget the part about the creek."

Carley scribbled on the pad. "Creek. Got it."

Norm interjected, "My son's been doing some research. The place is an old vehicle graveyard. The heirs of the late owner want to sell."

"Any EPA issues?" she asked.

Skip's face was plastered with irritation. "Nothing for you to worry about. We'll deal with any environmental issues on our own later."

Geneva eyed both father and son. "If not my advice, gentlemen, what do you want from me?" Not that she didn't know already.

Skip blurted his answer before his father could open his mouth. "We'd like to renegotiate our rent-to-own deal with you and refinance to include the price of the land."

She ignored him. "Norm, is that what you want?" When Skip started to answer, she held up her hand. "Son, my contract is with your father, not you."

Geneva controlled a snicker when Carley mumbled audibly as she wrote, "Contract with father *not* son."

Norm fiddled with his hat. "The thing is, we've been working hard, eh, but the profit's not enough to keep up with our expenses. My son—I mean, we—thought this might be a decent investment as well as a solution to our financial concerns."

She nodded. "On your say so, Norm, I'll look into it."

Skip muttered to Carley. "Did you write that down?"

Geneva stood. The men followed her lead.

"I appreciate your consideration, Miss Geneva," Norm said. "Now, we've taken enough of your time." He reached into his shirt pocket and handed her a folded check.

"Thank you." She turned to Carley. "Could you please write a receipt for Mr. Fournier?"

When Skip opened his mouth again, his father kicked his son's boot.

They said their goodbyes. Geneva watched from her library window as the younger Fournier hopped into the driver's seat of a new luxury SUV. His license plate read, "ARRIVED."

Little snit.

She turned to Carley. "How about some tea?"

Carley's eyes widened. "And maple crème cookies?"

"Perfect. I'll join you in the kitchen in a minute." She glanced at the legal pad and read the notes Carley had written. *Land on creek. Vehicle graveyard? EPA nightmare. Renegotiate what? Speak up, Mr. Fournier! Contract with father NOT son. It's MISS Geneva to you, sonny-boy.*

That girl is a chip off the old DNA block, she is. Chuckling, she called out on her way to the kitchen. "You know, Carley, I don't believe Skip Fournier is married. I could put in a word for you if you don't mind a younger man."

Carley remained steady as she poured their tea. "How nice of you to offer, but I'd rather eat mud from the creek abutting his contaminated vehicle graveyard, thank you."

She tried to sound serious. "Are you sure?"

Carley pinned her with a stare. "Quite."

"What would you say to T-bone then?" *Agh!* She wished she'd bitten her tongue.

Carley thought for a second or two. "I'd say you were getting warmer, but—"

She managed to get her cup to her lips. "Forget I said that, dear. I hope you're not offended."

"Offended? Hardly. Knowing how you feel about him, I take the hint as a compliment."

She patted her niece's hand. "I meant it as such."

Carley started to say something but stopped.

Geneva leaned in. "What is it, dear?"

She squiggled in her seat. "Do you mind if I ask you a personal question?"

"Not at all."

"Why do you think your husband chose Mr. Fournier to manage his tree farm?"

"Otto always said Norm was honest, hardworking, and faithful. But I'm sure my husband's main reason for choosing him was because they shared the same passion for farming."

"Do you think Otto would have said the same about Skip?"

"Not for a minute. What are you getting at?"

"I don't know. Seems like Mr. Fournier needs to remember why Otto selected him. He might have to stand up to his son."

"Maybe." She drained her cup. "I've never been a parent, so I'm not sure how a person would do that."

Carley almost choked on a cookie. "You? I have a feeling you'd have no trouble at all."

Chapter Seventeen

Carley: Present Day

A few mornings later, Carley removed the stiches from Miss Neva's hand as promised. "I don't think you'll even have a scar."

Opening and closing her hand, her patient said, "Super, because my hand-modeling gig is coming up soon."

Carley snickered. "Now that would *not* surprise me."

"Still, watching me as a lefty won't be pretty—especially when I eat."

"You'll do fine with a little help."

"Speaking of help, after breakfast could you get me set up at my laptop? I'm way behind on some of my work."

"Sure thing."

Once her aunt was settled at her desk in the library, pecking away one-handed at the keyboard, Carley headed outside. Dubber and Warren showed up to help with gardening minutes later. The three of them attacked more weeds, then picked enough produce to make salads for the week.

Dubber set down his full basket. "Why don't we put some rhubarb aside for Miss Eversall? If she makes her strawberry rhubarb pies, sure as shootin' the bakery will be busy tomorrow."

"I like the way you think," Carley said. "I'll even put in an order for one myself."

They filled the "Fresh Picked. Help Yourself" stand at the end of the driveway. Neighbors would make quick work of their harvest. When noontime arrived, Carley offered to make the men lunch.

Warren declined. "Nice of you t' ask, but we brung our own. Our workdays don't allow much time for fancy eatin' breaks." He pulled out a tarnished pocket watch and checked the time. "Fact, we're due over at Cooper's place in a half hour."

Dubber yanked on his overall straps. "Yep, he needs a shed teared down, and we need the reclaimed wood." He snickered. "'Sides, we get to use his mini dozer to do the job."

Warren nudged his brother. "Come on, we'll eat in the truck on the way."

Carley waved the duo off and then checked on her aunt. She found her sound asleep on top of her made bed, her Bible open by her side. A plate with cracker crumbs and a half piece of cheese was on the nightstand. Too tired to prepare much else, she retreated to the kitchen and mimicked her aunt's light meal.

She sat at the table with her muddled thoughts, twirling her straw in her iced tea.

Hmm. The Antoine sisters. How could I help them preserve their legacy?

She thumbed through the copy of the *American Philatelic* magazine Miss Josette and Miss Lorette had lent her, not without Miss Josette's admonition: "We only have two copies of this issue. Please do not dog-ear the pages." Under that sort of pressure, Carley grabbed her laptop and moved on to the American Philatelic Society's website instead. She was happy for a decent Wi-Fi signal for a change.

Since the society's main jobs were "to promote the hobby and serve its members," maybe her online research would reveal an idea the sisters hadn't discovered in the monthly magazine. She clicked through the site's main menu, looking for clues. Under *About*, one sentence stood out: "To assist its members in acquiring and disposing of philatelic materials." Reading further, she learned about APS's fellowships which promoted stamp collecting to young people and connected collectors with those more knowledgeable.

The site listed the society's numerous clubs. However, the club presence in this region of Maine was limited to towns more than two hours away from Andover. She gathered a few more bits and pieces from their list of events and blog posts until a vague idea floated around her head, seeking a place to light.

Though Carley didn't know much about stamps, she had a feeling the value of the sisters' collection lay more in nostalgia than cash. She also sensed *nostalgia* was a higher value in their minds and hearts. Would others feel the same? Contacting the society to ask a few questions couldn't hurt.

She perused the staff directory. Still not sure who could help, she emailed the Education Coordinator, the Shows Coordinator & Youth Assistant, and the Director of Expertizing, whatever that was. About to close out, she clicked on *Board of Trustees*. A familiar face stared back at her from the top row. She tried to shake sense into her head. The name under the photo read: Geneva Kellerman, Treasurer, Andover, Maine.

What on earth?

Vern stepped into the kitchen. "Hi. I knocked, but no one answered."

"Sorry." She turned her laptop screen in his direction. "Tell me, did you know about this?"

He shrugged. "The sisters asked if Neva would be willing to serve a term when the last treasurer got sick." He smirked. "Of course, that was about three years ago."

"I thought Miss Neva said she didn't know much about stamps."

"She doesn't, but she's a whiz with dollars and cents."

"When does she find the time?"

"In this case, her role is more of an advisory one."

Carley raked both hands through her hair. "My aunt trims her own trees, tends a huge garden, makes the best apple crisp around, deals with problem tenants, reads books on the stock market, oh, and makes her own preserves. Is there anything this renaissance woman can't do?"

Geneva rounded the corner. "Apparently, I can't carry three jars of preserves up the stairs without falling. Oh, and nurse myself back to health. That's all you, dear."

"Surprisingly, you've been an easy patient." Carley stood. "Now, what can I get you?"

Vern got a couple of glasses from the cupboard. "Iced tea, Neva?"

Her aunt held her hand up, palm out. "Stand back to be amazed." She filled the two glasses and set one down in front of him. "Not bad for a southpaw."

"Impressive. Let me see." He put his glasses on, took her hand in his, then ran the tips of his fingers over the place where the stitches had been. "Can hardly tell where they were."

His tenderness with her aunt made Carley feel like she was intruding.

A few seconds passed before Miss Neva pulled away and looked at the clock. "I see you're keepin' banker's hours now."

"Your wit never disappoints." He wiped the grin from his face. "As it happens, my last client of the day didn't have much of a legal problem. I thought maybe I could treat you two ladies to an early dinner out for a change. That's if Carley hasn't already, um, planned something."

Carley crossed her arms. "He's a diplomat, you've gotta give him that. Vern, if you're asking if I've ordered takeout yet, the answer is no."

"What do you say, Neva? I thought we could ride over to Bethel. I know how much you enjoy the Millbury Inn."

Even when Vern didn't have a hat in hand, he always *looked* like he had a hat in hand when he addressed Miss Neva.

"You're a thoughtful man, Vern Beckham. If my niece agrees, then we accept."

"Works for me," Carley said. "I didn't feel like chili and cornbread for the third time this week anyway. When do you want to leave?"

"Is five thirty okay?" He peered at Carley over the top of his glasses. "Leaves plenty of time for someone to take a shower."

She almost choked on her tea. "Subtle. I think you've been hanging out with my aunt too long."

"That's not possible," he said. "Not possible at all."

Though she had more than enough time to get ready, Carley excused herself. Mostly, because she wanted to give them space. Was she reading the signs correctly? Since her aunt's accident happened so soon after she arrived, Carley had no way of knowing if all this attention from Vern was new or normal. Since Miss Neva seemed embarrassed by all his fussing, she suspected new. But were they strictly friends? Did *they* sense the awkwardness she sensed tonight?

Guess those two would have to figure things out for themselves.

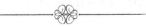

Before Carley got in the shower, she called her attorney whom she hadn't heard from in three weeks.

"Ms. Jantzen! I've been meaning to call you. We've had some new developments in the case."

"What do you mean?"

"I'm not at liberty to discuss them. Suffice it to say, what we've learned makes our investigation more complicated."

She sighed loud enough for him to hear. "*Our* investigation? Whose attorney are you, anyway?"

"I work for you, but I've got to abide by the federal investigator's rules."

"Um-hm. What does all this mean for my situation?"

"Trust me when I say, since you didn't go straight to the government, the settlement will be worth the wait."

"For the umpteenth time, Mr. Yeager, I'm doing this for the patients not the money. How long will I have to put my life on hold?"

"I can't give you an exact date, but I'll keep you posted."

"Do that, please." A question surfaced as she hung up. What would she do once her life was *off* hold?

A long, hot shower cleared her mind and relieved her stress.

She chose her dressy black slacks, royal blue silk top, and strappy heels. She checked herself in the mirror and realized this was the first time she'd worn anything feminine since she'd left Philly—including makeup and jewelry. Besides, this outfit was more suitable for an *inn*. *Why?* She couldn't say. At least it wasn't another diner.

Vern whistled as she joined them on the front porch. "Very pretty."

Miss Neva stared at Carley. "Remind me to show you a picture of myself at your age."

"Is there a family resemblance?" Carley hoped there was.

"None I can see." She huffed. "You'll agree when I show you the picture."

"Don't let your aunt kid you. She was as pretty then as she is now. So, are we ready ladies?" With a hand at her back, he guided Miss Neva to the front seat of his SUV. Once she was settled, he asked Carley to finagle the seatbelt to work with her cast. "I'm too clumsy. I might hurt her."

Her aunt gave Carley one of her eyerolls.

On their way through town, Vern pulled into the gas station.

Since dinner was Vern's treat, Carley reached for her wallet. "Let me take care of the gas."

"No need. My tank's full."

"Oh?" *Then why are we here?*

As if her aunt had read her thoughts, she said, "We're waiting on T-bone."

Before Carley could say a word, T-bone exited the front door and hopped into the back seat. He was cleaned and polished and smelled nothing like gasoline or motor oil.

Why did she feel like she'd just been set up?

CHAPTER EiGHTEEN

CARLEY: PRESENT DAY

If this was a veiled attempt by the older couple to fix her up with Andover's gas station owner-veterinary assistant-EMT, Carley decided to play innocent. "Glad you could join us on such short notice, T-bone."

"Me, too." He buckled his seatbelt. "Look how nice you clean up!"

"Thanks." She could have said the same about him ... but didn't.

"Sorry if I made you wait," he said. "I had to give Dubber and Warren last minute instructions on how to close up."

Vern eyed him through the rearview mirror. "Haven't those two closed up for you plenty before?"

"The station, yes, but not the post-op. Faith's Husky is recovering from another intestinal obstruction. Since the diner's open late tonight, she can't come by for him until near eight."

Her aunt shook her head. "What on earth is she feeding that poor creature?"

"'Poor creature?' Hardly. That dog isn't named Houdini for nothing. He ate her granddaughter's plastic tea set and a full bag of ponytail ties before they could move to stop him." He shivered. "Let's just say the two of us had a very long night."

Vern snickered. "We can guess the rest."

Carley's curiosity won over T-bone's privacy. "I've heard the plan is for you to take over Doc Quimby's practice when he retires."

He shifted in his seat. "I've been hearing those rumors myself for years now."

Miss Neva turned and faced him.

"Sorry if I'm being nosey," Carley said—but didn't mean. "Have you applied to any veterinary schools yet?"

He shook his head. "This whole vet thing started when I nursed my dog Zulu back to health. Poor guy had contracted a virus in the shelter before I adopted him. Anyway, around that time, Doc Quimby hired me to care for his post-op patients—mainly because I had the space. Somehow everyone assumed I was a shoo-in to replace him."

Her aunt frowned. "You're allowed to speak your mind, you know."

He shrugged. "Part of me figured if enough time slogged by without me applying to a school, people would figure things out. Another part of me wondered if they were onto something."

"So, what's the verdict?" Vern asked.

"Seems all I want is to have another dog someday—but not one like Houdini."

On the thirty-minute trip to Bethel, Carley awakened to her new appreciation for the area's winding, hilly roads. Back in Philly the roads were flat and forced to comply with a civil engineer's cold calculations. Here in Oxford County, the mountainous topography dictated a more natural, more serene route.

The sign entering Bethel boasted a population of 2,607, over three times Andover's. Large painted colonial-style homes and commercial buildings—none in disrepair—lined both sides of Main Street. Mature shade trees, clean-swept sidewalks, and bright, rippling OPEN flags (or NEPO flags, depending on how you read them) added to the town's New England charm.

Carley commented, "Bethel seems a bit more affluent than Andover."

Vern pushed the windshield visor up. "You caught that, huh?" He turned around on a side street and parallel parked directly in front of the Millbury Inn, a quaint, three-story white colonial with dark blue shutters. Rocking chairs, hanging geraniums, and an American flag welcomed guests onto the deep front porch.

Once inside, sunlight brightened every corner of the expansive dining area. Classical music intermingled with breezes floating in through half-open windows. Tables were dressed in crisp white linen, polished flatware, and glistening crystal. At six o-clock, only a few tables were occupied.

Carley was glad she'd 'cleaned up real nice.' This eating establishment wasn't like any she'd seen in Andover. She stepped toward the host's station.

Miss Neva called to her, "This way, dear," and motioned to a doorway.

"Oh?" Carley was confused. A sign on the door read, "Downstairs to Mill's Pub."

T-bone led the way down the narrow, angled staircase.

Carley's vision adjusted to the dark room. The paneled walls and dropped ceiling made the room feel closed-in. Metal signs covered the walls, advertising local attractions or brands of beer and ale. A large horseshoe-shaped bar filled the center of the pub. The rest of the place was furnished with rustic tables and chairs—none of which were "dressed in crisp white linen, polished flatware, or glistening crystal."

After hellos were exchanged with some local folk at the bar, Vern led them to a booth in the corner. "What do you think, Carley?"

She mentally compared the fancy, mostly vacant dining hall upstairs with this casual, full pub. "By the people and the aromas circulating, I'm guessing this place serves great food."

He gave her a thumbs-up. "Then you'd be correct."

Her aunt slid across a bench, her cast to the wall. Vern slipped in beside her before Carley could. The arrangement left T-bone and her side by side in the chairs facing them.

A server dropped off menus and took their drink order.

Carley got sidetracked by the décor. Business cards were stuck in ceiling tile grids, and flyers welcoming campers, bikers, and skiers were tacked to adjacent beams. A sign above their table read *Bethel Regional Airport*. She pointed. "An airport?"

"Small one, but yes." T-bone chuckled. "Gus Eversall's squadron of drones is the closest Andover has to an airport. You're likely to see them flying around during Olde Home Days."

"When is that anyway?" Carley accepted an iced tea from the server. "Thanks."

Miss Neva answered, "First weekend in August."

A shadow fell across their table before they could continue their conversation.

Wilda Weikert sauntered closer, one fist on her hip. "Well, well, look who we have here."

Her aunt responded, "A surprise to see you as well."

Wilda snapped a nod in Miss Neva's general direction, then gave Carley a saccharine smile. "Miss Merrill, I hope you weren't thinking about applying for that part-time librarian's position Linda mentioned to you. The town officials agreed I was best-suited for the job."

"I'm certain they made a wise decision, Miss Wilda."

Wilda tried in vain to fluff her wispy thin hair. "I overheard you folks mention Olde Home Days. T-bone, remember when you dedicated your poem to my niece, Izzy, last year?"

T-bone tilted his head. "Miss Wilda, you do know I wrote that poem *before* I met your niece, don't you?"

"Of course, I know. Everyone does. That's why we all say your encounter was kismet." She poked him in the shoulder. "I'm sure Izzy would love to accompany you again this year in between her shifts at the sausage and pepper booth." Wilda shot Carley a stern glance.

"'Again?'" T-bone looked confused.

Vern's reading glasses balanced in the middle of his nose. "If you're not careful, Wilda, you'll fill your niece's head with so many of *your* ideas she won't be able to form one of her own."

"Pfft." Wilda ignored him and turned back to T-bone. "I'll tell Izzy to expect your call."

As soon as Wilda was out of sight, Carley teased, "'Well, well, look who we have here.' From the color of your face, I'd say a medium rare T-bone."

He kept his eyes on his menu.

Miss Neva picked up her glass. "To be fair, Izzy did seem like a sweet girl."

Vern quipped. "Nothing like her sour old aunt."

"Whether she's sweet or sour is a moot point," T-bone said. "For all her aunt's efforts, I never heard a word from her after that night."

"Sounds like you wished you had." Carley narrowed her eyes. "I think Wilda might be on to something."

Her aunt's eyes crinkled. "Is what Carley is saying true?"

Vern whispered, "Do tell. We can keep a secret."

T-bone raised his hands. "Look, can we please move on to our meal?"

"One more question about Miss Wilda," Carley said. "Is there a *Mr.* Weikert?"

"Used to be," Miss Neva said. "Sadly, he died years ago after falling off their roof."

Vern kept a straight face. "Some say he jumped ... with his hands in his pockets."

"Vern Beckham!" Her aunt slapped his hand. "Is that a Christian thing to say?"

He hung his head. "No, ma'am. Not rightly, I guess."

The four of them tried not to laugh but failed.

The fancy upstairs dining room would've been too reserved for their lively conversation—much of which stemmed from her tablemates' description of Olde Home Days and the townspeople who made the event unique. Carley had to admit she'd never seen lawn tractor races, skillet tosses, or arm-wrestling in New Hope or Philadelphia.

After her last bite, she wiped her mouth with her napkin. "This was some of the best pub food I've ever had. Reminds me of the underground bistro Roxy and I found near our office."

Vern tapped the rim of his coffee cup. "Speaking of your friend, today's Friday. Is she expecting your call this evening?"

"Ooh. Thanks for the reminder." Carley checked the time. "I'd better call her now before I forget again."

T-bone pushed his chair back and stood. "You'll have to go upstairs, maybe outside, to get a signal." He pulled her chair out.

"You don't have to come with me." She smirked. "I'm pretty sure I can find my way."

"Uh, I was on my way to the men's room."

"Oh." Now it was her turn to blush.

T-bone was right about the weak signal. Carley ended up on the far end of the front porch.

Roxy answered, "What's cookin', good-lookin'?"

Carley scoffed. "Sheesh. You sound like an old geezer."

"Gee, thanks, exactly what I was going for. How's everything in Maine?"

"Okay." Carley caught her breath. "Wait. How did you know I was in Maine?"

"I didn't, but we'd eliminated Connecticut already, which left me one chance in four to guess correctly." She sighed. "If *I* can trick you so easily, how about others? Or maybe they've tricked you already?"

"No one has tricked me. I'm here of my own accord." She changed the subject to Roxy's nephew. "How's my little buddy doing?"

"He's as sweet as ever, but he still has cerebral palsy, if that's what you're asking."

"No, that's not what I'm asking." *How* Hunter had contracted CP had never been confirmed, but Roxy still needed to place the blame. Carley switched gears. "What's happening at work?"

"Is that secret code for what's happening with your Dr. Nichols?"

"I'll pretend I didn't hear you." Did she sound nonchalant? "Speaking of secrets, find any more bugs in the office?"

"No, and we found out the one in the breakroom was placed there by a jealous spouse, hoping to catch her husband cheating. Someone from the night maintenance crew."

"Has anyone asked you to fire me yet?"

"I'm sure your doc won't let that happen. He can't wait to get you back. The nurse I assigned to him is driving him nuts."

"He's not *my* doctor. I was his NP, nothing more."

"*Was* his NP? Why would you say *was* if you're planning to return?"

"Roxanne Ingram, has anyone ever told you you're a pain?"

"Shall I give you a list, or are you looking for one name in particular?"

She laughed. "I wanted to call to let you know I'm okay before you sicced your cop-uncle—" She was distracted by T-bone, standing beside her with a finger pressed to his lips.

He whispered, "Shh."

"Something's come up, Rox. Gotta go. Give Hunter a kiss for me. I'll call you next week." Carley hung up, questioning him with her eyes.

He led her back into the building and down the stairs to their table. He checked behind them before he spoke. "Wilda was seated at a window table. The window was open, and she had her ear pressed to the screen."

Carley thought back over her phone call. "We didn't talk long. I'm not sure what she could've heard." She paused. "I asked her how she guessed I was in Maine. I supposed Wilda could make something of that ... Uh, oh."

He leaned in. "'Uh, oh,' what?"

"I used her full name, I think, and mentioned one of the doctor's names too."

T-bone waited until the server refilled his coffee cup. "Do you think your friend has already guessed the reason you're here?"

"She's pretty adept at putting two and two together, but I think she suspects my leaving has something to do with Dr. Nichols, but not in a whistleblowing way."

"In what way then?" Miss Neva asked.

Carley faltered. "Um, uh, she might think it's personal."

Vern tilted his head. "Personal?"

T-bone sat back in his chair, smiling. "What Vern means is was there a romantic link between you two?"

"No, there wasn't." Carley twisted her napkin until the paper shredded.

T-bone raised a brow. "But you wanted there to be?"

Carley frowned at him. "I didn't say that." *First, Roxy, now T-bone. I need to do a better job of concealing my feelings.*

Her aunt shrugged. "No sense worrying about what Wilda did or did not overhear. We'll know soon enough once she starts strutting her tongue, perhaps as early as tomorrow morning at the corner table at the Red Rooster."

Chapter Nineteen

"Vern, mind taking a little detour on our way home?"

"Anything for you, Neva."

"'Anything?' I'll keep that in mind, but for now take your next left, please. I want to show Carley the Haven Academy campus."

The scent of fresh cut grass wafted in through her open window as Vern drove down Church Street, past three-story brick buildings and lush grounds. The campus was bustling with students.

"For over a century, Haven has been attracting families who want to give their children an excellent education." She glanced over her shoulder at Carley. "I've told you how I spent years as a mother's helper for the Emerson family. Well, Daniel, their youngest, is the Head of School now."

"Impressive," Carley said. "So is the campus. I bet the tuition is pricey."

"Yes, but Haven maintains a substantial scholarship fund for worthy applicants." She steered the topic away from finances. "In addition to traditional subjects, they take advantage of their proximity to the White Mountains to incorporate on-snow programs into their curriculum."

"On-snow? As in skiing?" Carley asked.

She nodded. "Both Alpine and Nordic. Snowboarding too. The school partners with a ski resort nearby."

Her niece pulled herself forward. "Miss Neva, did you ever learn to ski?"

"My main job was to stay in one piece so I could watch over the children." She held up her cast. "Guess I'm making up for that now."

"Don't let Neva fool you." Vern slowed the car as they wound through a narrow backroad. "She skied with the best of them up until ... well ... a few years ago."

Her niece asked, "Do you still ski?"

Geneva had no desire to explain why she hadn't skied since Otto passed. "No, I don't." She hoped to end the discussion.

T-bone whistled. "Can you imagine how much the property value has increased over the years? Anyone who bought land back in the '70s could've made a bundle."

"I don't know much about real estate," Carley commented, "but my father always said the most important investment a person can make is in people."

Geneva cut her eyes to Vern and caught his approval.

"Seeing as your dad's a foreign missionary," T-bone said, "sounds like he puts feet to his words."

"He always has," Carley said. "I used to think he and I were so different, but once I started nursing, I realized the best part of my job was interacting with the patients."

Geneva raised her hand. "I, for one, can testify to your excellent skills and bedside manner."

"Thanks. Maybe that's why this whole Medicare fraud thing at work makes me so angry."

"You're doing the right thing," Geneva said. "Blowing the whistle will go a long way in preventing others from doing the same."

At home later, Geneva and Carley relaxed in their comfy nightclothes, chatting about their evening out.

Carley said, "Were you surprised by T-bone's news tonight?"

"You mean his decision not to pursue a veterinary degree?"

"Yes." Her niece pulled her legs up underneath her onto the couch.

"Not really. He loves animals, but I've never heard him say he wanted to be a vet."

"Well, he seems to be an accomplished auto mechanic. And I've seen him in action as an EMT, so he has other choices."

"He does." She hesitated before sharing more. "Between you and me, T-bone has another passion—writing. His poems aren't the only words he puts on paper. He's been scribbling in journals and making up stories since he was a boy. He majored in English at Bowdoin."

"Bowdoin College?"

"Yes. Are you surprised?"

"He never mentioned college to me at all. Is his writing any good?"

"From what I've read, yes, but he keeps most of his work to himself. I've tried my best to leave developing his gift between him and the Lord"—she winked at Carley—"but there's nothing wrong with lending a hand here and there."

Carley's eyes brightened. "Do you have something specific in mind?"

"For starters, adding more categories to the Olde Home Days writing competition so he can submit in multiple genres."

"What makes you think he'll enter?"

"He will, especially if he wants to encourage others to do the same."

Carley squinted. "You didn't just come up with this idea, did you?"

She studied the fingernails on her good hand. "Not exactly, but I have prayed about it."

Carley drew in a breath. "I was thinking, what about this for the Antoine sisters?" She outlined a plan whereby the sisters would mentor youth members of American Philatelic Society. Part of the sessions would include cataloging the balance of their stamp collection.

Neva peeked at Carley over the top of her reading glasses. "And *you* didn't just come up with that idea either, did you?"

Carley grinned. "Well, no." Her eyes grew wider. "Maybe they could even rent out their upstairs bedrooms to a few of the mentees in exchange for their cataloging work."

"Remember, these women are in their nineties. Change isn't always easy for us older folk."

"Maybe mentoring a few local teenagers who love stamp collecting would fill their days with *purpose,* not work." Carley glanced sidelong at her. "By the way, not for a second do I buy *you* being classified as 'older folk.'"

She and Carley spent the next hour sorting out details and overcoming any possible objections either T-bone or the sisters might have.

When they awoke the next morning, Carley could barely contain herself. "I don't know why I didn't think of this last night. Asha Kumar, the daughter of one of my patients back in Philadelphia, is an editor at a publishing house. When I gave her dad a little extra attention, she told me to call her if I ever needed editorial services. What do you think about me asking her to serve on the panel of judges for the writing contests?"

Geneva finished pouring their juice. "Mercy, wouldn't that be like the Lord to set things up way before we need them?" She was pleased Carley's enthusiasm had not waned. "In the meantime, since I know most of the people on the Olde Home Days committees, I'll call to suggest they add some new genres. Then, I'll email my contacts at the philatelic society for a list of possible mentees."

Carley filled their bowls with raisin bran. "I'll contact Ms. Kumar."

After breakfast, Geneva called Vern. "Will you be coming by this afternoon?"

"Planned to, why?"

"Carley and I have a few ideas we'd like to discuss with you as our legal counsel."

"I'm liking this girl more and more," he said. "Are you thinking what I'm thinking?"

"Let's wait on that a little longer, Vern."

That afternoon, Carley joined Geneva on the sofa in the living room. She held a silver-framed photo of Otto in her hand. "Tell me about Otto. I'd love to know him better."

The photo was one of Geneva's favorites. He was leaning on a hoe at the edge of the garden, wearing his prize bib overalls, a beat-up straw hat, a sly smile, and a twinkle in his eyes.

She blew a bit of dust off the glass. "Why is that, dear?"

"I don't know. Maybe because he was such a huge part of your life." Her eyes waltzed around the room. "His handprint is all over this homestead and your business."

"That's true." She gathered her thoughts. "Otto was a good man, a faithful husband, and my best friend. He was an extremely talented farmer whose ethics were beyond reproach." She paused to remember. "Some people accused him of being a bit too stern—which I attribute to his German heritage. He found satisfaction and fulfillment in physical labor. There was no room for nonsense in Otto's days."

"How old were you when you started dating?"

"Near as I can figure, nineteen or twenty." She chuckled at the memory. "You see, Otto and I never made a conscious decision to *date*. Up to then, Otto, Vern, and I were a band of three. Sometimes Faith joined us. When Vern left for college and Faith went off to culinary school, Otto and I continued to pal around together. People began to assume we were a couple. After a while, neither of us minded their assumptions."

Carley scrunched up her face. "No offense, but that doesn't sound very romantic."

She chuckled. "If you're searching for grand gestures or a whirlwind courtship, you'll be disappointed. Neither of us were the type to exchange poems and love letters. He never *claimed* me as his own like some bare-chested hero in those silly romance novels. If he had, twenty-year-old me would've run away."

"Why?"

She shrugged. "I'm not sure. Maybe I was comfortable with our relationship because I didn't grow up in an atmosphere of fiery emotions. My parents were kind to one another, but I never witnessed too much affection between them."

"Sounds a little sad."

"They weren't so much sad as exhausted. Life in Kingdom Come, a hollow in Kentucky, was physically demanding, I don't believe they knew what they were missing."

"And you and Otto?"

"Compared to what my parents endured, Otto and I had it easy. Mostly, we were content."

"Content? No glamour and romance?"

She smiled, knowing something this young person couldn't. "Contentment in itself can be romantic, don't you think?"

Carley sighed. "I wouldn't know since romance and I are virtual strangers."

She treaded lightly. "Had you hoped to have a relationship with your doctor friend?"

Her niece took a long second to answer. "Any hope I might have had with him was lost in the prenatal stage."

"This may sound like a platitude, but God isn't finished writing your story." She tapped her niece's hand. "You'll see."

Carley didn't respond.

"Speaking of God,"—Geneva raised her free arm—"now that we've figured out how to dress me in something other than Vern's old T-shirts, I'd love to get back to church. Would you care to join me?"

"I'd love to. You attend that little church way down on South Main, right?"

"Yes, Grace Bible. Until *you* came into my life, the people there were the only family I knew."

"Sounds like the church Dad and I belonged to before I moved to Philly for college."

"And your church in Philadelphia, what was that like?"

Carley pinched her lower lip. "Big city big. Don't get me wrong, the pastors were excellent teachers, the music ministry had more talent than they could use, and there were ministries for every age. But I missed that family feel."

Geneva chuckled. "I hope you can say the same after church on Sunday. There's a potluck luncheon following the service. Prepare yourself for more *family feel* than any one person can handle!"

Chapter Twenty

CARLEY: SEVENTEEN YEARS OLD

NEW HOPE, PENNSYLVANIA

With high school graduation only three weeks away, Carley needed to find a well-paying summer job. Her scholarships would cover her room and board and tuition at the University of Pennsylvania, but there was still the matter of books and other incidentals. Her father's salary as a geography and Spanish teacher didn't allow for many extras. Besides, if she earned enough to cover her miscellaneous expenses, that might free up funds for him. Dad never did a thing for himself.

She fought off envy when she remembered how her friend Braden had boasted. "With the money I get from family and friends for graduation, I can take the whole summer off *and* cover my extra expenses at college."

Family and friends? She and her father were the *only* members of their family, and their friends had even less than they did.

That reminds me, I promised to go to the market for Mrs. M. this morning ... and pick up Mr. Zalinsky's prescription.

Her dad came in the back door after an elders' meeting at church. "Morning, cariño. What's on your schedule for this beautiful Saturday?"

"I've got a few errands to run, and then I'm job hunting." She handed him a copy of her résumé. "What do you think?"

He read the single sheet. "Succinct yet professional." He laid the résumé on the counter. "Before you start pounding the pavement, I have something that might interest you."

"Like what?" She tried to read his face. "Is your friend at the ice cream stand looking for help again? Dad, they barely pay minimum wage."

He crossed his arms. "Yes, but don't forget about the family discount."

She rolled her eyes.

He kissed her forehead, then handed her a sealed envelope. "Pastor asked me to give you this."

Their church's address was printed on the corner of the envelope. "Dad, I've worked in the church daycare for the past three summers. I can't afford to work there again."

"I'd call this an all-expense paid situation."

She grunted. "To where?"

He shrugged. "You won't know until you open it."

She unfolded the letter and read out loud, "The Board of Elders of Grace Fellowship Church is pleased to award Carley Rae Jantzen the Luke 6:38 Scholarship in the amount of $2,500." She stopped reading to look at her father. "What? Dad, did you know about this?"

He leaned against the counter, grinning. "Not until an hour ago."

She kept reading. "This scholarship is given yearly to a high school senior who has achieved academic excellence as well as shown themselves to be an example of Luke 6:38: 'Give, and it will be given to you. A good measure, pressed down, shaken together, and running over, will be poured into your lap. For with the measure you use, it will be measured to you.'"

She paused to swallow the lump in her throat.

"Also, in appreciation for your dedication and service to the family of God at Grace Fellowship, we hope you will accept our invitation to accompany your father on an all-expense paid mission trip to Bolivia this summer."

Her hands shook. "Is this for real? Bolivia? *This* summer?" Carley had participated in local outreach programs, but this would be her first time out of the country—and to Bolivia!

He laughed. "Seems like the idea excites you, cariño. So, what do you say?"

"Yes! Yes!" She bounced up and down and hugged him. "When do we leave? What will I be doing? Do I need to get shots?"

"We'll learn everything we need to know at the meeting Monday night, but my guess is they'll assign you to the mission school or clinic since you're so *fluid* in Spanish."

She gave him a raised brow instead of her usual eyeroll. "Dad, don't you ever get tired of teasing me about the mistake I made during a second-grade show and tell?"

He tapped his cheek. "Nope. It's a dad thing."

Her eyeroll made a comeback. "So how long will we be there?"

"Um, do you think you can handle a four-week commitment?"

"Of course, I can. Besides, aren't you the one who always says missionaries need more than two weeks to make a lasting difference?"

He chuckled. "I have said that, haven't I?"

Before she left for Bolivia, Carley lined up her best friend Selena to run errands for Mrs. M. and Mr. Zalinsky while she was away. Since Mr. Money-Bag-Lazybones-Braden had 'the whole summer off,' she guilted him into taking care of the lawns she usually mowed. She also kept her promise to help Big Moses, aka the honorary mayor of their neighborhood, finish his disability claim letter to the Veterans Administration.

LA PAZ, BOLIVIA

After a half-day of travel, their plane approached El Alto International Airport in La Paz, the highest capital in the world, two miles above sea level. In one direction, the Andes loomed over expansive lowlands, where red brick buildings lined a crisscrossing maze of streets. In another, stacked houses, packed in tight, clung to the hillsides.

Carley's parents had first met in La Paz while on mission trips from their respective churches. Almost from the day Carley took her first step, her dream was to follow in her mother's steps by becoming a nurse and by using her skills in the mission field. She hoped her efforts would bring her closer to the woman she'd never gotten to know.

Their team's itinerary included spending their first night in the city. The hostel sent a shuttle bus to pick them up. After they checked in and freshened up, her father met her outside. He'd promised to take Carley to the exact spot her mom was standing when he met her—on the seventh step of the staircase of the National Museum of Ethnography and Folklore.

The air was thin and the temperature cool as they started out on their three-block walk. July in Bolivia was like December in Pennsylvania. She zipped her coat and stuck her hands in her pockets. "Dad, do you realize, outside of when I was born, this will be the only other time I will be in a place where my mother has been before?"

He put his arm around her shoulder. "I know, cariño."

When they approached the Marquis de Villa Verde Palace which housed the museum, Dad walked her up to the seventh step. "This is the very spot." He kissed the top of her head. "Now stand just like that, and I'll take your picture."

Inside, Carley perused the displays of pre-Hispanic relics, festival masks, Andean ceramics, colorful fabrics, feathered costumes, and all manner of weaponry. She learned a lot about the many different and independent cultures of Bolivia. But mostly, Carley had questions. *Did my mother see this? Did she touch this? Did these weapons freak her out?*

Around midmorning the next day, their team arrived at the mission center. Several large buildings were arranged in a circular fashion on the property. Separate dormitories for men and women. A dining hall. A chapel with seats for a hundred. A clinic. A good-sized school with grades kindergarten through senior high.

Carley was assigned to work in the clinic her first two days. "*Que necesitas que haga?* What do you need me to do?" she asked the nurse in charge.

Nurse Gomez smiled and gave her a list of chores and administrative tasks. "*Trabajo tedioso pero vital para administrar una clínica.*" She switched to English. "Tedious work but vital to running our clinic."

"I understand." Carley set about organizing the large medical supply closet, labeling each shelf for ease of use. She refilled supplies in the three treatment stations and washed down the exam tables, then stepped back to survey the room.

Half-smiling, half-crying, a little boy with a bloody knee stood in the doorway.

She called to the nurse. "I see we have a young patient."

Nurse Gomez sat him up on the exam table and checked his wound. "You'll be fine." She placed a bottle of alcohol on the counter. "Senorita Carley will fix you up in no time."

Though his injury was minor, Carley was pleased with the woman's trust. She smiled at the boy and wiped his tears. Adding alcohol to a cotton ball, she said, "*Esto picará un poco. This will sting a little.*"

She blinked back a few tears herself. *If only my mother could see me now ...*

A few days later, the principal showed her around the school. "Carley, I'd like you to meet Señor De Lorenzi and his daughter Señora Adelina, our vocational instructors. You'll be working closely with them during your stay here."

For some reason (probably her American pride), she had expected the teachers to be foreign missionaries, not an elderly Bolivian man and his married daughter. She shrugged inwardly. *Who better than locals to teach students the skills they need to live in this part of the world?*

She greeted them in Spanish.

Señor De Lorenzi wagged a finger. "We *teach* English here, so we *speak* English here. We already know how to speak Spanish."

She bobbed her head. "That makes sense."

Señora Adelina added, "My father's theory 'teach in English, execute in Spanish' is one of his more creative concepts."

"Why not?" he said. "The concept works! By the time our students understand our lessons in *English*, they have mastered them in Spanish." Señor De Lorenzi stared at her. "I think you've been here before, yes? You look familiar."

"No, my first time ever. Although this is my dad's third trip."

"Your father's name?" Señora Adelina asked.

"Philip Jantzen."

The woman's eyes lit up. "Philip! We worked with your parents many years ago. I was a little older than you are now. Papa, remember Carley Rae, the young American who loved to cook?"

His eyes widened. "Yes, yes, I see the resemblance!" He shook his head. "Your mother was quite kind to me, to all of us. We were saddened to hear of her death."

His words almost made her cry. "Thank you. She's the reason I wanted to come. Dad says I'm a lot like her."

"Then we shall get along well." He walked around her. "Now for your initial lesson!"

Initial lesson? I thought I was here to help teach?

Señor De Lorenzi led the way into the large vocational classroom where a couple dozen students, close to her own age, worked at various stations around the room. "Class, Miss Carley is here from the United States. She'd love to see what you're working on."

They greeted her with huge grins and loud hellos.

He turned to Carley. "Are you ready?"

"What would you like me to do?"

"Get to know our students. Ask questions. Then, as they say, plug in." He winked. "Don't worry. There is no wrong answer."

She walked around, peeking over the students' shoulders. Each seemed to be involved in a different aspect of a single construction project—a house floor plan, a plumbing schematic, a lighting design, an art piece, a landscape sketch.

She spotted a loom in the corner where a girl wove with bright-colored yarn. "What are you making?"

"The fabric for Miguel's upholstered furniture." The girl motioned to the boy at a table nearby, whose furniture renderings were fanned out before him.

Carley picked up a sketch. "You will actually build these pieces?"

He nodded. "Yes, but not without help. I am better at design than I am at carpentry."

She wandered back to Señor De Lorenzi, glancing from one focused student to another. "What is the main project?"

He gazed at the students like a proud father. "A home for Nurse Gomez and her family."

"A *real* home?"

He grunted. "We can't ask Nurse Gomez to live in an imaginary home, now can we?" He rocked on his heels. "Last year, our class built the clinic ... and you've been there, so you know it's real."

Her face burned. "It's just that I've never seen or heard of anything quite like this before. How do you decide who does what?"

"I don't decide, *they* do. The first six years of school are mostly academic. The next six include practical application in our vocational classes. By the time they reach this stage, most of them have discovered their gifts and talents. Next, they wait upon God's calling."

"Isn't God's calling the same as our gifts and talents?"

"Not exactly." His jowls jiggled. "Gifts and talents may determine *what* we do, but God's calling determines how we use them, where we use them, when we use them, and for whom."

Yes! Like me following my mother into nursing and the mission field.

Midway through their flight home, Carley mulled over her four weeks in La Paz. The biggest lesson she'd learned from the Bolivian people was relationships were more important than events and activities—even if that meant you were late for everything. The more these gracious people showed Carley how they cared for one another, the more her heart had turned to the people back home.

So why would that trouble me?

Carley nudged her dozing father. "Dad, I'm worried about my calling to the mission field."

He struggled to open his eyes. "Huh? What do you mean?"

"It's hard to explain." She pulled in a breath and let it out slowly. "Like when that old Bolivian couple needed someone to go to the market for them, I thought of Mrs. M. And when Señor De Lorenzi tutored the grown-ups in English, I wondered if Big Moses needed my help with another letter. Then, at Nurse Gomez's blood pressure clinic, I prayed Selena hadn't forgotten to pick up Mr. Zalinsky's prescription." She sighed. "Dad, how do these feelings fit with my call to the foreign mission field, you know, like Mom?"

His eyes opened wide. "Is that what you think, cariño?" He put his seatback up. "I named you after your mother to honor her memory. But if you believe you're supposed to be just like her, then I may have done you a grave disservice."

"I *want* to be like her, Dad."

"Well, you shouldn't, because God takes pleasure in our uniqueness." He held his hand up to stop her from interrupting. "You need proof? Your mother was a homebody, an introvert. But you? You flit about town and make friends with everyone you meet. Your mom loved to knit, sew, and cook. As far as I can see, you're not interested in any of those activities. Your mom was an excellent nurse, and I believe you will be too. However, as for a call to foreign missions, she saw plenty of need in the USA. She is the reason we were home when you were born."

Lord, how did I not know this after all these years?

Chapter Twenty-One

Carley: Present Day

Since Carley had cut her call short with Roxy on Friday, she half expected to find several frantic emails waiting for her that morning. Nope. Though she did find one from her father.

Dear Cariño,

We're so busy with our work here, I don't have time to list all the things I miss about you in this email. Your laugh, your hugs, your scolding, your smarts, your caring, your fantastic eyerolls, and most especially our chats. (Notice I didn't say cooking?)

She laughed amid a few tears.

Though you're probably back at work by now, I hope you enjoyed some quality time with your aunt. I never got to meet Geneva myself, but I kind of like the idea of having more relatives. Our family won't grow any other way—unless you get married and have children of your own. (No, that is not a hint. Okay, so maybe a little one.)

Don't hold your breath, Dad.

As for me, the workload in La Paz keeps growing. You'll be happy to hear Señor De Lorenzi is still strong and active in the vocational school. I've joined forces, so to speak, with his daughter, Adelina. Perhaps you remember her from our mission trip? Sadly, her husband died in a car crash a few years ago.

As soon as Addy and I feel our teams are making a difference here, we hear of another village in need. Currently, we're trying to secure funds to purchase a complex bio-sand filtration system. (Love the work, hate the begging.) Thankfully, one of our tech-savvy team members set up one of those fundraising sites online with a goal to raise $12,750. With my skills and wallet, my contribution is to pray. Would you please add your prayers to mine?

Lord, how can I whine so much when so many people have so little?

Her dad wrote more on his faithful coworkers, the grateful people they helped, and their makeshift but lively church. When the widow Addy's name popped up a few more times, Carley smiled. *Could it be?*

He signed off abruptly, saying someone had rung an alarm.

Carley found the fundraising site and made a small donation. Without a paycheck, her funds were dwindling. She closed the computer and met her aunt in the kitchen for breakfast.

Miss Neva set two mugs on the table and then poured their coffee. "Why the worry-brow?"

"Thinking about my dad. He emailed me today ... just when I was missing him."

"God knew." Her aunt dished out their oatmeal. "What did he have to say?"

"He's glad I got to meet you." She smiled. "Says he likes the idea of having a bigger family."

"Your father sounds like a kind man."

"He is."

Over breakfast, Carley unfolded memories, bragged a little, and talked about her dad's passion to help his Bolivian brothers and sisters. "His main concern now is raising enough money for a water filtration system for a neighboring village."

Her aunt listened attentively, then joined Carley in praying for his team's fundraising efforts.

At the end of their prayer, Carley's heart didn't ache ... as much.

After breakfast, Carley helped her aunt load Rylee Cooper's ATV with food items for Appalachian Trail hiker boxes.

"What exactly is a hiker box anyway?" Carley asked.

"In this case, they're storage containers set in trees along the trail. We fill them with food items and whatnot, like socks, tee shirts, matches, gloves. We're pretty close to the trail's end here, so we want to make sure the thru hikers get the nourishment and encouragement they need to reach the finish line."

"Mount Katahdin, right? How far from here?"

"A little over two hundred miles."

Carley's eyes widened. "Two hundred miles? I thought you said we were near the end?"

"Ha! We are if you consider the trail begins about 2,000 miles south in Springer Mountain, Georgia."

"Wow. I had no idea. The longest hike I've ever taken was when I sold Girl Scout cookies on a tree-lined street in the ritzy neighborhood in New Hope, Pennsylvania."

Geneva chuckled. "The foliage might be a bit denser up this way, and the mountains higher."

Carley handed her a pack of granola bars. "If I was only sixteen like Rylee, I'd be afraid to travel in the woods alone."

Her aunt whispered, "We've got a few spotters watching out for her once she heads for the trail off South Arm. That girl's capable enough, but she's a little too daring for her own good. Takes after her father."

No sooner had Rylee taken off than Faith Eversall pulled in. She called out her car window, "Mornin', Neva, Carley. Thought I'd stop by on my way to the diner and speak to you two before someone else did."

They walked over to her car.

"What's up?" her aunt asked.

"Over the past few days, the rumor mill's been grinding out theories about your niece's sudden appearance in town. As usual, Wilda's been turning the sluice wheel. She suggested you might be running from the law, escaping creditors, or hiding from an abusive boyfriend."

Miss Neva shook her head. "We've got to give that woman a purpose before her gossiping causes irreparable damage."

Carley asked, "Should I be worried that people will believe her?"

Faith chuckled. "Nah. You would've loved the comebacks she got. Every time Wilda spouted one of her ridiculous theories, the locals added another for kicks. Mary said she thought she'd seen your mugshot on an FBI Most Wanted flyer in the post office. Leo said he heard you were working undercover for a rich land developer who planned to build a waterpark on the town common. That one had her apoplectic!

"Then, when Linda whispered the words 'WITSEC' and 'drug cartel,' Frank came up with a story about a whole town in New Mexico being wiped out for harboring a rat. They got poor Wilda so frightened *she* made them all promise to keep their mouths shut whenever strangers were around."

Her aunt snickered. "How is that even possible this time of year in a town inundated by strangers vacationing from all parts of the country?"

Faith smirked a little. "Exactly."

Though Carley was grateful to the townspeople for misdirecting Miss Wilda, she knew full well their actions were more out of respect for her aunt than for her.

That afternoon while dusting a framed sampler hanging in the library, Carley read the cross-stitched King James Scripture verse out loud. "Verily I say unto you, inasmuch as ye have done it unto one of the least of these my brethren, ye have done it unto me." Having this verse, one she knew by heart, hanging in a prominent position in her aunt's house made her feel even more at home. In a flash, Carley realized she'd felt that way since her very first day. She smiled.

Her aunt entered the room. "Does housework always put a smile on your face? If so, I can make a longer chore list."

She chuckled, then explained about the verse. "We had a pillow with that same embroidered verse."

"This is one of the few treasures Mama gave me when I moved up north." Her aunt pointed to the corner of the framed needlework. "Tell me, did your pillow have the initials EJN stitched in the corner?"

Carley leaned in closer. "Yes! I remember that. My dad thought they might be my great-grandmother's initials."

"He was right. Your great-grandmother was my mother, Eleanor Jane Newell."

The sweet connection warmed Carley's heart. "Sometimes, the simple things make a person happy."

Miss Neva smiled. "And enough simple things over the years can add up to a productive, abundant, and contented life."

Carley motioned to the sampler. "Like doing for 'the least of these?'" She glanced sidelong at her aunt. "I've seen what you do for others. No fanfare, no grand gestures, no expectations of repayment. And you *care*, which adds a whole new dimension to good deeds."

"I heard this axiom recently, which sums up my goal. 'Do for *one* what you wish you could do for everyone.' The Lord has blessed me. If I'm able to help a few people here and there, then God is due the praise, not me."

"I get it, really. I'm not trying to puff you up. Truthfully, I've been missing work, thinking that was the only place I could make a real difference. But your manner of giving back has shown me I don't have to wait until I go back to work to help people. Like the sisters, for instance."

Her aunt embraced her with her free arm. "I'm so glad you're here."

The catch in her own voice matched her aunt's. "So am I."

"How 'bout we sit for a spell?" Miss Neva took the desk chair. "I'd like your opinion on a business matter."

"*My* opinion?" Carley sat across from her.

"Yes. As I might have mentioned, Otto used to handle most of the decisions concerning the various farms. Since I no longer have his input, I would appreciate your insight on Norman Fournier's request. I need to give him an answer soon."

She didn't hesitate. "I'm certain you already know what to do, and I'm guessing my answer will confirm yours. No, I would not lend them the money to invest in that parcel of land. Come to think of it, I wouldn't lend them the funds for any parcel of land Skip would be responsible to care for.

His priorities seem to be in attaining toys and status—not in hard work."

"I see."

"He has no respect for his father or you, for that matter. I wanted to box his ears every time he called you Geneva. Before he's put in charge of anything, he needs to develop some common sense and common courtesy!"

Miss Neva slapped the arm of her chair and laughed. "Mercy! I see I'm not the only one in this family who doesn't pull her punches."

"Am I wrong?"

"No. You're right on the nose. I feel bad for Norm, but I'd feel worse if I helped him enable his son any longer."

Carley added, "My gut tells me Mr. Fournier is depending on you to give him the answer he *needs,* not wants."

"Astute observation. Thank you. I'll call him this morning."

Carley's thoughts twisted and turned as she ran errands later that afternoon. The last cryptic message from her attorney suggested "multiple people" might be involved in the fraud. While Dr. Green-Eyed-Monster had been her prime suspect, she wouldn't be shocked to discover his partners had colluded with him. She decided to do some research on Drs. Peter Stryker and Bryce Reinhart.

She parked at the public library to use their Wi-Fi. Though her aunt's signal could be fair to middling, her attorney had told her sticking to a public connection was best. Carley had no idea if that were true, but she figured she would do what he said—most of the time.

Once she found the Federation of State Medical Boards website, she clicked on Find a Doctor. Dr. Nichols's and Dr. Stryker's career overviews were virtually identical.

Education: University of North Carolina School of Medicine, UNC, Chapel Hill

Year of Graduation: 2010

Active Licenses: North Carolina, Pennsylvania

Certifications: Family Medicine

Actions: None

Dr. Reinhart's overview was similar, although he'd graduated a year earlier and held certifications in obstetrics and gynecology as well as in pediatrics. Under Actions, a few years back, a malpractice lawsuit had been filed against him when he'd been practicing as an ob-gyn, but the suit had been dismissed.

She was relieved with her findings.

But what if the FSMB website had more on the doctors than was visible to the public? She wanted to delve deeper, but without the proper authorization, she was blocked. Even if she were able to circumvent the site's safeguards, she couldn't risk the government's case by revealing herself.

Now what? Maybe Vern could apply his legal expertise.

CHAPTER TWENTY-TWO

CARLEY: PRESENT DAY

As Carley edged her car out onto South Main from Church Street, an SUV whizzed by. The tag read ARRIVED. *Skip Fournier*. Where was he going in such a panic? She followed him. When he clipped a sign careening onto South Arm, she sped up. Rounding the corner before her aunt's house, she caught him fishtailing into the driveway.

She scrambled for her phone. "T-bone, you need to get to Miss Neva's—now!"

When Carley pulled up to the house, the front door was wide open. She tiptoed in and heard Skip's voice booming from the kitchen.

"Why are doing this to me? You have some nerve telling my father I'm not up to the job! What makes you such an expert?" Papers rustled. "Here! Sign this loan agreement—NOW!"

Miss Neva spoke a little above a whisper. "Settle down, son."

His rage flared, he cursed. "I'm not your son, Geneva! Just sign the papers!"

Carley stepped lightly toward the kitchen. A hand on her shoulder held her back.

Vern.

He walked around her. "Everything all right here?"

She snuck in behind him and stood off to the side. Skip's appearance startled her. Bloodshot eyes, unshaven face, wild hair, torn shirt.

He pointed a thick finger at Vern. "This has nothing to do with you! Business is between me and her!"

Miss Neva flinched as he yanked her arm and pulled her closer.

Carley cringed.

Vern eased forward but kept his voice calm. "Skip, is it? I'm Vern Beckham, Miss Geneva's attorney and personal advisor. May I help?"

Though still in the young man's grasp, her aunt continued softly. "Why don't you let him take a look at the papers? Your father knows I always run my business decisions by my attorney."

He glared at Vern. "You've got no say in this decision. Neither does my father. Now get out, old man, before someone gets hurt!" He shoved Miss Neva away and raised his fists.

In a few rapid moves, Vern flipped Skip over and held him face down on the floor, his knee pressing against the much younger man's back. "If I were you, I'd stay down."

T-bone sprinted in. "Miss Neva, Carley, are you all right?"

Her aunt massaged her arm. "We're fine. Senior superhero here pulled a move out of his musty bag of martial art tricks."

Open-mouthed, Carley stared. "Well, the bag might be musty, but the trick wasn't. I've never seen anything like that in my life."

Vern shrugged. "I guess forty years of practice finally paid off."

Skip squirmed, trying to free himself. His face was contorted, a picture of rage. "Get off! I'm gonna kill you!"

T-bone stooped and took hold of his face. "Look at me. What are you on? Cocaine? Crack? Meth?"

He bellowed, "Nothing! Let me up!"

Carley reached for the phone. "I'll call 911."

"What'll it be, Fournier?" T-bone asked. "The hospital or jail?"

When the ambulance arrived, the EMTs restrained Skip before they loaded him in.

As soon as they were gone, Vern's focus was back on Miss Neva. He lifted her aunt's chin with the tips of his fingers. "Did he hurt you, Neva?"

She shook her head. "A little, but he scared me more."

He shook his head and closed his eyes. "I don't know what I'd do if anything—"

"Let me check you out." Carley moved toward her.

Her aunt shushed them. "I'm fine, you two. Don't fuss."

"I do have a question, Vern," Carley said. "I called T-bone. How did you get here before him?"

"He was filling my tank at the station when your call came in."

T-bone put his hands on his hips. "Yeah, and he almost got away before I could get the hose out of his tank. By the way, Vern, you owe me nine dollars and twenty-three cents."

"I've got a question for you too." Miss Neva grinned. "Would you prefer your superhero name to be Vern the Valiant or Vern the Victor?"

He laughed. "As long as it's not Vern the Vegan."

Carley said, "Then you'll be pleased to know I've got ground beef, hot dogs, and potato salad in the car." She turned to T-bone. "Plenty, if you wanna join us."

"Do I have time to run back to the station and close up properly? There's probably a gaggle of locals hanging out, wondering where I disappeared to so fast."

"Oh, we can wait." Carley smiled a little too sweetly. "Mainly because you'll be manning the grill."

Carley left Miss Neva and Vern seated in the living room as she hurried out back to light the grill. Vern was an easy read. She knew he'd appreciate the privacy. Her aunt was another matter. Not that she had rebuffed the man's attention following the episode with Skip, but she hadn't encouraged him either.

When T-bone returned, he joined her on the back porch.

Carley chin-nodded in the direction of her aunt and Vern. "*Those* two."

"I know." He poked at the red-hot charcoal briquets. "His feelings for her are obvious. I'm not certain if she feels the same."

She set down a platter of beef patties. "Maybe his feelings are obvious to us, but has he told *her*?"

"He *shows* her, doesn't that count for something?" He placed four patties on the grill.

"Yes, but a woman needs to *hear* the words." She tore open a package of hotdogs. "Are you ready for these yet?"

"Need a few more minutes." He poked at the briquets. "Would written words do?"

"Why? Are you going to act as Vern's Cyrano de Bergerac? Didn't that idea backfire?"

"Initially, but he got the girl in the end." He stared at the fire. "That's not why I asked though."

"Why, then?"

"General information purposes." He chuckled. "Guys need all the inside tips they can get."

She leaned against the railing. "Have you ever talked to either of them about their feelings?"

"I came close with Miss Neva about six months ago. She gave me one of her you-better-back-off looks, which was quite effective. Now, I'm hoping they figure things out for themselves."

"Well, I'm not as patient as you are." Carley held up a hotdog. "Now?"

"Boy, you are impatient, aren't you?" He poked the coals again. "Go ahead."

She placed a half dozen dogs on the grill. "Keep an eye on these. I don't like mine black."

"For someone who doesn't cook, you're kinda bossy." He flipped the burgers. "So, what do you have in mind concerning our esteemed elders?"

"I'm not sure yet, but I may need your help."

"*My* help?" He shook his head. "Uh-uh. No way."

She stomped her foot and pouted. "Oh, come on."

"Would you want someone getting involved in your personal affairs?"

"Depends." She thought back on how Roxy had pestered her to pursue Dr. Nichols. *What if I had listened to her?*

He rolled the hotdogs over. "Have you ever been in a situation like theirs?"

"What do you mean?" Carley fiddled with the paper plates while she searched for an answer.

He added cheese to half the burgers. "Not even with your doctor back in Philadelphia?"

"Why does everyone keep calling him *my* doctor?"

"Everyone?' He glanced around. "I'm the only one here."

"Okay, maybe I was thinking of Roxy."

"The friend who knows you almost better than anyone?"

She narrowed her eyes. "Oh, shut up."

"Look, Carley, I'm being serious. One friend to another, how does anyone know when or how to move forward in a relationship?" He took the hotdogs off. "I certainly don't want people talking behind my back like you and I are doing with our elders in there."

A bit of panic seized her. Was he referring to *them*? She studied his face. *No, I don't think he is.* She decided to give him an honest answer. "Truly, there was nothing romantic going on between Dr. Nichols and me. I confess there was some initial attraction on my part, but I can't speak for him. He was nothing but professional, no flirting or leading me on. Maybe that's why I feel so stupid and even a little scared that I could have been taken in by his unassuming, albeit false, charm—and he wasn't even trying."

He touched her shoulder. "You're a caring person. As often as not, caring people tend to be trusting."

"Maybe." She dragged the stainless-steel brush across the grate. "How about you?"

"I'm a thirty-year-old man who's lived in Andover his whole life, a town that's not big enough to hold too many bachelors. So, yes, I've been approached, used, and hurt."

Something made her ask, "Is Wilda's niece Izzy one of the ones who hurt you?"

"I didn't know her well enough to get hurt that bad." His voice said one thing, his eyes another. "Like you, I err on the side of trust instead of caution."

"Which makes us vulnerable to heartbreak."

He tilted his head. "Would you want it any other way?"

She sighed. "I guess not."

He shrugged. "Me neither."

"Hey, I just learned from my aunt that you graduated from Bowdoin College."

"I couldn't have done it without the Kellermans." He closed the grill cover. "They gave me a place to stay when I had nowhere to go. Otto put me to work on weekends and hired me full-time every summer." He chuckled. "Miss

Neva's mind is still probably fried from filling out all those college financial aid forms for me."

"Bowdoin's in Brunswick, Maine, right? I'm surprised you moved back here once you got the taste of a bigger town." She picked up the full platter. "With the odds as bad as they are of finding a partner in a place this small, why do you stay?"

He hesitated. "Have you ever gotten lost?"

She pursed her lips. "Yes. Once when I was about nine. Scared me to death."

"Do you remember what they told you to do if that ever happened again?"

She thought back. "To stay put."

"Yes, because someone's sure to come around and find you. That's the way I feel. Like if I don't move, the right woman, or maybe the right chance, is gonna come around and find me."

I'm not sure if that's sweet or sad.

Vern and T-bone left by ten, and her aunt retired soon after.

Midnight came and went before Carley got settled in bed. Her earlier conversation with T-bone had brought her Key State Medical days to the forefront of her mind. Not that she blamed *him* for that. She'd made that trip back on her own plenty of times before, torturing herself with the same question: What kind of professional caregiver was she to take so long to notice lies, deception, and fraud?

CHAPTER TWENTY-THREE

GENEVA: PRESENT DAY

What a night! Geneva crawled into bed, still aching from her tussle with Skip Fournier. She wasn't used to being attacked in her own home ... or anywhere else. The young man had scared her enough that she'd acted like some weak-kneed, wimpy female in front of Vern. He, in turn, had fussed over her the whole evening long. Thankfully, she'd managed to circumvent any attempt at serious conversation on his part by coming up with a silly idea for a Vern the Valiant comic strip.

What had her worried more was how his solicitous behavior had made *her* feel. She searched for the right words: off-center, warm, irritated, strong, weak, safe, odd, protected. Too many words fit, increasing her confusion. Was loneliness over missing Otto still wreaking havoc on her thoughts and feelings after all these years?

When Otto was living, the three of them seldom had uncomfortable moments together. Having Vern around all the time felt natural, like he was part of the family. Though she appreciated his continued friendship, something felt different.

Does he feel the same way as I do? Like our relationship is off kilter without Otto?

As the evening lagged, so had Vern's mood. He left earlier than usual. Had she offended him? Not her intention. The whole matter was disconcerting. She vowed to be more vigilant.

How about Vern the Vigilant?... Stop that!

At least one good thing had come out of the night's excitement—Carley and T-bone seemed to bond over the barbeque grill. Whenever she peeked out at them, they were head-to-head, like a couple of conspirators engrossed in secret plans. Not a hint of awkwardness between those two. Maybe ... No, she would not interfere.

Early the next day, Geneva opened the door to a wrecked Norm Fournier. "Good morning, Norm."

"Could be a better one, eh?" He fingered the brim of his hat. "I came by to apologize for my son's behavior. I don't know what got into—"

"Come in and have some coffee." She turned toward the kitchen. "If I remember correctly, you take yours black."

"Yes, ma'am." He shuffled behind her. "I'd understand if you don't want to—"

She held up her hand. "Stop, Norm. Skip is a grown man. You are not responsible for his behavior." She filled two cups and set them on the table.

He sat across from her. "I tried to show that boy a good example." He choked up. "I did everything to help him best I could, but I guess it wasn't enough."

She wrapped her hands around her mug. "Or maybe too much?"

His brow furrowed. "What do you mean?"

"Otto and I were never blessed with children, so I don't pretend to be an expert on raising them. But I know people.

Sometimes when we do too much for others, we enable them to do less for themselves."

"I thought my doing for him would make up for his mother dying so early." He dragged his thick fingers across his face. "As for the drugs, maybe I didn't want to believe he'd ever do that."

"The best thing you can do for him now is point him to a reputable recovery program and pray he's ready."

Carley entered through the back door with a basketful of vegetables from the garden. "Oh, sorry. I didn't know you had company. Hi, Mr. Fournier."

"Mr. Fournier's not company, he's an old friend." She reassured him with a quick nod. "Since Carley's kin, she won't repeat anything she hears here."

Carley raised her right hand. "I promise."

He wiped the corner of his eye with the heel of his hand. "I don't know how to thank you, Miss Geneva."

"I can think of a few ways. Most importantly, I recommend you find a support group for parents like yourself. Then, keep working the tree farm same way you've been doing for these many years."

"Appears I have some matters to ponder and decisions to make." He pushed his chair back. "Best be on my way."

"One more thing, if insurance is a problem for Skip's care, call me. I might be able to connect you with some financial aid resources." She walked him out, then returned to the kitchen. "Seems like you picked enough for the week in one morning!"

Carley emptied the basket. "What I hope to pick now is your brain. What else did Mr. Fournier say?"

Geneva turned the water on to rinse off the vegetables.

Her niece nudged her. "Aren't you going to tell me?"

"Hadn't planned on it." She snickered to herself.

Carley sighed. "I'm concerned. What if his son comes back?"

"If you must know, Norm came by to apologize for his son. He'll see that Skip stays away. No need for us to get involved."

"I see." Her niece smirked. "You mean unless insurance is a problem, and they need financial aid?"

She frowned to disguise her amusement. "Haven't you heard curiosity killed the cat?"

Mischief sparked in Carley's eyes. "And haven't *you* heard satisfaction brought it back?"

Geneva took a moment to formulate her answer. She shut the water off. "When the Lord prompts me to help, I do. Sometimes that takes the form of advice, encouragement, or a listening ear. Other times, garden vegetables or a little financial advice."

"Not to mention a safe haven for a notorious whistleblower like me."

She knocked on her cast. "As far as that goes, your timing, or rather *his* timing, was impeccable."

Carley caught her off guard with a peck on her cheek. "I don't know what I would have done without you!"

More and more I like this girl. "Speaking of timing, have you heard from your lawyer friend lately?"

Carley's brow wrinkled. "Why? Are you anxious to get rid of me?"

"On the contrary. The only thing better than your nursing is your company."

Carley swung one leg back and forth, skimming the floor with the toe of her shoe. "Aww, shucks, Miss Neva, you're making me blush."

"You didn't answer my question." She continued blotting the vegetables with a paper towel.

"Last time I spoke to him was the afternoon we all went out to supper at Mill's Pub. All I know is the original fraud investigator was replaced, as he put it, 'when the case took a wide turn.'" Carley reached for the box of gallon storage bags. "I don't know what that means, exactly, but if that medical practice is as messed up as Mr. Yeager inferred, I might not have a job when this is all over."

She gave her niece a quick squeeze. "Until God reveals his plan, you've got a place here for as long as you like."

Of the many viable outcomes Geneva had imagined for their relationship, Carley going back to Philadelphia had not made the list.

How did I miss such an obvious possibility?

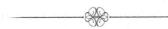

That afternoon, Geneva waited for Dubber and Warren to knock on her door once they finished their mowing.

The knock came.

"We're done for the day, Miss G. The front lawn seemed kind of thirsty, so we gave it a big drink of water."

"Speaking of thirsty, here you go." She joined them on the back porch and poured a couple of tall glasses of lemonade.

"Thank ya, ma'am." Two big gulps seemed to quench Dubber's thirst. "Anything else we can do for you, Miss G, before we go?"

"You two do so much for me already, I hate to ask you for another favor."

Warren downed half his glass. "Remember, favors between friends is free."

She lowered her voice. "Promise to keep this between us?"

They glanced at each other and answered in unison. "Yes, ma'am."

"For the past eight years, I've been watching Esau Cooper and that McPhee guy from away take turns winning the lawn tractor race. I'm certain Otto's John Deeres could do better. The thing is, I need the right driver. I know you both are busy, but maybe you—"

Dubber blurted. "Us? In the race? On one of Otto's JDs?"

"We could do that, Miss G." Warren cinched his belt tighter. "We sure could."

"You'll have to decide which mower to use because I don't have a clue. Maybe one of the newer ones with the wide mowing deck? No one would be able to pass you."

"No, no, not a new one, Miss G." Dubber tugged his ear. "An older model, a beater we can soup up—if we can find the parts we need."

Warren talked fast, his voice up an octave. "That course is rough. We'll need to reinforce the frame and customize the steering if we wanna last all twenty-five laps."

Dubber sighed. "I remember when Cooper traded a half cord of split firewood for that John Deere of his—a DL100 with a burnt out 17-hp motor. Nowadays, he'd have to pay three cords, split and stacked."

Warren grunted. "But he didn't start winnin' until he added that V-twin cylinder Briggs & Stratton 25 hp."

"I had no idea there was so much involved." She refilled their glasses. "Are you sure you boys have the time?"

Dubber slapped his leg with his hat. "Are you kiddin'? We live for this kind of work! Me and Warren'll take a gander through the barn and pick us a champion. You'll see."

Warren nodded. "We'll make you proud, Miss G, we will!"

"Don't be silly, boys, you already do."

Sometimes knowing how to bless people is easy.

The two men fast-walked in the direction of the barn, jabbering all the way.

When she turned to go inside, Carley was standing just inside the kitchen, arms crossed, a smug grin on her face. "Oh, you're good. They didn't suspect a thing."

Geneva eased by her. "I don't know what you're talking about."

Carley suppressed an eyeroll. "I'm talking about the way you help people without making them feel like they owe you something in return."

"Why on earth would I want to do that? The Lord has given me more than I need."

Carley tapped her foot. "I suspect there's way more to this story."

She challenged her niece. "Really? Do tell."

Chapter Twenty-Four

Geneva: Forty years earlier

The Emerson siblings entered the mudroom with Geneva, cackling simultaneously about their afternoon of skiing at Sunday River.

Their mother came around the corner. "What's all this noise I hear?"

Fifteen-year-old Noah's face was animated. "Mama, you should've seen Miss Geneva on the slopes! Coach said he'd like to hire her as his assistant."

Mrs. Emerson's eyes widened. "Is that so?"

Eliza responded with a level of maturity beyond her seventeen years. "He believes she has a natural ability, and with more practice and the right coach, she could be Sunday River's version of Isabelle Mir."

Noah hung his coat on a hook. "Yes, Mother, those were his exact words."

Mrs. Emerson helped Daniel off with his boots. "Does this Isabelle girl attend Haven with you?"

Disbelief covered on Eliza's face. "Really, Mother. Isabelle Mir is Austria's Alpine Cup Champion."

"I see." Mrs. Emerson straightened up. "The coach thinks you're that good, Geneva?"

She laughed. "I suspect Haven's coach is a bit of a flatterer."

Daniel frowned. "Mother, who will be your helper if Miss Geneva goes to help Coach?"

Geneva mussed his hair. "Don't worry, the only people I want to coach are you three."

"Dinner will be ready in an hour." Mrs. Emerson waved them off. "Showers all around, please."

"And, boys, remember to put your ski clothes in the laundry room this time." Geneva held her nose. "The odor of perspiration and mildew is overrated."

"When you're ready, Geneva," Mrs. Emerson said, "would you please join my husband and me in his office?"

"Sure. I won't be long."

Geneva knocked on Mr. Emerson's half-opened study door.

His soft-spoken reply followed. "Enter, please."

"You wanted to see me, sir?"

His wife was seated in one of the chairs in front of his oversized desk. "We both did." She patted the chair beside her. "Have a seat, please."

Bouncing his fingertips off each other, Mr. Emerson said, "How long have you been with us now, Geneva?"

"Seven years next month, sir." She fidgeted. *What is this about?*

Mrs. Emerson chuckled. "I remember the day Upton picked you up at the bus station. You were as skittish as a day-old fawn. I think we scared you a little."

Her face warmed. "Maybe a little."

Mr. Emerson walked around to the front of his desk, leaned against it, and crossed his arms. "Now you're all grown-up and married. You've got a good man in Otto Kellerman."

She blushed again. "Thank you, sir. I agree." *Are they trying to tell me they don't need me anymore?*

Mrs. Emerson picked up a photograph of their family. "You've done well by our three children. Seems like yesterday they were babes." She set the photo back on the desk. "Even though the youngest will be a teenager soon, we still believe they can benefit from your guidance. We hope you'll stay on, perhaps as a part-time tutor."

Poof! Her worries disappeared. She and Otto could use the extra income until his tree farming business turned a profit. "I would love that. The truth is I may have learned more from your children than they have from me."

Mrs. Emerson reached over and squeezed her hand. "Let's agree your position here has been a mutually beneficial one."

Her husband rubbed his chin for a moment before he spoke. "In raising our children, there's a verse that speaks to us as parents. Proverbs 22:6. 'Train up the child according to the tenor of his way, and when he is old, he will not depart from it.' Though many theologians relate this verse solely to discipline, the word *tenor* in the Darby Bible translation infers a natural bent. In your opinion, Geneva, what is the tenor of each of our three children?"

She worded her answer thoughtfully. "All three are bright and inquisitive. Eliza's strengths lie in language and literature. Do you know she is reading Victor Hugo's *Les Misérables* in French now?"

Mr. Emerson teased his wife. "She gets that from *your* side."

Geneva continued. "Even at twelve, Daniel plays school every chance he gets, long after his homework is done. He may make an excellent educator one day."

"Hmm, an admirable field." Mr. Emerson lowered his head, peering at her over the top of his glasses. "And Noah?"

She couldn't contain her grin. "Like you, sir, Noah has a natural affinity for finance. That boy knows how to get the most out of his allowance. He was the only one of the children who heeded my advice about money. He gives away a portion every week, saves another, and is careful how he spends. His bank account is larger than Eliza's and Daniel's put together." She chuckled. "He's even going to ask for stock shares for Christmas. I believe the 'tenor of his way' is quite clear."

Mrs. Emerson chuckled. "Noah definitely takes after *your* side, dear."

He walked back around to his desk chair. "If you don't mind my frankness, Geneva, you have a similar bent. From the very start, you grasped complex financial principles without any formal education in those subjects. I have a proposition for you to consider."

"A proposition, sir?"

"Yes. I've been contemplating hiring an assistant for a long time now. I was hoping to find someone whose passion for finance matched my own. I think that someone is you."

"Me?" Her mouth fell open. "I ... I don't know what to say."

"Why don't you discuss my offer with Otto this evening. If he is agreeable, I hope you'll say yes." Mr. Emerson winked. "You won't regret it."

Geneva rushed to the kitchen. "Mrs. Lankford, is Faith here?"

"She's reorganizing the pantry. Now don't you go interrupting her chores. That girl's been lollygagging all day long, scribbling fanciful recipes in that notebook she carries around."

Faith's dream of attending the culinary institute seemed to be more than her mother could grasp. Geneva had heard Mrs. Lankford lecture her daughter before. "What's wrong with helping me in the kitchen here until you get married and have children? You'll get your fill of cooking for your own family soon enough."

Usually, she stayed out of their business, but today she couldn't help but ask, "Mrs. Lankford, besides taking care of Otto and the children we'll have someday, do you think I'm suited for anything else?"

The cook turned, one fist on her plump hip. "You're a whiz with figures. You shouldn't waste that gift. While Otto's out working, you could take care of the books."

"Because I have natural abilities in that area?"

Mrs. Langford shrugged. "Why else would I say that?"

"As I see it, Mrs. Lankford, Faith has inherited your passion for cooking."

She scowled at her. "Your point is?"

She recounted her meeting with the Emersons. "They believe everyone has a natural bent. *Tenor* is the word they used ... from the Bible."

Mrs. Lankford grunted and pushed her way past Geneva to the dining room.

Faith came around the corner and hugged her. "I heard you, Neva. Thanks. Think Mom will ever change her mind about letting me go to culinary school?"

"Maybe ... if you get a scholarship. I can help you fill out the applications."

"Why have you always believed in me, Neva?"

"How could I not? In high school English, your essays were always about food and entertaining. In math class, you were the first one to figure weights and measures. And when we got to world history, all you wanted to know is what the people ate and how to make it."

Faith laughed. "I can't take all the credit. You're the one who convinced me those boring subjects could actually be 'tools of my trade.'"

"I'm sure your mother will come around. In the meantime, you need to get yourself some business cards. More than a few of the guests at our wedding asked who catered the reception."

Faith's eyes grew wide. "They did?"

"Even Mrs. Eversall. And her family's been in the restaurant business in Augusta for years."

She nodded. "So that's why her son Gustav was snooping around the kitchen."

Geneva shook her head. "Gustav had more on his mind than food."

"What do you mean?"

She nudged her friend. "*You*, silly. He wasn't more than ten feet from you the whole afternoon."

In their early years of marriage, Geneva and Otto began every day chatting over breakfast, mostly about the work that lay ahead of them. She might have felt selfish for enjoying her position with Mr. Emerson so much if her husband hadn't felt the same way about his work.

After some basic cooking lessons from Faith, she managed to prepare a tasty supper each evening. Thankfully, she was married to a man who appreciated simple meals *and* leftovers. If she ever apologized, he'd say, "This meal was delicious the first time we ate it. No reason to believe it won't be delicious now."

They had most of their weekends together, often working side by side in the garden. What she hadn't learned about growing vegetables from her mama, she learned from her husband. Wasn't too long before their garden increased to a commercial size, and Otto had secured the business of the county restauranteurs.

Geneva did the accounting and applied the basic principles of financial management and investment she learned from Mr. Emerson himself and his extensive library of books on the subject.

One of her employer's favorite axioms was: "Put your money where your mouth is." If he believed in a company or cause, he would invest financially in that entity. Geneva discovered a word that described him well: *intuitive*. He had a knack for investing in winners. After seeing his success, she began to follow his example, although on a much smaller scale.

So, in 1981, when Mr. Emerson bought three hundred shares of the new home improvement retailer, Home Depot, she bought five. Later, when he bought five hundred shares of a little-known technology company called Apple, she put aside money each week until she could buy ten. As those companies grew, she bought more of their stock.

When they invested in Berkshire Hathaway, Mr. Emerson said, "You keep plugging away, Geneva. I believe this Warren Buffett fellow has some solid ideas."

If her mentor had only been interested in amassing money, she may not have been as passionate. However, Mr. Emerson invested to gain funds which he in turn poured into his local community.

"There are laws in the kingdom of God," he explained. "The law of reciprocity is based on the biblical principle of 'Give and it will be given unto you.' The law of use is about using what we have been given for the good of others. The law of responsibility teaches us how to be wise in all we do."

Geneva figuratively sat at his feet and marveled at the possibilities awaiting her. The day she realized she didn't have to wait until she had accumulated a large sum of money before she could invest in the lives of others was the same day she saw the need in those around her. A classmate of Eliza Emerson's with no funds to buy a prom dress. Mrs. Lankford's car in need of new brakes. Faith's tuition balance.

The most difficult part of investing in the lives of others was maintaining her anonymity.

CHAPTER TWENTY-FIVE

CARLEY: PRESENT DAY

"Vern, Carley here. Could you please pick up some whipping cream on your way over this afternoon?

"Sorry, I've got plans this evening."

"Again? This makes three days in a row. Have we offended you?"

His chuckle sounded more sad than amused. "No, but I feel I may be wearing out my welcome."

Now I know something's up.

"Why would you think that?" Of course, Carley guessed why—her aunt's coolness since the night of the incident with Skip. "Miss Neva's starting to think you don't like us anymore." Not that her aunt had said that, but she could have ... maybe.

"Then Neva doesn't know me at all. The way I see it, actions speak louder than words. I'll catch you later, Carley."

Yikes. That was it. Anyone with a speck of intuition could tell how Vern felt about Miss Neva by the way he studied her. As for her aunt, Carley was convinced the woman was in denial. But why?

Her aunt came around the corner. "Did you get ahold of Vern?"

"Yes, but he's got stuff to do tonight." Carley watched her face for a reaction. None whatsoever.

"Maybe T-bone can pick up the cream instead."

Really? Is cream all you care about? "I'll ask him. Back to Vern—"

Miss Neva cut in, "We haven't had Dubber and Warren to supper since you arrived. They're in the barn fiddling with mowers. Maybe they'd like to join us."

"We have plenty." Carley plowed ahead. "Now about Vern—"

Her aunt sped toward the back door as if she hadn't heard her. "Let me catch them before they take off."

Carley crossed her arms and sighed. In the past few days, she'd been stymied every time she attempted to broach the subject of a possible romantic connection between her aunt and Vern. On Wednesday, Miss Neva had had a headache. Thursday, she'd worked in the library until bedtime. Now she was shielding herself from Carley's questions behind dinner guests.

Coincidence? I think not. Or is this you, Lord, trying to tell me to mind my own business?

When T-bone arrived, Carley greeted him at the door, her arm making a sweeping arc across the entry. "How kind of you to join us for our evening repast, Mr. Stakes."

"Tis not kindness that draws me nigh, but the pleasure of your company." He bowed and handed her the pint of whipping cream.

She chuckled. "Thanks. Been reading Shakespeare, have you?"

"Oh m'lady, I doth not have the time for the bard, having to pumpeth the gas and all."

"You're crazy."

"I am." T-bone followed her to the kitchen, motioning to the table set for five. "Vern's coming?"

"Nope. And don't bring up his name either. Miss Neva invited Dubber and Warren instead."

"I'm not the one who wants to interfere."

"Well, if it makes you feel any smugger, I've had a change of heart on that matter."

"How so?"

She sighed. "I think God wants me to back off."

He flashed a grin. "Did he tell you that in so many words?"

"No, but I've been bumping into brick walls and slammed doors for the past three days." She handed him an empty platter. "The London broil's in the warming oven. Make yourself useful."

Miss Neva entered the back door. "How long before dinner's ready? These two men have earned themselves a hearty meal."

Dubber and Warren clomped in behind her, grease and oil smeared on their hands and faces.

"I can see that." Carley noted their appearance again. "Dinner will be on the table by the time you two finish washing up."

Once they were seated, T-bone leaned over to cut Miss Neva's steak.

Her aunt shook her napkin out. "A few more weeks and this cast will be off! Good thing, too, because my patience is wearing thin."

"Wearing thin? Near invisible if you ask me." T-bone managed to keep a straight face.

She raised a single brow. "No one asked you, Mr. Smarty-pants."

Warren stabbed a bunch of green beans with his fork. "You know, Dubber an' me are having a bit of trouble with patience ourselves. This year's Olde Home Days can't get here soon enough."

"Meantime, we've got plenty to do to get ready," Dubber added. "Miss G, what do you think about me and Warren bringing our entry tractor over to T-bone's garage?"

"That's fine with me, if it's okay with him."

T-bone scooped some potato salad. "Makes sense. I've got the tools and the room."

"We'll trade ya," Warren said. "You help us, and we'll let you be part of our pit crew on race day."

Nice try, guys. You don't really expect him to fall for that deal, do you?

T-bone said, "Well, who could pass up an offer like that?"

She studied him. *He really is one of the good guys, isn't he?*

Warren bounced his fist on the table. "This year we'll show 'em how a lawn tractor race is won, won't we, bro?"

"Or die tryin'," Dubber said. "Thanks to Miss G, we got us a real chance."

For a long twenty minutes, the three men prated about the race. They dissected their competitors' racing styles and choice of machines and discussed turn radiuses, fuel consumption, and boosting RPMs. The brothers decided on a name for their entry—The Lawn Ranger.

After a while, Miss Neva changed tracks. "I'm glad the committee decided to bring back the old favorites, like the frying pan toss and pie eating contest."

"Yeah, people love that sort of stuff," T-bone said.

Carley nudged her aunt's foot under the table. "Miss Neva, didn't you tell me they were adding some new categories to the writing competition?" She glanced at T-bone to see if he'd heard her.

"What do you mean?" He took his last bite of steak.

Her aunt rested her fork on her plate. "Since not everyone is a poet like you, they added essays, short stories, and the like to be fair. Mark my words, they'd get more entries for a cherry pit spittin' contest."

T-bone stopped chewing. "Why do you say that?"

"How many writers do *you* know in Andover?" Her aunt sputtered. "I mean, there's that weekly writers' group that meets at the Liar's Table, but no one cares enough to mentor those dabblers."

"Don't be so sure." T-bone leaned forward. "What night do they meet?"

"Not sure. Maybe Monday," Miss Neva she said. "Around seven, I heard."

T-bone helped himself to another slice of London broil. "I bet we could steer them in the right direction."

"*We*? I know numbers, not words. Go ahead and help if you want, I've got enough on my plate and only one hand to manage it."

Carley averted her eyes and smiled to herself. *Miss Neva is good, very good.*

Before dessert could be served, Dubber and Warren got a call from a neighbor wanting to get rid of an old Evinrude motor—a chance they couldn't pass up.

Her aunt sent them off with a container of cobbler with strict orders. "Remember, this is part of tonight's dinner. No need to send over another bucket of fertilizer."

T-bone offered to help Carley clean up so Miss Neva could finish some paperwork in her library.

Carley glanced over her shoulder to make sure they were alone. "Did you notice how Vern's name didn't come up once during dinner?"

He brought the dessert bowls to the sink. "I thought you said you weren't going to get involved?"

"I'm making an observation, that's all." She filled the sink and added detergent. "So, do you think you'll meet with the writers' group?"

He smirked. "That's what Miss Neva intended, isn't it?"

"Not much gets by you, does it?"

"Only when I want it to." He pulled a dish towel out of a drawer. "I'm no Hemingway, so I'm not sure what I can offer them. Sometimes getting together with folks of like interest can be fun."

"Have you ever been published yourself?" *What made me ask that?*

He stalled. "Well, I guess it depends on what you mean by *published*. After winning a few contests, some of my poems and shorts got published in a few obscure magazines as part of the prize."

"What was the other part of the prize?"

"A certificate or, if you hit the big time, a fancy plaque." He paused a few moments. "About six months ago, I self-published an anthology of my memoirs under a pen name—Adam Thomas. Thomas is my middle name."

Carley straightened. "I can't believe my aunt didn't mention that."

"She can't mention something she doesn't know."

Carley was incredulous. "If Miss Neva doesn't know, who does?"

He sighed. "Me and the ten other people who bought the book."

"Ten?" She sighed. "What marketing did you do?"

"I put it on Amazon." He shrugged. "Figured they'd handle the rest."

She put her hands on her hips. "You know, there are people who can help you with marketing."

"Maybe so, but I don't know any of them."

She finished putting away the dishes. "Have you ever thought of writing as a career?"

"I already have three jobs. From what I hear, if I become a writer, I'll have to get myself a fourth to pay my writing expenses."

She chuckled. "Do you have any copies of your book? I'd love to read it."

"Only my copy." He smirked. "But you can buy one on Amazon. That'd make an even dozen."

"I might just do that, wise guy."

"One more thing, let's keep Adam Thomas and his anthology between the two of us for now, okay?"

"Mind my asking why?"

"I've got a few brutal memoirs in the collection. My dad was a mean drunk with a penchant for using his fists. Miss Neva knew he was tough on me, but I don't want her to know *how* tough."

Yet another secret to keep? "I promise."

Later, Carley typed in "Adam Thomas + memoir" into her search engine. Once she found T-bone's anthology, she downloaded the e-book and ordered a print copy. About to close out, a link to a literary magazine caught her attention. The heading read, "Adam Thomas Crushes Essay Contest." T-bone had taken first place for his submission entitled "Orange Crush for the Strawberry Blonde." She was bummed when she couldn't find a link to read the essay.

More importantly, who was this mysterious strawberry blonde?

CHAPTER TWENTY-SIX

HARRISON: PRESENT DAY

Harrison sequestered himself in his office after seeing his last patient of the day. Every time someone knocked on his door, he imagined Carley entering. He missed seeing her earnest, albeit naïve, expression when she discussed each day's cases.

Another knock.

He shook off his thoughts. "Come in."

Roxanne entered. "Doctor, may I speak with you about something?"

"What's on your mind?"

She sat on the edge of the chair across from his desk. "Is there something going on I should know about as office administrator? Seems like ever since Carley left, the vibe has been weird. And finding that bug in the breakroom didn't help."

He sighed. "I'm not sure what you mean by 'weird,' but we believe that listening device was an isolated incident involving members of the maintenance company we have under contract. They've handled the matter to our satisfaction."

"Are you sure that's all? Carley left so quickly, and I feel like there might—"

He cut her off. "She left because of her father's illness. Speaking of her, has she contacted you again?"

"Nothing in the mail since her last letter."

Truth is, as the weeks passed, Harrison's concern had grown as well. But concern for what? That she would *not* return? That he thought about her too much? That she would come back and find out what he had done?

He was a few steps away from his car when he realized he'd left his phone in his desk drawer. The staff had gone for the day, so he had to use the security code to reenter. Halfway down the carpeted hall, he slowed. His door was ajar.

That's strange.

He froze when he heard his partners talking.

Peter's voice had an edge. "How much longer before we put an end to this?"

"Don't get your boxers in a twist," Bryce shot back. "This is Boy Scout Nichols we're talking about. We don't know anything for sure."

What do they know exactly?

Peter again. "Hurry! Stick the bug under his desk so we can get out of here."

"Yeah, sure." Bryce grunted. "Like we did in the breakroom so the maintenance man could find it? No, we can do better than that."

Harrison didn't need to hear anymore. Peter and Bryce might not know much of anything, but he did—like how to use that bug to his advantage. He tiptoed down the hall and out the door.

The next morning, he only needed a few minutes to find the bug on a plant stand near his desk. He even moved the stand closer for better reception, and then called his extension from his cell phone.

"Dr. Nichols speaking." ... "Yes, yes, Dr. Milton. Of course, I remember you. We met at the recent conference in LA. You're in New York, correct?" … "My partners? We've known each other since medical school." … "What? Of course, I trust them. I wouldn't have joined the practice if I didn't." … "No, they invited me to come on board a year later." … "I can assure you those rumors are unfounded. Drs. Reinhart and Stryker are above reproach and have my highest professional respect."

There. How about that for a little junk psychology?

Four days later, tired of monitoring his every word in his own office, Harrison made sure Peter and Bryce saw him carry the plant down the hall.

Pete called to him. "Hey! What are you doing with that?"

He held the pot away from his body. "Throwing it out."

Bryce, "Um … didn't you say you liked plants because they absorb toxins and produce oxygen?"

"They do." He frowned. "But this one is infested with bugs."

He could almost feel their eyes on the back of his head as he chuckled to himself.

Chapter Twenty-Seven

GENEVA: FOUR YEARS AND EIGHT MONTHS EARLIER

Geneva tried one last time. "Otto, please change your mind and come skiing with us. Norm can handle the tree farm for one weekend. You deserve some time off."

He pushed back from the breakfast table. "If I got what I deserved I might be dead by now."

She ignored his morbid attempt at humor. "This is supposed to be a couples' weekend with Faith and Gus and Frank and Linda. Faith's celebrating her return to skiing since her mastectomy. Please, Otto, I don't want to be a fifth wheel."

"Neva, it's four weeks 'til Christmas, the busiest time of the year. I'm needed." He put on his jacket."

When Otto made up his mind, nothing she said could sway him. "Is it wrong that I was hoping to spend the weekend with my husband?"

"Maybe next time." He gave her a peck on the cheek and started for the back door.

She spotted his flip phone on the counter. "Don't forget your phone. And please remember to turn it on this time."

He stuck the phone in his jacket pocket. "Will do."

Geneva plodded back into the kitchen to wash the breakfast dishes. "You can be such a kill-joy, Otto Kellerman, stuck in your fuddy-duddy ways!"

She sighed. *Maybe I should stay home. ... Nope. ... Not this time.*

Vern called a while later. "Gus invited me to go skiing this weekend. Is Otto going too?"

"What do you think?"

"Well, Gus said Faith reserved two rooms at Sunday River's Grand Summit Hotel. One room for the ladies, one for the guys."

"Was everyone that certain Otto wouldn't come?"

He chuckled. "Pretty much. Let me see. Christmas is a month away and they need him at the tree farm."

Plain maddening how predictable my husband can be!

On Saturday morning, the six of them piled into Faith's minivan for the eleven-mile trip to Sunday River Ski Resort in Newry, where more than forty years ago Geneva had learned to ski with the Emerson children. Sunday River's varied terrains and fairytale glades were some of her favorites.

Gus was at the wheel. "Faith, tell me again why we're paying for a room when we don't live that far away?"

"I haven't been skiing for two whole years. Are you trying to cheap out on me? You know darn well what would happen if we went back home. You'd get called out to check someone's furnace, and I'd end up back at the restaurant prepping for the week."

He shrugged. "You're probably right."

Faith untwisted her seatbelt. "No *probably* about it, Buster."

"I have to say, Gus, I agree with your wife," Frank said. "If we go back to our place tonight, Linda will pull out her to-do list."

Linda tapped her handbag. "Actually, I carry the list with me in case I need to add another to-do."

Frank groaned. "After all these years, I still have to remind my wife that the reason we bought the cabin is to relax and enjoy everything this area of New England has to offer."

Geneva gripped her pocketbook on her lap. *Relax and enjoy? Did you hear that, Otto?*

Vern pointed out the snow-capped peaks and white trails off in the distance. "Sunday River's got some of the best snowmaking capabilities in the region. Of course, I doubt they will have to prove it after the snow we got the last two days and the eight to ten inches predicted for tonight. Great skiing, either way."

"Tubing is more my speed," Linda said. "That way I won't slow down my husband."

Otto, see how Linda came on this trip for Frank even though she doesn't like to ski?

Linda bubbled from the back seat. "Last spring, Frankie and I took the lift to North Peak to hike the trails. Amazing views. Lots of wildlife too."

"Wildlife? Huh!" Gus teased, "Frank's idea of wildlife is birdies and eagles on the golf course."

"I don't deny it." Frank sighed. "Now if I could only turn my bogeys into birdies ..."

Linda sighed. "Of course, since you guys live up here year-round, you can do fun stuff every weekend."

Geneva crossed her arms, her whole body tensed. *Oh, yeah, Otto, we do "fun stuff" too—like pulling weeds in the garden, spraying trees for bugs, and fertilizing blueberry bushes.*

Vern scolded her with one of his looks and said under his breath, "What is your problem?"

She gave him one of *her* looks back. "*I* don't have a problem." She wished he weren't as adept at reading her face.

They checked into the hotel and changed into their ski gear. While the others took a less challenging course, she and Vern decided on Aurora Peak. No matter how you liked your terrain, Aurora had it all.

They hopped off the lift at the summit. Geneva told Vern to go on without her. "I'll catch up in a few minutes."

He sped off, calling over his shoulder. "Don't be too sure about that!"

She pushed her goggles up. A vast blue sky hung over the eight majestic peaks. Multiple stands of huge pines stood tall in the snow-covered ground. The scene humbled Geneva to tears. "Lord, you are a mighty God, *my* God. I feel as if you created this magnificent setting just for me."

A quiet voice spoke to her spirit. *As I have created gardens and tree farms for Otto?*

She recalled the last time Otto had joined them on a ski weekend—over three years ago. Neither of them had had a great time. When she'd asked him why he thought that was, he'd replied with a question, "Tell me, do you enjoy doing things you're not good at?"

She bowed her head. "Oh, Lord, my attitude has been stinky, hasn't it? Help me to be the wife Otto needs." She drew in a breath of fresh air, then started down. With a clearer head and a lighter heart, she picked up speed. The snow glistened in the sunny thirty-degree temperature. The brightness and clarity of the day made it easy for her to see the bumps and changes in the gradients well before she reached them.

Otto was right when he'd said Vern was the only one in their group who could keep up with her. Nevertheless, she breezed past Vern about twenty yards before the base.

He skied up alongside her. "Full disclosure, Neva, I took pity on you."

She laughed. "So that's the story you're sticking to?"

Since they had skied through lunch hour, Geneva was spent and hungry when she returned to the hotel room. Her call to Otto went directly to voice mail. After a quick shower, she tried him again. Still no answer.

As she entered the dining room to join the others, Faith called out. "Here comes our ski bum! The other one's not far behind her. I told you we wouldn't see them until dusk."

She pulled a chair out. "I hope we didn't hold you up."

"Not at all," Linda moved over to make room for her. "We weren't in a hurry to order since we ate earlier .... after we did a little shopping."

Vern sat across the table from her. "Get ahold of your hardworking husband?"

She shook her head and sighed. "He probably forgot to turn his phone on again."

"What can I say?" Vern shrugged. "He's a guy. Sometimes we're dumb."

Faith raised her glass. "Ladies, who are we to disagree?"

Gus asked the server for more rolls. "Tell us, Vern, did you keep up with Neva on the slopes?"

He snorted. "You'd think someone who'd been skiing these mountains his whole life would be able to outski a transplant from Kentucky, but no-o." He scowled at Neva. "I'm not giving up yet."

Faith said, "Those daily workouts of yours didn't help, huh?"

Vern laughed. "Apparently, martial arts don't translate to downhill speed."

"I've got way more speed," Frank blurted.

"Really?" Vern didn't hide his surprise well.

Frank grinned. "Yeah, *golf* is way more my speed."

Frank's penchant for humor and Gus and Faith's comical bantering helped lighten Geneva's mood. Wiped out from the fresh air, exercise, and full meal, they were all back in their rooms by nine.

Before turning in, she tried to reach Otto on their home phone with no success.

Where on earth is that man? He never ignores my calls ... but he has been known to sleep through the ringing.

The group had another full day on the slopes on Sunday. Geneva and Vern managed to ski three more of the eight peaks. Like the resort brochure promised, they "went steep and deep on White Cap," "nosed their way through the wooded trails on Oz," and "skied big and bold on Jordan."

Best ski weekend ever! One she would never forget.

When Geneva got home around six thirty, Otto's truck wasn't in the yard or the garage. The Christmas tree stand closed at five on Sundays, and Rumford was less than a half hour away.

Her jaw tightened. *Mercy, Otto, didn't you even miss me a little?*

She unpacked and got her clothes in the washer. Around seven-thirty she called Otto's cell again and the tree farm office. No answer at either. She punched in Norm Fournier's number.

He answered, "Hello."

"Norm, is Otto with you?"

"No, Miss Geneva. I've been in Boston since last evening. My boy got himself in a jam, so Otto told me to go. Said he'd close up and handle things on his own today."

She paced around the house as her irritation spun up into worry.

"Vern, it's me." She told him what she knew and what Norm had said. "The stand closed almost three hours ago. Otto's never been this late without letting me know. Do you know anyone who lives in that area who could take a ride by?"

"I'll pick you up." His voice sounded calm. "We can scold him together when we find him."

They reached Bountiful Acres Tree Farm around eight-thirty. But for the two streetlights a quarter mile apart, the tree lot and office were in darkness.

Her nerves began to unravel. "Drive around behind the office. That's where he parks."

The truck was there.

Vern got out. "Hand me the flashlight in my glove box. You stay here. I'll make a quick round of the area."

"No, I'm going with you." Otto's truck was unlocked. She found his camping lantern behind the driver's seat. "Let's go."

They checked inside and around the outbuildings. *Nothing.* They searched the cordoned off trees for sale in the lot. *Nothing.* They flashed their lights on the acres of live trees before them.

"Stay with me. I don't want you getting lost too." He tried to chuckle but failed.

Up and down, right to left, they walked through rows and rows of trees. They took turns calling out, "Otto! Otto! You here?"

Silence.

Vern voiced what Geneva had been thinking. "We need help. There's no way the two of us can cover this much acreage in below freezing temps. We'll freeze to—"

To death?

She shivered. "Call the sheriff, but let's keep going."

A few rows later, Geneva's lantern captured a patch of white on a tall Balsam Fir. She edged closer. Tied to one of the branches, a large tag read: "SOLD! For my Neva."

Oh, Otto.

Without thinking, she leaned over to take in the Balsam's comforting fragrance. Her foot hit a lump in the snow. She closed her eyes and shuddered.

No, God! Please, no, no!

Her voice quaked. "Ve-rn."

He wrapped his arm tight around her. Trembling, they stooped down together.

Otto lay dead under a blanket of snow at the base of the Christmas tree he'd tagged for her.

She removed her glove to brush the snow from her husband's peace-filled face. Clinging to Vern, she sunk to the ground and wept.

"Otto, my friend," Vern choked out. "What will we do without you?"

Five days later, Geneva buried Otto in the family plot, alongside the graves of the three children she had miscarried.

Chapter Twenty-Eight

Carley: Present Day

Carley made her weekly call to Roxy that evening. She heard Hunter in the background. "Aw, let me say hi to him."

Roxy snorted. "I think you'd rather talk to him than me."

"What can I say? Having adult conversation is nice for a change."

"Very funny. Hunter, do you want to talk to Auntie Carley?"

She heard the pitter patter of his bare feet across their wood floor.

Excitement in his voice, he asked, "Can you come over and see my new firetruck?"

Her heart ached. "Oh, honey, I'm too far away to visit, but I'll see it soon, okay?" She hated lying to him, so she switched subjects. "What else have you been doing?"

"Mommy and Daddy took me to a new lady doctor. She's nice. She gave me stickers."

"I love stickers! You're one lucky boy."

"Uh-uhn. Mommy says I'm blessed, not lucky."

"You have a smart mommy." Carley heard muttering in the background and had a good idea why. Roxy didn't think her nephew was blessed. She thought he'd been robbed of a healthy life.

Roxy got back on the line. "How long can you disappoint that little boy? You need to come home."

"I wish I—"

"Wish nothing! You've been gone for weeks. What's taking you so long, and what's such a big secret you can't share it with me?"

Carley was tempted but she knew Roxy. A champion of causes, with no fear or filter. She'd heard her rants about her sister's case against the doctor who'd supposedly botched Hunter's premature delivery. She'd even convinced her sister he was the cause of the child's cerebral palsy. If she got a hint of the fraud at the practice, she'd either march in and confront all three doctors or start snooping on her own.

She bluffed, "Friend or not, if you keep pressuring me, I won't call you anymore."

Silence, then Roxy said, "You mean it, don't you?"

"Yes, I do."

"Let me ask you this, how long do you expect Key State Medical to hold your position open?"

"I don't know." Carley sighed. "I'll get back to you in a day or two with my next step."

"Next step? What on earth is going on?"

"Bye, Rox."

Roxy's sigh sounded like surrender. "Bye."

Carley climbed into bed, exhausted after the challenging call with her friend. When sleep eluded her, she decided to read. T-bone's memoir came to mind. She grabbed her tablet and began reading.

The Flat Tire

On a moonless night, under a cold drizzle, I struggled to remove the lug nuts from the rear wheel of our rusty pickup.

Clarice G. James

From the driver's seat, my father (whom everyone called Del, including me) shouted over the rat-a-tat of the rain. "Your mother liked to brag about you bein' so smart. 'Adam this, Adam that.' But here ya're, too weak to change a tire. When I was your age ... nine years old, ain't you? ..."

He slurred his words like he always did when he drank too much whiskey.

"Yeah, sh-always thought you an' her wassh bettererin me. Then she up an' died before you was seven. How ssmart was-at?"

If I cried, Del would make fun of me, or worse, belt me one like he often did. No, I learned to save my crying for when I was alone, under the covers, on my cot at night.

Del's murmuring had an edge. "I never woulda married ssuch a snooty broad if she hadn't been so dumb as to get herself knocked up."

I'd heard him use the words "knocked up" before. Back then, I didn't know what they meant. And I never asked because I didn't want to know.

Once all six lug nuts were off, I pulled at the wet tire. My hands slipped, and I fell backward, landing hard in a cold, dirty puddle.

Cackling as he climbed out of the truck, he stumbled toward me and yanked my shirt collar. "Useless kid! Get up! I said, get up!" He wobbled and swayed, then fell face-first into the road.

Panicking, I struggled to pull him off to the side. If anything happened to Del, it would be my fault for not changing the flat as fast as I should have.

The third car I waved down came to a stop. I recognized the driver—Mr. Otto Kellerman. He and his wife Miss Geneva had a big house up the road from where my father and I lived. Once, they'd taken me to the emergency room when I needed stitches in my head.

Miss Geneva sat in the front seat of the car. The look on her face reminded me of my mother's face when my father got mad.

Mr. Otto got out and knelt in the road by my father.

Too late to stop him now. His pants must be sopping wet.

"Hey, son, can you tell me what happened here?"

Even Del never called me son. "My father fell. I tried to move him, but I'm not strong enough."

"That's okay. Always best to examine someone before you move them. The EMTs will take him to the hospital and make sure he didn't hurt his head too badly."

Having grown-ups here to help me felt good. I prayed Del wouldn't come to and start yelling at them.

"I suspect your father's a little under the weather." Mr. Otto stood. "Speaking of weather, Adam, why don't you climb into the car with Miss Geneva until we decide what to do next."

I obeyed because I always obeyed. Besides, Del was still out cold and couldn't tell me any different.

Mr. Otto leaned in and asked me, "Do you have family around here? Grandparents or aunts and uncles? Or maybe close friends?"

I shook my head. "No, sir. I have a sister, but she lives with our cousins up north."

Truth is my sister had run away from home the year before because, as she put it, "If I stay, I might do something that'll get me sent to jail." She promised to come back for me when she turned eighteen. As for friends? Del didn't like people enough to make any—or let me have any either.

"Don't you worry, son, we'll figure something out."

Before the EMT closed the ambulance doors, my father mumbled something.

Mr. Otto walked over to him. "Del, about your boy. Do you want me to call someone to stay with him until you get home?"

"We don't need nobody. Never have." He growled. "'Sides, shomeone's gotta stay with the truck."

"No, sir." Mr. Otto shook his head. "The way I see it, you've got two choices. You can give me permission to care for him until you're released from the hospital, or I can call the sheriff."

Good thing Del was strapped in or he might've swung at Mr. Otto.

"Take 'im then, but I want him home shoon as I get out. He's got chores to do."

The brief time I spent with Mr. Otto and Miss Geneva was the best time I'd had since my mother took me to the book fair at Bethel Public Library before she got sick.

Their house felt like a *home,* not like the two cramped rooms where I lived with my father. The closest thing I'd ever had to a *real* home had disappeared when my mother died.

Mr. Otto showed me around his barn and gardens. I even helped him pick carrots, radishes, and cucumbers. When he explained about plant food and fertilizer, I wondered if there was something you could feed a person to make them stop being mean. I was afraid to ask. What if the answer was no?

The Kellermans' kitchen had a stove with *four* working burners and a refrigerator three times the size of the one Del had bought at a yard sale. Theirs was stuffed full of food. That night, they had everything on hand to make supper *and* dessert.

Just like the families on TV, Miss Geneva ordered both her husband and me to wash our hands before we sat at the table.

Mr. Otto said a quick prayer before he took a roll and passed the basket to me.

The rolls were warm. I put one on the little plate next to the big plate like Mr. Otto.

He smeared butter over one half, then the other. "So, what does a boy your age do for fun these days?"

Fun? I wasn't sure how to answer. "I sorta like school. My favorite subject is reading."

"Reading, huh? Know what you want to be when you grow up?" He took a bite.

I buttered my roll, trying to think. "Del says I'll be working for him."

Mr. Otto asked, "Now, what does your father do again?"

"He's a handyman." I repeated what Del always said. "He's his own boss because he doesn't like people telling him what to do." I skipped the part about him saying, "Most people are too stupid to work for anyway."

Miss Geneva's face lit up. "You know, reading was one of my favorite subjects too. What types of books do you enjoy?"

Knowing I had something in common with someone as kind as Miss Geneva made me feel good—and smart. "Books about animals and boats and famous people. I get them from the school library."

She spooned mashed potatoes out on my plate. "You are blessed. When I was a little girl in Kentucky, our school didn't have a library."

I wanted to make her feel better. "Anyway, Del says reading is a big waste of time."

Sometimes, people looked at me funny when I shared my father's ideas or repeated what he said. Sorta like Mr. Otto and Miss Geneva did that night. In a weird way, their reaction made me feel better because Del's words didn't always sound right to me either.

After a helping of Miss Geneva's apple crisp, the three of us cleaned up the kitchen. Once we were finished, they asked if I wanted to play a board game with them.

They want to play with me?

"Um, sure, but I don't know how."

She chose a game called Operation. "This one is fun. The rules are easy. You'll see."

I'd seen pictures of the game in store sale flyers, but I'd never played before.

Mr. Otto and Miss Geneva were good at "operating," but I was better. Near the end of our hour of fun and laughter—something I never experienced at home—I suspected they might be letting me win.

Do they care about me that much?

A twinge of guilt broke through about Del being alone in the hospital. "Mr. Otto, do you think they'll operate on my father?"

"No, I think he needs to rest up a bit, that's all."

I had a real bed in a room to myself that night. The sheets smelled like the spring woods not like the oily insides of an old toolbox.

After a breakfast of sausage and blueberry pancakes the next morning, Mr. Otto drove me to where we left my father's truck so we could finish changing the tire.

I was embarrassed but mostly relieved when Mr. Otto was the one to discover the spare was flat too. If that had been Del, I would've gotten a whack.

"I know a couple of brothers who've got a yard of goods out past the landfill. They might be able to hook us up with a couple of used tires." When we got to their place, Mr. Otto said, "Let me do the talking, son."

When Mr. Otto said "yard" he meant junk. Old car parts, steel grates, broken furniture, scrap lumber, you name it.

Two men approached us. "Hey, Mr. Otto! What brings you out our way?"

"Dubber, Warren, pleasure to see you. Heard you were growing your business so fast you could use some labor around here to organize and catalog and what not. I bumped into this young man—Adam is his name. He might be just the person you need. Has handyman experience already."

"Is that so?" Dubber rocked back and forth on his heels. "Let the boy take a gander at our stock. We might could work something out."

Mr. Otto shrugged. "I'm not sure the boy needs anything in trade, but you never know when a deal can be made."

A deal? I had no idea what was going on, but I trusted Mr. Otto.

We meandered through various piles of stuff until I spotted tires covered by a big blue tarp. "Mr. Otto, look!"

"Keep walkin', son. We don't want to show our hand."

Show our hand? What did hands have to do with tires?

Mr. Otto walked back over to the brothers. "Nothing jumps out at us." He put his hands in his pockets. "Although Adam here works on cars, too, so he might be able to get rid of a few car parts or used Goodyears for you."

"We got plenty o' those. The parts need some degreasing, but we got some decent tires under the tarp over there— not a baloney skin in the bunch."

Who said anything about baloney?

I still don't know what happened or how, but by the time we left, I owed Dubber and Warren four hours of labor. They owed Mr. Otto two loads of loam, and he owed them the use of his lawn tractor for two full days. I promised to weed Mr. Otto's garden whenever I could get over to his place. And we left with four good used tires in the back of his truck.

We replaced the old tires with the not-as-old tires. Then Mr. Otto drove my father's truck to the hospital with me beside him. Miss Geneva followed in her car. They walked me to the hallway outside his room.

She whispered to me. "You come by and visit any time. There's always room for one more at our table."

Mr. Otto mussed my hair. "Mark my words, I'm gonna beat you at Operation next time!"

They hugged me good-bye. I'd forgotten how nice hugs felt.

I entered the room and found my father dressed, sitting in a chair. "Hey, Del, feeling better?"

"Better? What kinda son sends his own father off to the hospital when there's nothin' wrong with him? I'll tell you what kind. A do-nothing loser. That's what you are!"

I wanted to tell my father I was sorry, but that would've been a lie. "Here are the keys. Truck's outside. All four tires 're fixed."

"Better be."

I never mentioned anything to Del about my time with the Kellermans. I knew if he felt the least bit threatened by their kindness, he'd never let me see them again.

Carley wiped at her tears. What kind of man would treat his son like that? How did T-bone overcome such abuse and become the person he was today? She knew part of the answer: Mr. Otto and Miss Geneva.

By comparison, there was Dr. Nichols. Raised by loving parents in a decent home and given a good education with a promising future. What made this man so unsatisfied he would turn to greed?

CHAPTER TWENTY-NINE

CARLEY: PRESENT DAY

Monday morning, Carley steeled herself for a throw-down conversation with her lawyer. She was determined to get information out of this fee chaser—even if she had to resort to threats.

"Mr. Yeager, Carley Jantzen here."

"Ms. Jantzen, how are you?"

"Frustrated. Angry. Disappointed. Impatient. Fed-up. I could go on if you need more adjectives."

"No, no, that'll do. I really can't—"

"Please stop, Mr. Yeager. I don't want to hear what you *can't* do. I want to hear what you *can* do. Spill! What's holding up this case?"

Her aunt entered the room but retreated when she saw Carley on the phone.

Carley waved her over, then covered the mouthpiece and whispered, "My lawyer."

Miss Neva joined her at the table, and Carley put the phone on speaker.

"Ms. Jantzen, I can only tell you what the Medicare fraud team has told me."

"What have they told you besides the case has grown in size and may involve more than one person? What are my options at this point?"

"Options? What do you mean?"

She bluffed. "I'm starting to wonder if this whole whistleblowing thing was a big mistake. I'd rather have my job back."

Her aunt grinned and gave her a thumbs-up.

"But … you can't, I mean at this point—"

"Last time I checked, the United States was still a free country. I can do whatever I please."

Words gushed out of his mouth. "Now, now, settle down, Carley. Don't get ahead of yourself."

She pictured greedy beads of perspiration on his forehead. "The way I see it, I'm not *ahead* of myself or anyone else—least of all those who are still perpetrating the fraud. The longer the government waits to arrest the guilty party or parties, the longer they'll have to build up their offshore bank accounts and the longer my life is in limbo. I've reached my limit. Pass that word along to those who *can* do something before I pass my story on to the press!"

Miss Neva gave her two thumbs-up for her threat, idle though it may be.

His voice quavered. "The press? No. Wait!"

Her aunt scribbled something, then pushed the note toward her.

Carley read the note and stifled a giggle. "I've been speaking with another attorney. Beckham is his name. A fresh set of eyes might see what needs to be done to move things along."

"Now, now, let's not act hastily. Changing attorneys this late in the game will only complicate matters. Please, I promise, I'll have some news for you in a week."

"You've got three days, Mr. Yeager." She hung up, then high fived her aunt. "Me talking to a new lawyer scared him more than me going to the press."

"I'm pretty sure he got your message." She tapped her fingers on the table. "If he doesn't have an answer for you in three days, what's your next step?"

She sighed. "I guess I should have thought that through before I threatened him."

"Don't worry." Her aunt gentled her. "You're doing the right thing, dear."

"I doubt I'll have a job in the end." She sank down in her seat. "I'm tired of this whole mess. Blowing the whistle on people you've worked with and care about isn't easy. Many of them could lose their jobs. And what will happen to our patients?"

"I can only imagine how difficult this has been on you."

"In the meantime, I'll send another letter from La Paz, asking for an extended leave of absence and see what HR has to say."

She wrote the letters that afternoon, addressed the envelope to Roxy, and stuck the packet in the mailbox. Now all she had to do was wait.

A lot simpler in theory.

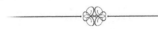

Carley's mood took an upturn when two vanloads of cackling kids from the homeschool co-op showed up earlier than their scheduled hour to work in the greenhouse. Their gardening class usually conflicted with the time she had to run errands, so they had often come and gone before she got back home.

A chorus of young voices called out, "Hi, Miss Neva, Miss Carley!"

She tapped a few bouncing heads. "You're here early today."

One of the moms said, "Academic classes are over for the summer, but we still maintain the garden and do weekly field trips."

Another woman let a border collie out of the back of the van. "Come, Kava, come." The dog bounded out and corralled the kids into a circle.

"Glad you're here," Miss Neva said. "I was beginning to worry those weeds would take over the place."

One little boy said, "We got to go to the fire station last week. Firefighter Camire let us climb on the truck and work the siren. He taught us how to drop and roll in case of fire." He raised his hand. "Kava! Fire! Drop and roll."

The dog dropped and rolled.

Carley shouted, "Bravo!"

Her aunt ruffled Kava's mane. "A very smart pooch indeed."

As the chaperones led the way to the greenhouse, Carley stared after the kids. Half to herself, she said, "I hope to have kids someday."

"I did too." Her aunt looped her arm through Carley's. "Then I got T-bone and now I have you."

That evening, for the first time in a long time, Carley wished her dad were around—and she felt selfish for doing so. The man had been called to the mission field when she was ten years old, but he'd waited to answer the call until after she graduated from nursing school and was settled in her position at Key State Medical.

And what a fine job I've done so far.

Though she emailed her father on a semi-regular basis, she never knew when or if he'd received her messages or if he would respond. Like a wink from God, that night he answered. His subject line read, *Jehovah Jireh!*

Hi, Cariño,

I had to share this answer to prayer. Remember the big chunk of money we needed for the new bio-filtration system? Thanks to a slew of modest donations and one in the amount of $10,000, we have only a few hundred to raise! You'll love the name of the ministry that donated the large amount: The Least of These. Ha! One of our favorite verses. How apropos, considering the people we're trying to serve in this part of the world. Jehovah Jireh! The Lord does provide.

The Least of These. That verse from Matthew 25 again. Was God trying to tell her something?

Carley sat in her car in the Andover library parking lot, engrossed in her online search for a new attorney. Not that she wanted to start all over again, but what choice did she have?

An imposing black SUV pulled up alongside her, casting a shadow over her car.

Irritated, she glanced up, wondering why the driver had parked so close in the near-empty lot. She shrugged and resumed her search.

A tap on the driver's side window startled her. A man in a dark suit flashed an FBI badge.

What on earth? She lowered her driver's side window and read the name on the ID. "What can I do for you, Special Agent ... Unser?"

"Could we have a word, Ms. Jantzen?"

How did they find me ... and at the library no less?

He continued, "Mind joining us in our vehicle?"

She checked his ID again. "Uh, okay." She got out of her car and climbed into their back seat. "What's this about?"

Agent Unser turned in his seat to face her. "We'd like to impress upon you the importance of not going to the news media about the Key State Medical fraud case."

She crossed her arms. "I see Attorney Yeager has been talking out of turn."

"Not directly to us, Ms. Jantzen, but we were made aware of your threat."

Carley snapped. "Threat? What has my lawyer told you?"

"I can't say, ma'am. Our assignment today is to encourage you to comply with the confidentiality clause and help us complete our investigation."

"Are you saying I can't take my complaint back?"

"Not at this point, ma'am. We're too far into the investigation, close to issuing arrest warrants."

"I guess I didn't expect things to take this much time."

Unser nodded. "We've heard that before, ma'am. The nature of these cases, especially when more than one perpetrator is involved, requires extreme care and thoroughness."

"So are all three of the partners involved?"

"We can't say, ma'am. Suffice it to say, your efforts will go a long way in preventing similar crimes. For that, the Bureau is grateful."

Carley sighed. "Tell me, does that lawyer of mine know I could have him disbarred for breaking my confidence?"

"Let me see your cell phone," Unser said. "I'll add my secure line to your contacts in case you need me to testify." He winked. "Until then, we'd appreciate your continued cooperation, ma'am."

The stocky agent, who hadn't said a word, opened the door and let her out. She got back in her car.

The black SUV backed up and headed out of town. Before Carley could stop shaking, someone opened her passenger door and slid in.

Wilda. Had she been watching from inside the library?

The wiry woman scooched down and put a finger to her lips. "Shh. I know all about WITSEC and the cartel. Those men were US Marshalls, weren't they?"

"I don't—"

"Never mind. Don't answer. As far as Andover residents know, you're Carley Merrill, Geneva Kellerman's niece from Pennsylvania."

"Wilda, maybe you should—"

"Shh. This case is on a need-to-know basis, and I don't need to know. Be aware we locals are keeping our eyes peeled and our ears open for strangers lurking about."

Carley gave up. "Glad to hear that."

Wilda leaned in closer. "There is one thing though. You need to be more careful when you speak on your cell phone. I heard most of your conversation with your handler when I was in the dining room at the Millbury Inn." She handed Carley a torn piece of paper with a number on it. "If you want to get one of those untraceable burning phones, my cousin's brother-in-law manages one of the few Radio Shacks left in New Hampshire." She slipped out of the car and practically belly-crawled her way back into the library.

No, nothing suspicious about her behavior at all.

CHAPTER THIRTY

CARLEY: PRESENT DAY

Carley was surprised when Miss Neva exited the doctor's exam room without her cast. "I thought for sure the doctor would keep the cast on longer." She examined her aunt's arm. "It's been less than five weeks."

"You're not going to mess with my freedom, are you?" Her aunt sprinted out the door and hopped into the driver's side of her truck.

"Now I know why you wanted to take your truck. Don't you think—"

"No, I don't. I'm taking the afternoon to visit the sisters, shop for groceries, and cook us dinner."

"Are you sure—"

"Yes, I'm sure. Besides, you need a break from tending to my needs."

Carley grumbled. "Sounds more like you need a break from me."

Miss Neva wagged a finger at Carley. "That is not the case, nor will it ever be. Haven't you picked up on the fact we're both cut from the same independent cloth?"

"As a nurse practitioner, I still think you should—"

"See these?" She held up both arms and then crossed them. "I'm not gonna and you can't make me."

Carley tried not to smile or worry or argue the rest of the way home.

When they got to the house, the homeschool co-op vans were parked at the edge of the field.

"Perfect timing," Miss Neva said. "I need to speak with them. One of the children left the hose running last week." She downshifted and started toward them.

Near the greenhouse, the school's mascot Kava herded a little girl.

"That border collie is so good with these kids," Carley said.

"Kava cares for them as she would sheep."

The dog left the girl's side, charged toward the woods, baring its teeth.

Her aunt hit the brakes, climbed out, and got her rifle from behind the seat.

Carley bailed out after her. "What's wrong?"

"Coyote ... near that copse of pines." She raised her rifle. "When they look that disoriented, usually means they're sick."

The young girl skipped over to the collie. "Don't be scared, Kava. I think that doggie wants to be friends." She took a few steps toward the coyote.

The coyote stumbled to the top of a mound, then growled.

Miss Neva yelled, "Kava! Drop and roll, drop and roll!"

The border collie dropped and rolled, pushing his charge to the ground.

The coyote sprang. A shot rang out. The animal fell with a thud.

Carley caught her breath, then hurried over to usher the girl into the greenhouse.

Miss Neva notified animal control.

Forty minutes later, the animal control officer arrived and examined the dead coyote. "By the foam around its mouth, my guess is rabies, but we'll know for sure after the test. Good shot, Miss Geneva. That critter could've done some real harm here."

Before Carley could react to all that had transpired, the officer, the dead coyote, and both co-op vans had left, and Miss Neva was back in her truck. Her aunt called out, "See you when I get back."

"You're still going?" Carley crossed her arms and stared at her. "One hour after your cast is removed, and you shoot a coyote?"

"You didn't think I kept those rifles around for show, did you?" She stepped on the gas and pulled out of the driveway.

Carley marched back to the house, grumbling. "Two can play at her game!" She trumped her aunt's stubbornness by calling the two people who might convince Neva to take it easy—T-bone and Vern.

Getting T-bone to stop by was simple. "Miss Neva's cooking again? I'll be there."

Vern was a bit trickier. They hadn't seen nor heard from him since the incident with Skip Fournier a few weeks earlier. What could she say to convince him? She decided on the truth.

"I'm worried about her. The doctor removed her cast today—much too early in my opinion. Then she shoots a rabid coyote, and she's off and running."

"She shot a coyote?"

"Yes, but more importantly, she has no idea what damage could be done if she rushes her healing."

"Where is she now?" He sounded alarmed—exactly what she was hoping for.

"I'm not sure. Said she'd be back to cook dinner."

"I've got an appointment at four thirty, but I can be there soon after."

"I'll set a place for you at the table. We'll call it a cast-off celebration."

Her aunt got home a few hours later, carrying grocery totes and bubbling with news. "Truck ran fine. ... Found some deals at the grocery store in Rumford. ... Oh, and you won't believe this! The sisters are already working with two college-aged girls they found in a local chapter of the American Philatelic Society. Lovely young women. They're even rooming there on the weekends."

"So happy for them." Carley helped unpack the groceries. "Looks like you emptied a few shelves at the market."

"Got some items we haven't enjoyed for a while."

Carley raised a brow. "You mean like items the local restaurants don't offer on their takeout menus?"

"No, that's not what I meant. Periodically, even I need to change up my own meal plan."

"Speaking of meal plans, I thought a celebration was in order." Carley broke the news about their dinner guests. "I hope that's okay with you."

The pace of Miss Neva's unpacking slowed. "Are you sure they're both coming?"

"Yes, I'm sure." Carley tried to read her face.

Eyeing her purchases, her aunt said, "I was going to marinate some chicken—or do you think we should have roast pork loin?"

Her aunt was consulting her on what to fix for dinner? "Pork would be nice for a change."

"Okay, yes, pork loin ... with cornbread and bacon stuffing. I've got some homemade applesauce in the larder too." She started and stopped. "Carley, could you check the garden? Fresh broccoli would pair well and add color."

The two of them spent the next hour prepping for supper and tidying the kitchen. They even set the table with good china.

Miss Neva glanced at the clock. "What time did you say they'd be here?"

After Carley repeated the time, her aunt removed her apron. "I think I've got time for a shower." She held up her cast-less arm. "My first in over a month without your assistance or a plastic bag over half my body. Besides, the humidity was a killer today."

At noontime, the local meteorologist had described the day as "dry as an Arizona dog bone," but Carley didn't contradict her.

Miss Neva paused on her way to her room. "Carley, do you know if that pale blue blouse of mine is clean? The one with the embroidered top?"

"Hanging in your closet next to your white slacks." Something or someone had her aunt flustered. Carley doubted that someone was T-bone.

T-bone arrived. "Ahh. What is that mouthwatering aroma?"

Carley kept her voice low in case her aunt was within hearing distance. "Miss Neva went all out. No offense, but I don't think her efforts were for you."

His eyebrows shot up. "Vern?"

She nodded. "He should be here—"

"What are you two whispering about?" Her aunt came around the corner. She'd found her outfit and had added a coral necklace. Her face and lips held a touch of color. She'd blown dry her shoulder-length hair, letting the thick streaks of white frame her face in soft waves.

Carley almost shouted, "Wow!" but caught herself. "Feel better?"

"Your hair looks nice," T-bone said. "Did you go to a fancy hairdresser or something?"

With alarm on her face, Miss Neva fiddled with her waves. "Why? Is it too much?"

"Ignore this guy." Carley gave him shut-up daggers. "You look as nice as you always do."

A knock at the door.

Her aunt sputtered, "Oh, uh, will you get the door, dear?" She headed to the kitchen. "I need to check on the chicken."

Chicken? What chicken?

Carley opened the door. "Come on in, Vern."

A fresh haircut, a clean-shaven face, and a creased oxford shirt. Hmm. Am I sensing a theme here?

T-bone shook his hand. "Hey, Vern, I'd say I missed seeing you around Miss Neva's supper table, but you being too busy left more for me to eat." He patted his stomach.

Vern chuckled. "At least you're honest." He tilted his head and glanced around the two of them. "So, how's the patient doing?"

Miss Neva walked in. "No longer a patient as you can see." Her eyes passed by his but didn't linger.

"So I hear." He walked over to her. "Mind if I take a look at your arm?"

"No, I mean, okay, if you want."

Vern scrutinized but did not touch. "I suppose the doctor gave you pesky warnings about not overdoing yourself."

"Of course." She huffed. "You know how they can be."

He locked on her eyes. "And I know how you can be. You'll behave, won't you?"

Carley and T-bone exchanged worried glances. This could go either way.

Her aunt spoke above a whisper. "I'll do my best."

Phew.

"That's my girl." He led her into the kitchen. "Now, anything I can do to speed supper along? My appetite is acting up."

Once they were seated around the table, the conversation turned to the meal before them. Carley hoped any uneasy moments would be left behind.

Vern reached for a serving dish. "Neva, is this your famous cornbread and bacon stuffing?"

She nodded. "I thought I'd make it for Carley."

Me? Oh, sure.

T-bone stuck his hand out. "Vern, pass that over here. Leave some for the rest of us."

Carley pretend-pouted. "Isn't anyone going to compliment the mashed potatoes? I peeled them myself."

"You did a fine job, dear. Carley picked the broccoli specifically for you, Vern."

I did? News to me.

Talk traveled from Olde Home Days to Dubber and Warren's big race to Wilda's covert efforts at keeping Carley's presence a secret from strangers. They steered clear of the incident with Skip Fournier, and no one asked why Vern hadn't been around. Carley was certain everyone knew why anyway.

Chapter Thirty-One

GENEVA: PRESENT DAY

Geneva's cooking had garnered praises. Coffee and dessert had been served. The evening had been a social success—up to the moment she asked, "May I get you anything else, Vern?"

"Yes." Elbows on the table, he folded his hands under his chin. "You."

"I'm sorry, come again?" She fumbled the sugar bowl.

Vern spread his hands flat on the table. "Neva, I want you."

Lord, please tell me he didn't say that.

She cut her eyes around the table. Carley seemed frozen, while a grin turned up at the corner of T-bone's mouth.

Neva's face warmed, her hands shook. "Perhaps we should have this discussion later."

"No, Neva, now." His voice was kind but firm.

Carley slid her chair back. "T-bone, why don't we go—"

Vern stretched one arm out toward Carley, the other toward T-bone. "You two, stay. I have something to say, and I want witnesses."

Carley wriggled back up to the table.

Geneva's voice trembled. "Vern?"

He cleared his throat. "Neva, I think you'll agree things have changed between us."

She started to get up. "I don't think now's the time—"

"Sit, Neva. Please."

She did ... slowly.

"I've loved you as a friend for forty-seven years. When you married Otto, who was like a brother to me, I loved you as family." He inhaled and exhaled evenly. "For the past few years, the desire to love you as my *wife* has grown."

She teared up. "But Otto was my husband and your best friend."

"I've thought long and hard on that and came to this conclusion. Otto had more practical sense than most. Not only would he approve, but he'd also be wondering what took us so long."

"Do you truly believe that?" She wrung her hands.

Vern reached across the table and covered her hands with his. "I do, with all my heart. Neva, I'm not asking you to trust me. I'm asking you to trust the Lord."

She met his gaze. "Vern Beckham, are you asking permission to court me?"

He shook his head. "No. We've known each other too long for that." He circled around to her and got down on one knee. "I'm asking you to be my wife—and I don't want to wait too long either."

Her heart rate slowed long enough for her brain to catch up. She sought confirmation in his clear brown eyes. Her soft "Yes" caught her by surprise. She cupped his face with both hands. "Yes, Vern, I will marry you."

"You will?" His brows shot up. "With no argument?"

She laughed. "I think I've exhausted the ones I had."

"Good." After staring into her eyes for a long, few seconds, he said in a thick voice, "Neva, I want to kiss you ... now. May I?"

She swallowed hard and nodded.

He stood and helped her up, then leaned in slowly before touching his lips to hers.

Her knees buckled. *Oh, my ... oh, my...*

Vern backed away. He inhaled and smiled.

Carley and T-bone made a general ruckus. "Way to go!" ... "About time!" ... "Hallelujah!"

Geneva had almost forgotten they were there.

T-bone bear-hugged her. "I'm so happy for you, Miss Neva, I'll even lease you my garage for your wedding reception and throw in some free latex gloves."

She pinched his cheek. "You're too kind to me, son."

He turned to Vern. "Hey, Vern, since Miss Neva calls me son, does that mean I can call you Pa?"

"What about me?" Carley protested. "If T-bone gets to call Vern *Pa*, I get to call him *Uncle*."

Geneva planted her fists on her hips. "You'll need to call me *Aunt* before that happens!"

"I'd be honored, *Aunt* Neva." Carley embraced her, then said, "Now, vamoose, you two. You have a lot to talk about. T-bone and I will do the dishes."

T-bone scrunched up his face. "We will?"

Carley snapped a dishtowel at him. "Yes, *we* will."

Vern winked. "Seems like these two want to be alone."

"You may be right." Geneva struggled against a grin.

Carley pointed to the screened porch. "Out!"

"Okay, okay." Vern led Neva out to the porch swing. "You don't know how often I've imagined myself sitting in this swing beside you." His voice sounded husky. He put his arm around her and exhaled. "It's even better than I'd imagined."

The nearness of Vern warmed her, both body and spirit. The scent of his spiced aftershave mixed with the drycleaner's starch on his pressed shirt tickled her nose. Light-headed, her mind swooned at this new reality. *We're engaged.* Shyness overcame her and left her speechless.

Me? Speechless? That can't be good. She snuggled closer. *But it is.*

Without warning, the swing jerked to a stop.

"I almost forgot." Vern patted around his pockets until he retrieved a small white envelope. He turned the envelope on end. A ring tumbled into his hand. "This was my mother's. Ever hopeful I would find a wife one day, she left her engagement ring to me in her will. I'd be honored if you'd accept it."

Geneva stared at the vintage piece, the diamond sparkling against the white gold. "It's beautiful." She chuckled. "I see you had tonight's proposal all planned out."

He tipped his head from side to side. "Not exactly. I've been carrying that ring on me for the past seven months. I was beginning to think I'd missed my chance." He put the ring on her finger.

Her smile widened. "A perfect fit."

"Like you." He kissed her temple. "I meant it when I said I didn't want to wait long. How about a month from now?"

She thought quick. "Make it three months and you've got a deal. A girl has to plan, you know."

They nestled together for a long while, lulled by the creaking of the swing.

She was stirred by the wonder of a God who would bring them together after all this time. She trembled.

"Are you cold?" He pulled her closer.

She shook her head. Tears plump with joy gathered in her eyes. She managed one word, "Blessed."

He wiped the tears from the corner of her eyes with his thumb.

"My turn." She caught his tears on her fingertips before they reached his chin.

They kissed.

He broke away. "Three months, huh?"

She quivered. "Perhaps two will do."

Chapter Thirty-Two

Carley: Present Day

Vern's comment about T-bone and her "wanting to be alone" had made Carley squirm. A quick check of T-bone's face found no sign he'd even heard the man. Conversation between them was flowing smoothly. No need to add any awkwardness. Not that she had anything against this guy—wasn't much to dislike about him at all. She just wasn't in a healthy state of mind to start any kind of relationship.

Carley hurried him along as they cleaned up after dinner. She wanted to be ready and waiting to hear all the details when the happy couple came in from the porch. Thankfully, T-bone knew his way around her aunt's cupboards and pantry almost as well as she did.

She put the last of the pots and pans away. "I've been meaning to ask, how's the Liar's Table writer's group going?"

"Kinda cool." He hung a damp dishtowel on the oven door. "I've met with them twice so far."

"Would I know any of the other members?"

"A few. I think you met Cynthia Giroux at the Red Rooster. She has a lyrical way with words, natural not forced." He leaned against the refrigerator and crossed his arms. "The one I was most surprised to see there was Rylee Cooper."

"The same teenage girl who flies around town on her ATV?"

"The one and only. She's working on a superhero fantasy set on the Appalachian Trail."

"Really? Is she any good?"

"A little early to tell, but she's got some interesting characters." T-bone's phone rang. "What's up, Doc? ... How many? ... Again? ... No problem. I'll be there in five."

She sighed. "'Doc' as in Quimby?"

"Yes, he's got another menagerie for me to watch over tonight."

She growled. "I was hoping you'd be here when they came back inside."

He chuckled. "Why? Worried they'll start kissing again?"

"That's not what I meant." *Was it?*

"You'll do fine." He grazed her upper arm with his fist. "Thanks again for dinner. I'll go out the back door and sneak past the lovebirds."

Carley closed the door behind him, then walked through the living room as the grandfather clock chimed nine. Something niggled at her, but what?

Oh, well.

She sat back on the couch, her mind whirling with questions. Would her aunt and Vern have a long engagement? What kind of a wedding would they have? Where would they live?

For that matter, where will I live?

Carley glanced out at the porch. The swing was still moving. She darted upstairs to change into her pjs and check her email. Mostly junk. As she was about to close out, a new email popped up. Attorney Yeager. What did he want this time of night?

Dear Ms. Jantzen,

I've been informed by the FBI they reached out to you recently —against my wishes—about not contacting the news media about your case. As your legal counsel, it's my duty to advise you to heed their command. They can be a stubborn lot to deal with if you cross them. We wouldn't want to jeopardize your sizable settlement in this landmark case, especially since we've worked so diligently to get to this stage. I'm sure we won't have to wait long now.

Against my wishes? Liar. The only *sizable settlement* he was worried about was his percentage. That's what I get for searching the term "whistleblowing attorney" in a major search engine. Whoever can afford to pay for the ads at the top gets the clients. How could I have been so naïve?

And why do I keep annoying myself with that same question?

Back downstairs, the porch swing was still creaking. Carley picked up the weekly paper to keep her impatience at bay. Andover's local rag diligently reported on high school sports, civic and fundraising events, and milestone occasions. Of course, much of the actual news was old by the time the paper was delivered on Fridays—

Friday! Uh, oh. I forgot to call Roxy. She glanced at the time. *Too late now. She's probably home already.*

She called T-bone instead. "In all the excitement, I forgot to call Roxy. Do you think I could call her cell phone now? If she doesn't hear from me, she's liable to freak and send out an Amber Alert."

"I don't recommend you doing that. If *she* doesn't use her cell to receive your weekly calls, that tells you something."

"What if—"

"If you really need to contact her, I'd use your burner to call her direct line at work on Monday. They get multiple calls so yours won't stand out. But don't talk long."

"Thanks." Monday would have to do.

Carley *happened* to be peeking out a window when Vern headed for his car. She hustled across the room and plopped back into her easy chair seconds before her aunt came through the door. "Vern gone already?" She yawned and stretched.

Her aunt gave her a sidelong glance and pointed to the grandfather clock. "Didn't you hear grandpa chime at eleven? Speaking of the time, why did T-bone leave so early?"

"Doc Quimby had some patients for him to babysit."

"I see." She paused in front of Carley's chair. "Kitchen all cleaned up, is it?"

"Yes, and everything's back in its place." Though Carley held her nosiness in check, she followed her aunt's every move and waited. Surely a newly engaged woman would want to talk.

"Thanks. Well, I guess I'd better turn in."

Carley hid her pout. "Yeah, sure, if you want."

Aunt Neva stepped toward the hallway. "Today was quite the day though, wasn't it?"

Finally! Carley bolted upright. "Sure was."

"I never would've guessed"—her aunt hugged herself—"that I'd get my cast off so soon."

Carley squinted at her. "Your cast?"

"Why? Something else you want to talk about?" The twinkle in her eyes was hard to miss. "Maybe the coyote incident?"

Tapping her chin, Carley played the game. "Hm, let me think. I've got it. How about we talk about romance?"

Her aunt laughed as she sank onto the sofa. With dreamy eyes and a smile to match, she said, "My heart was pounding right out of my chest when I asked Vern if he wanted anything else and he said 'You.'" She fanned her face. "Oh, I thought I was going to swoon."

Carley sat on the edge of her seat. "That caught us all by surprise."

"And when he knelt down to propose ... mercy! ... I admit I've never felt so treasured."

"I'm so excited for you, *Aunt* Neva. You don't mind, do you?"

"I would've suggested that sooner, but I didn't want to assume a role in your life I hadn't earned."

"Oh, you've earned it! Especially after I got to witness the whole proposal."

They chatted like contemporaries for another half hour, discussing venues, guests, and refreshments.

When Carley asked if there was a bridal shop nearby, her aunt said, "I have a cute print dress that'll do just fine."

Carley frowned. "Haven't you ever watched 'Say Yes to the Dress?' Shopping for a wedding dress is fun!"

She shook her head. "Why would I spend all that money on something I'll wear one day?"

"Let's table the discussion for now," Carley said, "but so you know, I don't give up easily."

"Neither do I, dear." She smiled. "I would like to get one thing settled tonight. Will you be my maid of honor?"

"Me? What about Faith? Isn't she your best friend?"

"She is, but you're family."

Carley choked up. "I'd be honored."

"One more thing, you'll be glad to know I finally understand the difference between love and contentment and love and *romance*." Aunt Neva made googly eyes. "I never knew what I was missing."

As her aunt floated off to bed, Carley whispered, "Lord, will I ever know that feeling?"

Chapter Thirty-Three

Harrison dropped his car off for its scheduled maintenance and caught a ride to the office with the dealership's complimentary transport. He was late, and his overbooked morning did nothing to relieve his stress.

His break didn't come until one thirty. Sinking into his desk chair, he stared out the window, not seeing a thing.

Why did I start this whole mess? How did I not realize I'd lose more than I'd gain? Too late now.

He'd been so anxious to *act* he hadn't made the effort to *think* about his exit plan. Now the ramifications of what he'd done—was still doing—swung toward him like a wrecking ball. He exhaled nervous energy.

How long do I have before my medical practice—and life—come crashing down?

For months he'd been living two lives. One as a respectable doctor treating his patients as if they had a future under his care. Another as a man sneaking behind his partners' backs, knowing his actions would ruin all they had built. Maybe he should have thought more about the long-term consequences.

What baffled him was how both his personas had the audacity to imagine a relationship with Carley Jantzen. Who was he kidding?

A knock on his door.

He faced front and straightened his glasses. "Yes."

Roxanne stepped in. "I thought you'd want to see this before our staff meeting tomorrow. Came by international courier a few minutes ago along with a letter to HR." She handed him a small white envelope.

Frustration flared as he recognized Carley's handwriting. He'd clung to hope, refusing to believe she would not return. Over two months had passed. His nerves were frayed. "I take it she's not on her way back."

"That's the gist of it." She fiddled with the cuff of her sweater. "All I can tell you is the situation with her father must be dire for her to stay away this long. You know how much she loves working here, especially with *you.*"

"She does?" That sounded pathetic. He cleared his throat. "We value all our staff members here." *Blah, blah.*

Roxanne winked. "If you like Carley a little more than the others, it's okay. I do too."

Afraid he'd give himself away, he held up the letter and stalled before he spoke. "Thanks for dropping this off." He knew he'd failed to keep his face blank.

Carley's letter was almost a duplicate to the one she'd sent earlier.

Guess that's that.

Once Harrison finished with his afternoon appointments, he secluded himself to update his patient records. New to this habit, he jotted down potential physicians to take over where he would leave off. He copied everything to a stick drive in the event he lost access to the office computer files. Just because his life was falling apart didn't mean his patients had to suffer.

When the staff bid each other goodnight, Harrison had a half hour before the car dealership was due to pick him up. He spent the time entertaining thoughts of his prodigal nurse practitioner, wondering if he should've been honest with her. Would she have understood? She was a reasonable woman, wasn't she? Maybe he wasn't too late. With no way to contact her, that idea proved impotent.

An inside line rang. Their service would pick up.

He'd thought everyone had left for the day until he heard Roxanne in the next room.

"I waited the whole weekend for you to call. Are you okay? ... Sarcasm. Really? ... With all the stuff going on, I was worried about you. ... What do you mean *why*? Your mysterious departure for one. ... Everything's fine here other than your doctor's long face."

He stepped closer to his near-closed door. *Could she be talking to Carley?*

"So you keep saying." ... Roxy grunted. "Yes, but will he get over *you*?" ... "Yes, I gave the letters to him and HR." ... "As for those frat-brother doctors, why should I inform them? Stryker's oblivious to what goes on here. And if you haven't noticed, Reinhart's inflated ego doubles as blinders. He probably doesn't even know you're gone."

Her voice trailed off ... then nothing. From what he overheard this was not their only time speaking since Carley had been gone.

What's going on?

He bided his time until she had left the building, then entered the office the nurses shared. Carley's desk looked much the same as it always had. A framed quote to the left of her monitor: *They may forget your name, but they will never forget how you made them feel.* A phone charger. The snarky mug a patient had given her which read, *Please don't confuse your Google search with my nursing degree.* A hand-carved wooden pencil holder made in Bolivia, stuffed with all manners of colorful writing instruments. A dead potted plant ... which he hoped was not an omen.

Sitting in her chair, he switched on the computer. While waiting for the device to wake up, he peeked in Carley's desk drawers. Most everything he found was work related. The few personal items included a box of engraved notecards and a package of peppermint candies.

All the file names and document titles in her directories seemed to be related to patients, general offices practices, or the software classes she'd led for their staff—including him. Ironic that she'd been the one who had given him the key to access the billing modules. Little did she know ...

Harrison checked her search engine history on the off chance he'd find a clue as to why she left and where she was. The history was blank. *Odd*. The main reason people erased their history was if they didn't want someone else to see what they'd been searching. *Knowing her, she probably preferred to start each day with a clean slate.*

About to log-out, he noticed the download directory. He scrolled down a list of files, recognizing the software training videos as well as articles from various medical journals. A download from a travel club caught his interest ... until a file titled "Medicare Fraud" stole his attention. He swallowed, trying to stop the queasy feeling in the pit of his stomach.

He stiffened. "What have you gone and done, Carley?"

Chapter Thirty-Four

Geneva: Present Day

News of Geneva and Vern's engagement spread around town like a gale blowing through a barn full of chicken feathers. All that was needed was one praise report at Sunday service, one Monday morning breakfast at the Red Rooster, and one Tuesday afternoon at the Liars' Table.

On Wednesday, Vern and T-bone joined Carley and Neva for supper.

"Neva, I don't want to be one of those grooms accused of not taking part in his wedding plans, so I've been thinking. What do you say we have our wedding ceremony in the gazebo on the town common during Olde Home Days weekend? Everyone will already be there. We won't have to feed them."

Geneva filled his glass. "You know what I love about you the most?"

"Let me guess," Carley said. "His brains?"

T-bone flexed. "No, it must be his brawn."

Clearing his throat, Vern said, "I believe the woman is referring to my sex appeal."

She grinned. "Close. Your sense of humor."

He stuck his bottom lip out. "No wedding on the common then?"

"Actually, I like your idea of the gazebo and the common—just not that date." Geneva turned a page on the wall calendar. "What about the Saturday after Labor Day?"

"Perfect." Vern reached for her hand and kissed it. "There's another matter we have to settle." He turned to T-bone. "What do you say to being my best man?"

"I better say yes, because who else are you gonna ask?"

Vern laughed. "I expect a bachelor party out of this, you know?"

"I'll get Dubber and Warren working on that pronto."

Geneva sat near Vern on the leather sofa in the anteroom of his law office. "Carley hasn't mentioned anything about her living situation once we're married, but I know she's thinking about it." She sighed. "The girl's gone through so much already, I hate to uproot her."

He covered her hand with his. "Even if we suggest she keep her room at the house, she'll say she doesn't want to intrude on us newlyweds."

"Yes, and I can almost hear her use those very words."

Vern pulled back a little, a smile forming. "I have an idea. Since none of us know what Carley's plans will be once the fraud case goes to court, how about I offer her my place as a temporary solution? Might not be the Ritz, but it's clean."

Cluttered is more the word Geneva would use. When Vern's mother passed a decade ago, he'd placed an inflated value on her furnishings and added most of them to his own eclectic collection. Last time she was there, the walls appeared as if they would buckle under the load and spill over into the orderly front rooms which housed his law practice.

"I don't know ..."

"I can read your face." He chuckled. "I need to get the place ready to rent anyway. I promise, you can fix it up any way you want. There's truly little I care about now that I have you."

She snuggled closer as relief tamped down a smidgeon of guilt. "If you're sure?"

"I've never been surer of anything." He lifted her chin. "Why not call her to see if she's free to come by now?"

"Now? Um, I don't think we need to hurry."

"Afraid my place will scare her away?"

"I didn't say that."

He brushed her cheek with the back of his hand. "As I said before, this pretty face is an easy read."

When Vern excused himself to prepare for a meeting with a client, Geneva perused his quarters. She visually thinned out the mishmash in each room, trying to envision a comfortable home for her niece. She walked out to the backyard. A small cobblestone patio with plenty of shade and privacy lay outside the French doors off the master suite. A perfect place for morning coffee or afternoon tea. The area had potential, once the grounds were trimmed and weeded, and the outdoor furniture had a fresh coat of paint.

If this idea is to work, we'll need help—and fast.

Meandering around to the front, she nearly bumped into Wilda Weikert coming down the steps of the law office. "Oops. Sorry, Wilda. I knew Vern was meeting with a client, but I didn't know who."

"Why would you?" Wilda huffed. "I expect nothing less than one hundred percent confidentiality from my attorney—even after he gets married." A smile slipped out as she adjusted her purse. "You caught yourself a fine man there, Geneva."

She smiled back. "And I didn't even know I was fishing."

Wilda wagged a finger. "Of course, your engagement came as no surprise to those of us who've been watching you over the years."

Geneva's brows shot up. *I guess the 'one hundred percent confidentiality' doesn't apply to watching others, huh?*

"As I mentioned to your fiancé today, my niece Izzy is with an exclusive interior design firm over in Bethel. They also do event décor. If you need help with your wedding venue, she's the one to call." She reached into her purse. "I already gave Vern a card, but here's one for you too."

"Thanks. We're still in the initial planning stages, but we'll keep her in mind."

"With the wedding planned for the weekend after Labor Day, I wouldn't wait too long if I were you."

No need to send save-the-date cards in this town.

After bidding Wilda goodbye, Geneva returned to the anteroom. Vern's private door was open. She peeked in. He was seated at his desk, fingers steepled, eyes gazing off in space, a wan smile on his face.

"Okay to come in, or are you contemplating a legal matter?"

He stood, his smile widening. "Yes, to both. The legal matter is our wedding. I'm contemplating our honeymoon." He winked. "Where would you like to go?"

"Um, uh, I hadn't really thought about it much."

"No? How disappointing."

She fiddled with her collar. "I mean not that I haven't thought ... well, you know ... I should be ..."

I'm a sixty-two-year-old woman and I'm blushing—again. This must stop!

"Come here, please. I want to tell you something."

She stepped closer. "Yes?"

He lifted her up and sat her on the edge of his desk. "Do you know why I'm not a courtroom attorney?"

"No, why?"

"I lack the verbal skills to sway female jurors. To counter that shortcoming, I plan to spend the rest of my life *showing* you how much I love you." He cupped her face and kissed her softly. "Starting with our honeymoon."

She slid off the desk, her knees barely able to hold her. A sound between a squeak and a whimper escaped her lips from somewhere deep inside her.

Oh, Lord, please tell me he didn't hear that.

He laughed and held her in his arms. "Now, about that honeymoon you haven't been thinking about ..."

The next morning over breakfast, Geneva commented to Carley, "I had hoped to squeeze in a visit with the sisters today, but my schedule is a bit tight."

"Why don't I stop in and see them after I run my errands?" Carley refilled their coffee cups. "Anyway, I'd like to see for myself how their mentoring program is working out."

"Thank you, I appreciate that." Neva pushed her breakfast plate aside and slid her coffee cup forward. "As for your mentoring idea, don't worry. I believe that plan was ordained by God."

With her afternoon redeemed, Geneva called Wilda's niece. Bottom line, the work had to be done whether Carley moved in or not. If the do-over of Vern's place was to beat the speed of town gossip, she could not afford to delay.

The "exclusive interior design firm in Bethel" had one full-time employee—Izzy—who also moonlighted at a franchise home goods store thirty miles southwest in North Conway. Despite Neva's doubts, she agreed to meet the budding entrepreneur at Vern's that afternoon—but not before she swore her to secrecy.

She was pleased when Izzy showed up dressed neatly and on time. Her portfolio was impressive, filled with professional quality before and after photos of all her projects, no matter the size. The girl got bonus points for not wincing at the sight of Vern's quarters.

Neva accepted Izzy's proposal to declutter and design all five rooms and the patio. "As for liquidating assets you don't want to reuse or repurpose, I'd appreciate your working directly with Dubber Polaski and Warren Churner. I'll give you their number."

"No need. I've worked with the brothers before," Izzy said. "They've got some invaluable connections with local antique dealers, consignment shops, and auctioneers." She ran her hand over the top of a flawless mahogany console table. "Have you thought about incorporating some of Mr. Beckham's furnishings to make *your* home feel more like *his* too?"

She and Otto had fully outfitted their home over years of living there together. She couldn't think of a thing she needed.

She and Otto ... their home ... she needed. The girl made a point she hadn't considered. "What do you suggest?"

"I've heard your home is lovely, Miss Geneva, but I find a refresh of the main living areas is wise when one person is moving into a home that has been shared with a previous spouse. Perhaps bringing in some of Mr. Beckham's artwork and appropriate pieces would do."

"Hmph. And I thought all I had to do was set another place at the table."

"For both your sake and Mr. Beckham's, I also recommend a makeover of the master bedroom." Izzy waved her hand in the air one way and the other. "Tuck the old memories away safely to make room for the new."

What a nice way of saying that.

Geneva tapped her upper lip. "Do you think Vern should be included in the design decisions?"

Izzy's brows lifted as she picked up a large martial arts trophy, one of a dozen clustered on the sill of the bay window. "That's one option." Next, she opened a curio cabinet filled with Vern's mother's collectibles and dangled a Victorian figurine in front of Geneva. "Mr. Beckham may have some creative ideas ... or I could surprise you both on the return from your honeymoon."

Geneva thought about all the work she would *not* have to do, all the decisions she would *not* have to make, and all the chances she would *not* have to take on Vern's "creative ideas."

"You've got a deal—as long as the trophies and the tchotchkes don't make the cut."

Izzy extended her hand. "Deal."

Chapter Thirty-Five

Carley: Present Day

Carley reread the rental ads in *The Bethel Citizen* and *Uncle Henry's Weekly*. A couple of listings sounded promising. The one in the *Citizen* listing read: 2 BR home, furnished, 5 minutes from Sunday River Ski Resort. No price was mentioned, which concerned her. The *Uncle Henry's* ad read: 1 BR. Heat, hot water, close to stores. Non-smoking. Pets welcome. Andover. $700 a month.

Her goal was to find a place before Aunt Neva found out she was looking.

Preferring a house over an apartment, she decided to call the number for the Bethel rental. If the rent were too high, she would scratch that place off her list and save herself a trip.

"Rent's $450 a month startin' in September," a man said. "Heat, lights, and water included. Gotta get your own satellite dish."

Two bedrooms with utilities included for $450? She tried not to sound too anxious. "I plan to be up that way in about an hour. I might have time to come by."

"Sounds fine. Watch for a sign and some balloons at the end of the driveway."

Signs and balloons? Must be a real estate open house.

With the scarcity of listings, she'd need to act quickly.

Carley arrived at the address in less than forty minutes. Home for Rent was written with black spray paint on a scrap piece of plywood leaning against a tree. One limp and two deflated balloons languished on the ground. Taking a deep breath, she turned down the overgrown driveway. About thirty feet in, she reached the home ... the *mobile* home ... the *rusty* mobile home, leaning about ten degrees to the left and held together by a heavy net of briars.

Maybe the inside is better?

The screen door hung off to the side by a single hinge. She held desperately to her wishful thinking ... and knocked.

A man yelled, "Door's open!"

She stepped into the main room, piled high with cardboard boxes and all manner of tools and equipment. She flinched when a gray cat scampered by. "Ah!"

A thin bearded man came out from behind a stack of boxes. "Pay Kitty no mind. She's after the mice."

The mice?

"I'm the one's been renting the place. I go by Quonset. You the one that called?"

She nodded.

"Come on in so's I can show you around." He waved his arm across the room. "What we got here's open concept living. That's when the kitchen and living room are joined together."

"Huh, uh." She'd completely missed the kitchen, because the entire area—including the stove, sink, and refrigerator—was either under or behind layers of junk.

"This here's the half bath." He slid a vinyl woodgrain accordion door open. "The toilet flushes. The sink here's clogged, but the one in the full bath works fine."

The toilet listed to one side on rotten floorboards, and the sink basin was caked with rust. She'd need a tetanus shot when she left this place.

Carley followed the man down the hall, sidestepping a trail of used fabric softener dryer sheets.

Quonset must have seen the question on her face because he picked up a sheet and said, "Keeps the mice away."

Oh? Then why do you need the cat?

He pointed to the small bedrooms on one side of the hall, both packed to the ceiling with plastic tubs, boxes, and mismatched furniture pieces. "Two bedrooms is more than I need at this stage in my life. I'm comin' up on retirement so my plan's to downsize to something cheaper."

Downsize? Cheaper? She was speechless.

He detailed a few more amenities the rental had to offer. "There's plenty of free deadwood layin' around for the stove if you chop it yourself. There's a big ol' patch of blueberries a ways up the road, too, if you get to them before the black bears. I'll even get my cousin—he's the one that owns the place—to throw in this here roll of industrial plastic to tape over the windows in the winter. How 'bout it?"

She cleared her throat. "Thank you for showing me around, Quonset. But now I'm thinking I'd like to be a little closer to town."

"If ya change yer mind, don't waits too long 'cause someone's gonna snap this beauty up quick."

I'm sure.

A quarter mile away, she pulled off the road and called the number for the Andover apartment.

A woman answered. "Sawmill Market, how may I help you?"

"Sawmill? Is this Pauline? Uh, I may have called the wrong number ... unless you have an apartment for rent."

"I will soon. My brother's moving to Florida. Place is out back."

Sounds perfect, in the center of town, not far from the people I know. "Any chance I can come over to see it this afternoon?"

"If you wait until three, I'll be finished cleaning up after the midday rush."

With a couple of hours to spare, Carley headed for the Antoine sisters' house.

Miss Lorette and Miss Josette displayed the energy of women twenty years younger. Working with their junior philatelists seemed to have revived their spirits. They had also made headway in organizing their stamp collection after an anonymous stamp enthusiast had donated several wood and glass display cases like you find in a museum.

Miss Lorette could hardly contain herself. "You must see! Once we moved Papa's old furniture out, the cases fit perfectly in our front parlor."

Though Carley's part in the outcome was small, the satisfaction of making a difference in someone else's life was huge. Especially since everything in her own life was on hold—the fraud case, her career, a place to live.

She headed for Sawmill Market about three o'clock. The cashier directed her to a door in the back where she found the owner, Pauline.

"Hey, Carley. Looking to get your own place for after Miss Geneva gets married?"

"Yes, but I'd like to keep it hush-hush for now if you don't mind."

"In this town?" Pauline laughed. "Let me know how that works out for ya."

Carley ignored her. "Is the apartment still available?"

"As I said, will be soon enough. My brother's moving south to get away from the cold." She motioned for Carley to follow her down a hall and up a half flight of stairs. "Come in, come in."

The main room was large, the ceiling high. She tried to overlook the curated collection of mounted animal heads displayed on the walls and their matching skins arrayed on the floor. A strong odor of something wafted by.

She couldn't help herself. "What's that I smell?"

"I can't honestly say for sure. Might be the borax or alcohol or formaldehyde, whatever my brother uses for his taxidermy. He handles the bigger carcasses in the garage out back, but he does the smaller creatures, like bob cats and beavers, in here."

Her eyes grew wide. "Inside the apartment?"

Pauline shrugged. "The tagging station is right outside that double window over there. Good fit for a taxidermist. Lots of people only hunt for meat, so my brother trades his butchering skills for the rest of the carcass." She motioned to the décor of heads and skins. "As you can see."

Carley turned to the double window in time to see a pickup truck back up with a huge brown-black lump half-covered with tarp in the bed. "Is that ... a bear?"

"Hope not. Bear season doesn't start for another few weeks."

Carley glanced down at the truck bed again. "What kind of gun would you use to shoot a bear?"

"In season, *your* rifle. Out of season, someone else's." Pauline sized up the load in the truck and chuckled. "But that species down there is what you call bark mulch."

"Oh." Carley's imagination mixed with the smells made her queasy. "You know, I think I might prefer a place in a less busy part of town."

"I get that." She tapped her chin. "You know, my husband's cousin is downsizing and might have what you're looking for—a sweet mobile home set back in the woods in Bethel, not far from a huge blueberry patch."

Carley almost choked. "I'm thinking now I might wait on finding a place for a while longer."

She got in her car and put the AC on high. *Well, that was a bust.*

On her way home, she took the corner at Vern's place. Her aunt's truck was out front.

Probably the only place they can go for privacy without me hanging around.

A white compact SUV sat in his driveway. A colorful logo Carley couldn't read was painted on the side.

Oops. No privacy there either.

Carley drummed her steering wheel with her fingers. "God, do you have an update on that romantic relationship I asked you for? Might I add I'll be thirty in less than two years?"

T-bone crossed her mind. He was a decent guy, smart and talented too. A good catch, by all accounts. She sighed. *Too bad we've become more like siblings.*

About a mile up the road, she approached his service station. On a whim she pulled in and got out of her car.

He met her at the open bay, removing his signature latex gloves. "What's up?"

"I stopped to tell Adam Thomas how much I'm enjoying his anthology."

He hooked his thumb on a belt loop. "You actually bought a copy?"

"Two, actually. I downloaded the e-book, then ordered a print copy so I could get it autographed."

"Take a seat." He pointed to a turquoise and white striped lawn chair. "Autograph'll cost you extra, you know."

"One of my better investments." She accepted a bottled water from him. "I haven't finished yet, mainly because some of the sections are a bit tough to read."

He grunted. "Try livin' them." He hopped up and sat on the tailgate of the truck he'd been working on.

"Del, your father, is he still around? What about your sister?"

"Cirrhosis of the liver claimed Del's life when I was sixteen. I moved in with my sister until college. She was married by then with a couple of kids. Still lives up north."

"Your writing is raw, sweet, and heart-wrenching—but filled with hope. I have a feeling you'll be famous one day."

"Aren't you full of compliments." He gulped his drink. "Is my future fame the cause of those worry rows on your forehead?"

"No." She slumped. "Everything's in flux. I'm not sure what my next step should be or where I fit in."

"Do any of us?"

'*Do any of us*? That's all you've got? I expected more wisdom from a guy who writes like you do and runs a successful business."

"Let me clue you in on a few things. Writers write because they're trying to figure things out. And wisdom isn't included with auto service manuals." He finished his soft drink. "Perhaps, you could start with what's bugging you the most."

She drew in a breath, then emptied her lungs in one big whoosh. "Me being under foot while Aunt Neva and Vern need time alone. If I say anything to them, they'll insist everything is fine the way it is. I need to get out on my own."

"Have you checked the classifieds?"

"Yes ... today ... with no success. Until I find a suitable place, I need to find something to do *apart* from them."

"I might be able to help with that."

Hopeful, she asked, "How?"

He tapped the truck bed. "This baby here could use a good wash and wax before I give her back to her owner."

She stuck her tongue out at him. *Yup. Bratty brother.*

"No?" He laughed. "Then how about we get a bite and bowl a few strings one night? That should get you out of the old folks' hair for a few hours."

Not the best offer she'd ever received, but she'd take it. "Sure, why not?"

Ding, ding.

T-bone slid off the tailgate as a car rolled over the hose at the pumps. "Hold that thought." Halfway there, he slowed his steps ... like he was just learning to walk.

Carley checked out the car, which looked a lot like the white SUV she'd seen in Vern's driveway. The sign on the car door read Interiors by Izzy. She scooted closer to the threshold so she could see and hear them better.

"Izzy, been a long time. What brings you by?"

'What brings you by?' She's at your gas pump. And why is your voice so deep?

"Hi, Adam. A fill-up, please, regular." She leaned out the window. "I think one of my tires might be low too. My car's pulling to the left."

Carley caught a glimpse of the pretty strawberry blonde.

T-bone locked the fuel nozzle, then walked around the car, checking all four tires. "The front passenger tire is almost flat. Are you sure the car was pulling to the left?"

"Um, well, it might have been the right. I'm not sure now."

"No problem. I can put some air in it for a quick fix, but I can't guarantee you'll make it home to Bethel ... uh, I mean if that's where you still live."

"I do." She pushed a wisp of hair off her face. "And the long-term fix?"

"I take the tire off to check for punctures. If the leak is minor, I patch it. If not, you're lookin' at a new tire." He pointed to the garage. "Pull in there after I back the truck out." He started half-jogging toward the bay.

Izzy glanced back at the pump. "Adam! Shouldn't we wait until you finish filling my tank?"

He half-tripped and then tugged at his ball cap. "Yeah, sure, of course. I'll do that now."

Carley wasn't sure if she should show herself or hide. However, once Izzy pulled into the garage, she had no choice. "Thanks for the cold drink, T-bone. I'd better get going."

"What? Oh. Carley."

Yup, he forgot I was here.

Instead of waiting for T-bone's manners to kick in, she introduced herself. "Carley Merrill, Geneva Kellerman's niece. I've heard good things about you from your aunt."

Izzy grimaced. "In case you haven't noticed, Aunt Wilda is a bit prone to exaggeration."

"Never hurts to have someone brag about you, especially when you're in business for yourself." Carley pointed to Izzy's vehicle. "Nice logo. ... Hey, tell me, was that you I saw at Vern Beckham's earlier?"

Izzy fidgeted but didn't respond.

"I'm sorry," Carley said. "I didn't mean to pry."

"No, that's okay." She sighed. "Sometimes I'm asked to keep confidences, which I find quite difficult to do in a town where everyone knows one another."

Carley chuckled. "Isn't that the truth?"

T-bone had retrieved a soft drink from the old-fashioned cooler in his front office. "Here you go, Izzy. Is Orange Crush still your favorite?"

"You remembered?" She reached for the can. "I'm impressed."

He stood nearby, unmoving and mute.

Carley caught his eye. "T-bone, how's that tire coming along?"

He sprang into action. "Tire. Right. Won't take long."

Watching him around Izzy reminded Carley of every crush she'd ever had, most recently the one on Dr. Nichols. *Painful* was the word to describe their clumsy moves, awkward chitchat, and goofy stares. She was almost afraid to leave them alone for fear they'd trip over each other and get hurt.

When the title of T-bone's essay popped into Carley's head—*An Orange Crush for a Strawberry Blonde*—she decided to act. "Izzy, I hope you don't mind if I borrow T-bone for a second before I go. I forgot to get a copy of my aunt's last invoice."

"Not at all." Izzy placed her soda on the floor by her feet and folded her hands in her lap.

T-bone's brow wrinkled. "Invoice?"

Carley pointed in the direction of his office. "Yes, back there."

He scratched his head. "Sure, yeah, of course."

When they reached his office, Carley poked him in the chest and shout-whispered, "Numbskull! That girl isn't here to get her tire fixed. She's here to see you. Now what are you going to do about it?"

He shuffled his feet. "You think so?"

She rolled her eyes. "I know so. Now get back out there and make things right!"

Carley found Aunt Neva in the kitchen when she got home. "Need some help with supper?"

"Sure. You can snap these beans while I prepare the chicken."

Carley sat at the kitchen table with a colander and an apron full of green beans. "So, how was your day? Get a lot done?"

"I did. Thanks again for filling in for me at the sisters' this afternoon. Tell me, are they still making progress?"

"Since you were there last, the parlor has been turned into a museum of sorts, display cases and all, thanks to an unnamed benefactor."

"God works in mysterious ways, doesn't he?" Her aunt dipped a piece of chicken in an egg mixture. "Makes me happy to know that burden has been lifted from them."

"On my way home, I noticed your truck at Vern's place. Izzy Weikert's car, too. I met her at T-bone's when I stopped by. She seems really sweet."

Her aunt's mouth dropped as did the chicken leg in her hand.

"Don't worry, Izzy was too busy trying to get T-bone's attention to divulge any of your secrets."

"A person can't get away with one thing around here!" Aunt Neva wiped the egg mixture and flour off her hands. "We need to talk. Sit, dear."

"Um, I am sitting."

"So you are." Neva got two glasses out of the cupboard. "Blueberry lemonade?"

Carley chuckled. "I thought you saved that for special occasions."

"Well, this might be one of them, depending on how you see it." Her aunt confessed the plans she and Vern had concocted with Izzy.

Carley was stunned. "That's way too much work for you, especially with your wedding coming up."

Chuckling, her aunt said, "I won't actually be *doing* the work. Izzy has people."

Carley shook her head. "What about the expense?"

"Vern's paying, and he can afford it." Her aunt crossed her arms. "Any other objections?"

"But I don't even know where my plans will take me yet."

"Dear, there is no obligation on your part. One way or the other, the place has to be cleared out and readied for a tenant."

Carley choked up. "Why would you go to so much trouble ... for me?"

"I'm not totally selfless. If you'd seen Vern's furnishings and collectibles, you'd understand why I don't want them to end up over here. More importantly,"—she emphasized each word with a rap of her knuckles on the table—"because ... that's ... what ... family... does."

Carley's eyes teared up. "You know, other than Dad, no one has ever cared that much."

"Get used to it, dear, because no matter where the Lord leads you, we'll be here when you need us." She shifted in her seat. "So, what were you saying about T-bone and Izzy?"

CHAPTER THIRTY-SIX

HARRISON: PRESENT DAY

Harrison tossed and turned, ruminating over the incriminating Medicare fraud downloads he'd found on Carley's computer. Coupled with her abrupt leave of absence, he could no longer override his suspicions. If only he could speak with her. Maybe it wasn't too late.

But where had she gone? Certainly not La Paz. What other lies had she told him? His thoughts wandered back to her computer files. He was missing something, but what? The name of a travel club scrolled across his mind.

Could that be it?

He arrived extra early the next morning so he could get to Carley's computer before the staff arrived. Roxanne's car was already in the lot.

That's what you get for hiring a conscientious administrator.

His morning schedule was so full he saw patients well into his lunch break. The afternoon was even busier. Waiting for everyone to go home for the evening seemed to take forever.

Roxanne stuck her head in his door. "You're working late today, doctor. Everyone else is gone."

"I'm finishing up a few things." He hoped she didn't ask what they were.

"Need any help?"

"No, thanks. Personal stuff." *I can lie too, Ms. Ingram.*

"Okay, then. See you tomorrow."

"Will do."

He waited at least five minutes before he headed down the hall to the nurses' office. He booted Carley's computer and downloaded the travel club directions and printed them out.

Seems weird she wouldn't use her phone's GPS.

As he was exiting the room, Roxanne popped up out of nowhere. He pulled back. "Sheesh. You startled me. I thought you'd gone for the day."

"I was straightening the waiting room. Is there something I can help you with?"

He held up the papers in his hand. "Needed to make some copies." He could feel his face turn red. "I'm embarrassed to say the only copy machine I know how to operate is the one in here."

"It worked?" She put her hands on her hips. "That's weird. That copier's been out of order all day. I scheduled repair service for tomorrow."

"Uh, no it didn't, actually." He pretended to wipe his brow. "Phew. I thought I broke it."

"Fortunately for you, I know how to work all the copiers." She plucked the papers from his hand before he could protest. "Follow me." She walked around front to admittance and placed the papers face down in the tray. "One copy enough?"

He started to sweat. "That's fine."

She pushed a button. "That should do it."

"Thanks." He chuckled. "I'm pretty sure I can handle it from here."

Even though he watched her drive out of the lot, he didn't trust Roxanne not to materialize out of nowhere again. He stuffed the printout and the redundant photocopy in his briefcase and didn't review them until he was safely behind his locked condo door.

The route's starting point was Philadelphia, the end was a residence in Andover, Maine. Couldn't get any better than this. Unless these weren't her directions? Her desk, her computer, her downloads. What were the chances of that? There was only one way to know for sure. He'd leave for Maine after work on Friday.

Chapter Thirty-Seven

Carley: Present Day

Andover Olde Home Days was set to begin in five days. From their front porch seats in the evenings, Carley, Aunt Neva, and Vern enjoyed hearing musicians rehearse in nearby garages and barns in preparation for the event's opening night concerts.

When Carley went by town hall on Monday to pay Aunt Neva's property tax, she got a sneak preview of some of the entries on display for the photography and art contests. One of the artists had mimicked the style and colors of Jean-Francois Millet's masterpiece *The Gleaners*. In place of women gleaning in a wheat field, the artist had painted Dubber and Warren "gleaning" in the dump. They'd titled the work *The Pickers*. Carley sensed a tenderness and respect on the artist's part, not an ounce of mockery.

Out back at the Liar's Table at Sawmill Market, folks drew Carley over to talk about the parade floats they'd been working on for weeks—sure their efforts would win them the cash prize this year. The owner, Pauline, bragged about the floral arrangement her brother planned to enter in the Historical Society's flower show. "He only used wildflowers and weeds, but his goat-skull vase is what will set him apart."

Andover's all-volunteer Fire and Rescue Department planned to show off their recent acquisition: a ten-year-old fully equipped rescue and emergency vehicle. Earlier that year, Oxford County had received a private million-dollar grant to purchase six new ambulances, straight off the production line in Massachusetts. The half dozen had been earmarked for the county's six largest towns, including Bethel.

When Bethel passed their old ambulance down to Buckfield, Buckfield passed their old one down to Hiram, which in turn passed theirs down to Andover. Barring any emergencies, EMT Leo Camire would be at the town common on Saturday and Sunday to reveal the not-quite-state-of-the-art vehicle.

Since lawn tractor race participants were not permitted to practice on the actual track, racers scrambled to find a place to hone their skills. Aunt Neva let Dubber and Warren test their souped-up tractor on the network of fire roads Otto had built throughout their property.

Tuesday afternoon, Carley and Aunt Neva took the golf cart down the wide pine needle path through the woods to the backroads. They found the brothers easily enough by following the sounds of their whooping it up on their tractor.

Aunt Neva waved to catch their attention. "Hidey-ho, boys. We brought you some ice water."

From the seat of the tractor, Dubber pulled his tee shirt up to wipe his face. "Thanks, Miss G, Carley."

"Pull your shirt down, Dubber. Have some class!" Warren gargled and spat. "These ladies don't be needin' to see your big ol' man boobs."

"Sorry." He yanked on his shirt. "Hey, Warren, why don't we let the ladies settle our argument?"

Carley frowned. "Argument?"

Aunt Neva held her hands up. "Whoa! Getting in the middle of a disagreement between brothers is dangerous."

Dubber got off the tractor. "S'more like a decision than an argument. See, we still haven't decided who's gonna drive the tractor on race day. Warren thinks he's quicker 'n me takin' the corners because he's lighter. I say the heft of me helps handle it better. One spill, and we're out."

Warren shook his head. "But the extra weight'll slow us down. I make better time in the straightaways."

Her aunt ran her hand along the hood of the tractor. "The Lawn Ranger here sounds powerful enough to overcome any of those conditions. Besides, calculating weight versus speed or skill versus experience is not in my toolkit. All that matters, boys, is that you work together to do your best and have fun—win *or* lose."

Dubber dropped his head. "Yes, ma'am."

Warren sighed. "Sorry, Miss G."

On their drive back to the house, Carley nudged her aunt. "King Solomon's wisdom is alive and well in Andover, Maine."

"I might not be wise, but I'm not stupid either."

Carley chuckled. "I'm really looking forward to Olde Home Days. The whole town is buzzing. And Dubber and Warren have put so much time and effort into practicing and in modifying their tractor, I hope they win."

"Me, too, but it's difficult to imagine those two any happier than they are now."

"I suspect you're right."

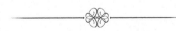

On Wednesday, Carley readied herself for a full day in the garden with Aunt Neva. Her aunt's contribution to Olde

Home Days was to provide fresh produce for the event's food vendors. This meant the oversized farm stand, built specifically for this occasion, had to be filled with fruits and veggies for vendors to pick up over the next few days.

When Linda Gregoire showed up at the crack of *yawn* to help, Linda was the one who set the pace. "Before we start in the garden, let me scrub out this stand. After it's dry, I'll apply a fresh coat of paint. Neva, do you have any of this green paint left? If not, I can run to the store for you."

"Um, I think there's a can in the basement."

While waiting for the paint, Linda untangled the hose and rinsed off the stand until there was not a spec of plant life or soil left behind "Now, where does your aunt keep her bucket and soap? This has to dry thoroughly before we paint, so we might as well wash our vehicles."

What do clean cars have to do with produce?

Aunt Neva returned with a half-full can of forest green. "On the shelf under the workbench, where I left it." She locked eyes on Linda. "Carley, why is wild woman washing my truck?"

Carley stared at the whirlwind that was Linda. "I don't think she can help herself."

After their cars were washed and the farm stand painted, the three of them picked the gardens clean. They rinsed off the produce and separated the varieties into covered crates.

By two o'clock, Carley was exhausted. "Don't you think we've earned ourselves some lunch?"

"Oops, I almost forgot!" Linda headed to her car. "I packed us a picnic."

Why does that not surprise me?

Aunt Neva looked over the feast Linda unpacked. "I'd say you shouldn't have, but I'm glad you did."

Carley offered to get some drinks.

"No need." Linda produced a gallon-sized Thermos and a stack of plastic cups. "I brought raspberry iced tea." She reached into the cooler. "And ice!"

They sat at the picnic table in the shade of an old maple tree to enjoy their meal.

After a total of twenty minutes, Linda began to fidget. She wrapped the leftovers and collected the trash. "So, what's next on our agenda?"

Carley was about to suggest they quit for the day when Frank pulled in. "Looks like your husband's been missing you."

"Frankie?" She waved him over. "Nah, my coming over here was *his* idea."

Why does that not surprise me either?

Linda greeted him with a kiss. "Frankie would've been here earlier, too, but when Gus begged him to play golf, I told him not to say no to the poor guy."

Carley restrained from snorting.

Frank shook his head and crossed his arms. "Looks like I got here in the nick of time. Hon, these two ladies have work to do. They can't sit around chit-chatting all afternoon, can they?"

Linda tried to protest. "But we still have to—"

"Come along now. I've got a fun project we can work on together at home." He jiggled his eyebrows.

"Frankie!" She blushed and gave him a swat.

Frank helped his wife load her car, then sent her off. "Thank you, ladies." He tipped his hat and winked. "Now you can rest."

She and Aunt Neva groaned as they struggled to their feet and hobbled to the porch.

Carley plopped down in one of the rockers. "Phew! I thought *you* were a hard taskmaster!"

Her aunt shook her head. "That woman has enough energy for three people half her age."

For a while, Carley rocked quietly, resting, and thinking. "Something on your mind, dear?"

"Sort of. In all my twenty-eight years, I don't remember ever being around a lot of couples. It was always Dad and me. No grandparents, no aunts and uncles, no married cousins. Most of our family friends—Mrs. M., Mr. Zalinsky, Big Moses—were either single or widowed. Even Selena and Tammy, my best friends at school, had single moms."

Aunt Neva's eyes closed. "Since your dad never remarried, having single friends would not be unusual."

"I guess." Carley shook her head. "You know, I've never even had a boyfriend. Maybe a few crushes in college, but none that lasted more than ten minutes."

Aunt Neva opened her eyes. "Does that concern you?"

"Never did before." She smiled. "Now that I see you and Vern, I know what I've been missing."

Her aunt squeezed her hand.

Carley squeezed back. "Take Frank and Linda. I like the way they give each other the freedom to do what makes the other one happy. She has her projects; he has his golf. After all their years together, he still flirts with her, she still blushes."

"And that gives you hope?"

"Yes, I think it does."

Her aunt cleared her throat. "You're not disappointed about T-bone and Izzy then?"

Carley lifted her head. "Not at all. I think they're right for each other, don't you?"

"It's what they think that matters." Her aunt paused a half minute then asked, "Does it still hurt about your Dr. Nichols?"

Carley skipped her usual kneejerk denial. "Yes, it does." Her admission prompted tears to well up.

"You know that story God is writing for you?" Aunt Neva took her hand. "I forgot to tell you. His endings are the best part."

They were still rocking when T-bone showed up. "What a life! Lazing the day away on the front porch."

Carley and her aunt started laughing and couldn't stop.

Aunt Neva caught her breath long enough to ask, "How can I help you, son?"

He rested his hands on his hips. "I need some onions and peppers for the Italian sausage booth."

"Oh, you mean *Izzy's* booth?" Carley got no reaction from him whatsoever.

"Yeah, I volunteered to help, and that's where they stuck me." His stare was more like a dare.

Too tired to reel him in, Carley let him off the hook. "Now that the paint's dry, you can help me move the farm stand and the crates into the shade over by the barn. Then you can take all the onions and peppers you need."

He tipped his hat. "Deal."

They set the stand in place and loaded the crates on its shelves.

"So, did you submit all your entries before the contest deadline?" Carley's phone conversation with Asha Kumar a few weeks back was still fresh in her mind. Asha had agreed to serve as a contest judge. She'd even recruited a fellow editor to join her.

"Yup, this morning."

Her head jerked his way. "What? But the deadline was—"

The mischief in his eyes matched his grin.

"Brat. You know, rumor has it a couple of editors from a New York City publishing house agreed to be on the virtual panel of judges."

He raised a brow. "Yeah, where'd you hear that?"

She shrugged. "Around."

"Uh-uh. Haven't you been in Andover long enough to know rumors outnumber black flies?"

She wagged a finger at him. "You'll see, 'oh ye of little faith.' Anyway, black fly season has to end sometime."

Chapter Thirty-Eight

Carley: Present Day

High seventies, low humidity, light winds. The weekend forecast couldn't have been better, especially for Olde Home Days.

Friday midday Carley helped her aunt open all the windows to air out the house.

"Ahh. Love that breeze." Arms stretched wide, Aunt Neva stood in front of the open window. "Feels so good after that spell of still, hot weather."

Carley huffed. "I could *never* do this in Philly, no matter what kind of weather. Most of the windows in my apartment were painted shut, the others had no screens."

Open windows. Such a simple thing, really, but full of meaning. *Fresh air. Woodsy scents. Sounds of nature. The feeling of being unstuck.* The tail end of a passing breeze caught Carley's old longing for city life and whisked it away.

"That didn't take long at all," her aunt said. "And when Vern gets here, he promised to help me take down the porch screens now that black fly season is over."

Carley frowned. "Are you sure it's over?"

"Yup, every year around this time." Aunt Neva sat on the sofa and patted the cushion beside her. "With the Olde Home Days' festivities starting at six tonight, what time do you plan to be there?"

Tonight's kick-off would be Aunt Neva and Vern's first official social event as a couple. Carley had volunteered to work at the new first aid station to give them space and to keep herself busy.

She joined her aunt on the sofa. "Maybe about five. Once I organize my supplies, there's not much more to do."

"Now, dear, if that tent gets too stuffy, Leo will be nearby. I'm sure if you ask, he'll help you tie the flaps back."

"If I can tear him away from his pride and joy long enough. Did you know he plans to make people put on disposable gloves and booties if they want to go inside the ambulance?"

Aunt Neva shook her head. "Mercy, I hope he doesn't mean the patients."

Carley posed a question that had been rattling around her brain for a while. "Why hasn't anyone thought of having a first aid station on site before?"

"Oh, we've thought about it plenty," her aunt said. "You see, many of the small towns in Oxford County don't even have a doctor never mind a walk-in clinic. Those that do can't spare staff members for a whole weekend."

"Sounds like the county could benefit from a mobile clinic." She grinned at her aunt. "Did anyone happen to get the name of that private donor who supplied the million-dollar grant for the new ambulances?"

"Since the operative word there was *private*, my guess is no." Aunt Neva tapped her temple. "But I do like the way you think."

Dubber and Warren had made the signage for the first aid station from a used wooden pallet and some old two-by-fours. A large cross painted red was nailed to the top.

Adjacent to her tent, clean and crisp in his EMT uniform, Leo stood guard over Andover's *new* ambulance. Every inch of the vehicle, inside and out, had been washed, waxed, and sanitized.

Carley began her shift rearranging the limited medical supplies and sorting bandages and stickers. A sweet memory of her long-ago mission trip to Bolivia popped into her mind. She wondered if Nurse Gomez was still living in the house the graduating class had built for her and her family that year. She'd have to ask Dad in her next email.

Wilda drove up in Aunt Neva's golf cart. She had a whistle hanging around her neck and a walkie-talkie in her hand. "Keepin' busy this evenin', Carley?"

"Hi, Miss Wilda. No patients yet, but I guess that's what we hope for."

Wilda wagged a boney finger. "We OHD officials always say we can never be too prepared. Finally, that includes a place to care for the sick and injured. A few years back, a grandmother slammed her grandson's hand in a car door. Then a girl scraped her leg in the dunk tank. Last year, a guy from away choked on a chicken bone at the fire station barbeque. T-bone had to use the Heimlich maneuver on him." She paused, raising one finger in the air. "Oops, I forgot. The term we professionals have to use now is *abominable thrust.*"

Carley had to ask. "Do you mean *abdominal?*"

"Yeah, *abominable,* like I said." Wilda lowered her voice. "Anyway, some of us suspect the choking victim was faking since he went on to win the pie eating contest."

Carley didn't dare laugh. She pointed to the badge pinned to Wilda's Olde Home Days neon-lime polo shirt. "What else do your duties include?" She only asked because she knew Wilda would be pleased to tell her.

"Each official oversees a certain area." She waved her hand around. "Mine is the whole town common. That's why Neva lets me borrow her cart. We keep a close watch, lookin' for those who want to make trouble. Personally, I don't trust those skillet-throwing contestants. I swear some of 'em are aiming for each other." She held up her walkie-talkie. "See this? *My* idea. Remember my cousin's brother-in-law who manages the Radio Shack? He gave us a sweet deal on these babies."

"Looks like you're prepared."

"All part of the job." Wilda handed her a business card that Carley was certain had been printed on a dot matrix printer. "If you need anything, you call this number. I won't be far." She drove off, her head scanning the common like a prison yard spotlight.

Carley didn't doubt Wilda's ability to find trouble. What she did doubt was this hundred-ten-pound woman's ability to do much about it.

During the next hour Carley bandaged two skinned knees and packed an arm wrestler's "guns" with ice in preparation for his next big match. When an exhausted pregnant woman wandered in on swollen feet, she insisted the woman lie down on the cot for at least thirty minutes.

Later, with no patients in sight, she made a quick call to Roxy.

"With all your new friends in Andover, I'm surprised you remember me."

Carley rolled her eyes. "I've told you before, the guilt thing won't work. Besides, forgetting you is impossible."

Her friend chuckled. "Does that mean you've tried?"

"Apparently not hard enough." She got to the point of her call. "Anything new at work?"

"More weirdness. Even your doctor's been acting strange all week."

"What do you mean?"

"Before he left this afternoon, I helped him make some copies. Driving directions, I think, but he acted like he was handling top secret documents."

Top secret? Driving directions? Is he going to run?

"Carley, are you still there?"

"I'm here." She steadied her voice. "Maybe he had a speaking engagement."

"Since I'm the one who makes his travel arrangements, I would know. The guy's up to something, I tell you."

"Stay calm, Roxy. Things will be back to normal soon."

"How do you know that? What aren't you telling me?"

"Gotta go, Rox. Talk later."

Carley searched her phone contacts for the FBI agent's number. *Should I call him? What do I really know for sure?*

She stuck the phone back in her purse. *Please, Lord, help.*

On Saturday morning, Carley arrived for her shift at the first aid station before the start of day's festivities. She had a clear view of the parade from her vantage point at the edge of the common. Though Andover was even smaller than New Hope, the town where she'd been raised, they both had the same folksy feel—family, friends, faith, community, and country. Heartsickness stirred—not for Philly, but for her father, her friends, her patients.

Mostly, she missed what might have been with ...

'What might have been?' Get a grip!

When her shift ended at one o'clock, she headed over to the sausage and peppers stand. "Hi, Izzy. I've been tempted by this delicious aroma all morning. I'll take mine in a roll, please, and a bottled water."

Izzy handed her an overflowing sandwich in a cardboard container. "Here you go." She put the water on the counter.

The sausage snapped at her bite. "Yum. Even better than I imagined."

"Wouldn't be half as tasty without Miss Geneva's fresh peppers and onions."

"And T-bone made sure to get all we had." Carley peeked around Izzy. "Speaking of him, where is he? I thought he was supposed to be helping you."

Izzy's whole face seemed to grin. "He was here most of the morning, but his pit-crew duties for Warren and Dubber called him away."

"Oh, right." Carley checked the time. "I think I'll take in the art and photo exhibit at the town hall before I head over to the track. Will you be there?"

"My shift doesn't end until five." She blushed. "Which works out fine since T-bone asked if I wanted to listen to the band at the fire station tonight."

Carley peered over the top of her sunglasses and raised a brow. "Seems like someone is over his skittishness."

"Seems so." Izzy smiled.

"You don't have to answer if you don't want to, but did T-bone ever tell you what took him so long to reconnect with you?" *I am an unabashed nosey body.*

"It wasn't all his fault. I'd just started my interior design business when we met last year. When Aunt Wilda told me T-bone was moving out of state to attend veterinary school, I figured there was no sense beginning a relationship at that point."

"I see." Carley took a sip of her water.

Izzy shook her head. "No, you're wondering why I would believe my aunt."

"Is my face that easy to read?" Carley chuckled. "By the way, if you need help at Vern's place, I've got some free time. I might not know much about interior decorating, but I can paint."

"That'd be a huge help. I'll call you when we reach that point. I'm still decluttering."

Mow-Ta Speedway at Grimaldi Field was a four-hundred-foot dirt track hemmed in by a wall of used tires. Carley arrived in time. The place stank of gasoline, motor oil, and burnt rubber. Men hosed the track to keep the dust down, drivers revved their engines, and spectators gathered in preparation for the fan-favorite lawn tractor race.

Aunt Neva and Vern walked hand-in-hand across the field.

Carley waved them over.

Vern surveyed the field of racers. "I think we've got over a dozen entrants this year. Should be a fine time."

Aunt Neva pointed out Dubber and Warren. "There's our team."

Dressed in crisp John Deere-green coveralls, the duo was easy to spot. "The Lawn Ranger" was stenciled across the hood of their tractor, and green eyes and a black mask were painted above its nose.

Carley shook her head. "Where did they find those jumpsuits?"

"They're called *coveralls*." Aunt Neva corrected. "A person can find just about anything online if *she* searches long enough."

Carley chuckled. "I can't wait to hear what you got in trade for them."

Her aunt winked. "Let's say the ruts in my fire roads have been filled, the weeds whacked down to pure dirt, and the tree limbs cut back."

"Tricky to decide who made out better in that deal." Carley shielded her eyes from the sun. "How many laps in this race again?"

Vern answered, "Twenty-five or until there's only one tractor remaining."

Carley noted the track's twists and turns. "How fast do they go?"

"Depends," Vern said. "The guy to beat is from away. McPhee's his name. He's reached thirty miles an hour more than once, but Esau Cooper has beat him before."

"That fast? Sounds like the drivers could get hurt."

"Nah, they bruise their egos more than anything," Vern said. "These guys *and* girls are tough and agile."

One bang from the starter pistol and the race began with a roar from the engines and a cheer from the crowd. With every lap, a few machines stalled out or fell over. Warren was holding his own in the straightaways and around the curves. Dubber and T-bone jogged alongside him as he passed by, spurring him on. By the fifteenth lap, half of the racers were out, either from a fall, a flat, or engine failure.

Keeping score wasn't easy for Carley.

The hometown audience booed when McPhee rammed Warren's bumper, then cheered when the guy's engine sputtered around the next turn, and he had to drop out. By lap twenty-five, only four remained. Esau in the lead, the lone female in second, Warren in third, and a longshot two laps behind.

Carley chewed her bottom lip. "Warren might be guaranteed third place."

"There's a lot of racing between 'might' and 'guaranteed.'" Aunt Neva shook her head. "We've seen some unlikely outcomes over the years."

Carley, Vern, and Aunt Neva moved closer to the finish line.

Leaning into every curve with skill and experience, Esau whipped past the longshot, causing the guy to flinch and drive off the track. The female rider made her move, trying to pass Esau on the left, but he stayed the course. His front bumper hooked her wheel, and his tractor flipped over, tossing him into the air.

The spectators gasped, the woman driver rubbernecked, and Warren swerved around them for the win!

Dubber hurried over, seizing Warren by the shoulders. "Can you believe it, brother? We did it!"

When a race official presented Warren with a checkered flag for his victory lap, he handed the flag to his brother. "Victory lap's all yours, Dubber. You earned it."

Carley got a lump in her throat.

Esau Cooper dusted himself off and came by to congratulate Warren. "Slick move, Churner. Let's do this again next year."

"Was an honor to go up against you, Esau." Warren chuckled. "You deserve a prize for that somersault you did when your tractor threw you. Might could get you on the six o'clock news."

"That was a hoot, wasn't it?" Esau said.

When Dubber finished his victory lap, Aunt Neva hugged both brothers. "You've done us proud, men! If Otto were here, he'd be cheering the loudest."

Dubber held his hat over his heart. "Miss G, we wouldn't be here if it weren't for you."

Warren's voice was thick. "You had faith in us, and that means more 'an any ol' trophy."

"I agree." Dubber nodded. "But there will be a trophy, right?"

Chapter Thirty-Nine

Harrison had caught the last flight to Portland on Friday evening. He hadn't slept at all the night before, and with an hour's drive at the end of his ninety-minute flight, he'd decided to book a hotel room. Unable to find a vacancy in Portland *or* Andover, he'd found a one-star motel halfway between the two.

Besides, he wanted to see Ms. Carley Jantzen's reaction in the full light of day.

As he approached Andover around nine a.m. on Saturday, traffic increased and slowed to a crawl.

Must be an accident.

He reached a crest in the road. A half-mile of cars lay ahead of him. He'd seen the Welcome to Andover sign a few miles back. Was their total population of 821 all out at the same time? When he got closer to town, banners announcing Andover Olde Home Days gave him his answer.

He edged his way through the bumper-to-bumper traffic and animated crowds until he found South Arm Road. Matching the number on the mailbox to the one in the directions, he pulled into the long driveway. A red VW Beetle convertible sat in the yard with the blue and yellow license plates which read *Pennsylvania*.

What will she say? What will I say? He settled his nerves before he got out of the car. Taking the porch steps two at a time, he knocked on the door. He imagined her shock. Seconds passed before he knocked again. No answer. He walked around the house and rapped on the back door. Still nothing. He trudged across the field to the barn and greenhouses. All empty.

He headed back toward the center of town. By now, Main Street was blocked off with parade route signs stuck in the ground. He had no choice but to pull to the side of the road, get out, and watch.

An Oxford County Sheriff's truck led a long line of homemade floats, ATVs, antique cars, and too many army vehicles to count. Laughing children chased after drivers who tossed candy and trinkets to them.

I don't think the Macy's Thanksgiving Day Parade committee has anything to worry about here.

Just when he thought the parade was coming to an end, along came farm tractors, horses and their riders, trucks covered with political campaign signs, and at least a dozen firetrucks from different eras and towns. Country tunes and patriotic songs, like Brooks & Dunn's *Only in America* and Lee Greenwood's *God Bless the USA,* blasted from speakers. Seated in lawn chairs along the route, people sang, clapped, and cheered.

His years growing up in rural Pennsylvania looped around his mind. His mom and dad were middle-aged when he'd come along, their only child. He'd had a pleasant enough upbringing—not spoiled but not ignored either. He'd even participated in parades like this himself ... mostly on the Fourth of July ... his wagon decorated with flags and streamers, later his go-cart painted red, white, and blue.

Mom and Dad were practical people, the kind who didn't place much value in dreaming beyond their means.

Unfortunately, the cost of medical school fell into that category.

He shook off the dusty memories. They had no bearing on his patients, his practice, or his partnership with Bryce and Peter—a partnership that would end because of million-dollar fraud.

How could I have risen so high yet been such a fool?

The parade over, he edged his rental car back toward the town common. Signs for multiple events pointed in all different directions. Skillet toss, fly casting, tractor pulls, and buggy rides. Way too many for him to read.

If Carley *were* here, how would he ever find her? Hoping for a miracle, he slowed to a crawl and searched for her face. A car honked behind him, then a truck did the same. He would've pulled over, but there was no room. He drove around until he got lost, then tapped into his GPS to bring him back to the house on South Arm. Still no one there.

He continued down the road to Lower Richardson Lake. Rather than return to his dreary motel room, he decided to take a walk along the shore to keep himself awake. He'd only gone a few feet when a swarm of vicious horseflies attacked. Waving them off like a lunatic, he scrambled back to the car.

Even with his windows up, he swore he could smell sausage and peppers. He stayed put for another hour until hunger and thirst got the better of him. One more run by the house with no luck.

Carley Jantzen's day of reckoning would have to wait another day.

On his way out of town, he almost pulled in to watch the lawn tractor race—for kicks, not because he thought Carley would be there—but he got tangled up in traffic. Grumbling, he headed back to his motel, stopping at a convenience store to get something to eat.

Standing in line with a grilled hotdog and a bag of corn chips, he thought he'd go insane with the itch. "Do you sell calamine lotion?"

"End of the counter." The clerk looked at him. "Run into some moose flies, did you?"

He scratched his arm. "Yes, over by the lake in Andover."

"Andover?" The clerk motioned to his shriveled hot dog. "You should've stopped by Old Home Days and gotten yourself some of their famous sausage and peppers."

He sighed. "Yes, I probably should have."

Back in his room, Harrison took a lukewarm shower—not by choice—then fell into bed.

Chapter Forty

Every year during Olde Home Days, Andover Congregational held a Sunday Homecoming Service on the town common. Geneva always volunteered to help with the picnic lunch that followed.

Since Carley had the early shift at the first aid station again, Neva suggested they drive in together. "Mind if we take your car? I have to drive my golf cart back to the house this afternoon."

"If you can wrestle it away from Miss Wilda." Carley chuckled. "She certainly is enjoying her position of authority. I even heard her ask a few people for their IDs."

"You're kidding!" Neva groaned. "Again, I say that woman needs a purpose."

"I think she's found one—Grand Overseer of Others."

"Perfect." Geneva nodded.

They climbed into Carley's car and buckled up.

"So, how's the first aid station working out, dear?"

"Patients have been trickling in and pleased to find us. I'm not sure everyone knows about it yet." Carley pulled out onto South Arm Road. "As of now, we have a single cot, but I could have used two when the sisters stopped by yesterday."

"Were they ill?"

"No, I think they just wanted to take advantage of the shade." She stopped at the intersection. "That reminds me, this weekend has been unseasonably moderate, but I'm sure that won't always be the case. What do you think about adding Gatorade and Pedialyte to the menu next year?"

Next year? "Whatever you think is best, dear. You're the nurse." She hid her smile. "Will your shift be over before the winners of the writing contest are announced?"

"I don't want to miss any part of that presentation, so I asked Linda if she'd mind covering my last half hour."

"I heard the committee received five times as many entries than in any previous year. Multiple genres, too." She cracked her window. "Did T-bone tell you what he submitted?"

Carley shook her head. "Nope. He's holding his submissions close to his chest. When I mentioned there might be professional editors on the panel of judges, he pooh-poohed the news as rumor."

"Just as well. Otherwise he might accuse us of having something to do with his winning." She sputtered. "Creatives! Drives me bonkers when they think accepting practical help reflects negatively on their talent."

"Is Vern meeting you there?"

"He's giving the communion devotion at Grace Bible this morning, but he'll be there in time for the picnic." She smiled thinking of the last two days—how Vern had held her hand and introduced her as his fiancée to everyone who'd listen.

Carley glanced over. "Aunt Neva, are you blushing?"

She rolled her window down all the way. "It's hot in here, that's all."

Carley smirked. "I can fix that. She pulled to the side of the road and put the ragtop down. "Still hot?"

Aunt Neva raised her hands high and shouted. "See what that man does to me?"

Carley chuckled. "You're in love, that's all."

"That's all? Mercy, that's quite a lot for a woman my age to handle!"

Geneva stood with Vern, Carley, T-bone, and Izzy waiting for the winners of the writing contest to be announced.

The emcee began, "As many of you may know, our virtual panel of judges usually consists of English Literature professors from nearby colleges. This year, we were able to add two professional editors out of a publishing house in New York City. Now without further ado, I have their results."

Cynthia Giroux won first place in the essay category. Rylee Cooper won second place with her fantasy short story. Adam "T-bone" Stakes earned both first and second places in three categories—general short story, memoir, and poetry.

The emcee asked him to read one of his poems.

With Izzy in the forefront of his cheering fans, T-bone obliged. "This poem is titled 'Bound.' I started writing it during one of my less optimistic periods." He smiled at Izzy. "I completed the last stanza a few days before I submitted it."

> Bound within myself. Apart.
> Prisoner of a shielded heart.
> Rarely dare to venture out.
>
> Speak, and then be routed back
> Behind the walls that thwart attack,
> Learning silence, caution, stealth.

Dreams of contact slowly ebb.
Quiet habit weaves a web
Barring paths to other realms.

Then one soul perceives the key
To glowing dawn releases me
By whispering, "I understand."

About to step off the gazebo after a round of applause, T-bone was stopped by the emcee.

"We have one more little surprise for you." He handed T-bone an envelope. "This is a letter from one of the professional editors who served on our panel. She has invited you to submit the complete manuscript of your memoir to her New York City publishing house."

T-bone stared at the envelope, then back at the man. "Really?"

The emcee slapped him on the back. "Really."

Geneva's eyes brimmed with tears. *Thank you, Lord!*

Chapter Forty-One

For as long as Harrison could remember, his mind had been set on a career in medicine. His studies had always taken precedence over social activities. To keep his scholarship at Chapel Hill, he had to maintain good grades, all the while working a part-time job. The only on-campus activity he ever participated in was the debate club.

Enamored by Bryce Reinhart's and Peter Stryker's brains, charisma, confidence, and connections, he had always felt like the odd man out around those two extroverts. He recalled a conversation among the three of them about their respective futures after graduation.

Peter shook his head at something Harrison had said. "Nichols, I bet you were that guy in high school who'd raise his hand to remind the teacher when they forgot to assign homework."

Harrison shrugged. "Not quite, but it did concern me."

Peter pointed at him and laughed. "I knew it!"

Bryce pushed Pete's hand away. "Give the guy a break. Besides, someday when we start our own practice, we'll need an upstanding guy like him to keep us in line."

"Yeah, sure." Harrison couldn't imagine why either of them would ever need him, especially with all their frat brothers.

"We mean it, Nichols." Bryce said. "We've got the connections, but not your way with the patients or prowess behind the podium. Your speaking skills could prove valuable on the conference circuit. Never hurts in building a practice. You better be ready when we call."

Pete leaned in. "No bull, Nichols."

Back then, the notion that Bryce and Peter valued him in *any* way had boosted his underdeveloped ego and wimpy self-worth. He kicked himself now for believing their trash talk. Their opposites-attract relationship had been the impetus for this whole sordid mess.

Harrison got an early start on Sunday, hoping to find Carley at the house. An old pickup sat where the Beetle had been the day before. He knocked on the front door but got no answer.

Don't these people ever stay home?

With that Podunk-town fair still going strong, he had to assume she was there. He backtracked to Grimaldi Field and scanned the Park & Ride for Carley's red VW. *There!* He parked two spaces over from the car.

At the edge of the field, a man in a neon-lime vest directed him to the town common. He was about to begin his booth-by-tent search when a church hymn rang out from speakers mounted on polls nearby. A black-robed woman standing at a lectern in the center of the gazebo began to speak.

A sermon? Wonderful.

He tried to skirt around the common without drawing attention to himself. After a few scowls, he stopped and pretended to listen. The brief message ended with an invitation to stay for a picnic. People queued up for box lunches, then sat on the grass in small groups.

Harrison wandered, slowing long enough to check faces. He zigzagged his way through the maze until he was back where he'd started. Refusing to give up, he stood in the open and scanned the area one last time.

A golf cart came up alongside him. An older woman— high forehead, squinty eyes—spoke. "Morning, sir. Hope you don't mind my saying so, but from the concern on your face, you're either lost or you've lost someone. Maybe I can help."

"No, just meeting a friend, but thanks." *Am I that obvious?*

"If your friend isn't here, you might find him over at the covered bridge for the canoe float or on Airport Road for the Ellis River Riders horse show."

"*Her*," he said absentmindedly.

"I see." The woman checked her watch. "My money says she's at the horse show. More to see there." She looked up. "There's the shuttle van now! Let me flag it down for you." She sped away, waving her hand madly at a slow-moving Dodge Caravan.

He had no clue whether Carley was interested in horses or canoes, but he had to continue his search somewhere. He jogged to the van, thanked the golf cart woman, and climbed in.

Banners announcing the open English and western horse shows were strung up on a semicircle of horse trailers. Fans lined the fences. Harrison do-si-doed through the spectators, stopping long enough to see snapshots of the dressage and barrel racing events. Still no sign of Carley.

Idiot. The only place she's sure to be, eventually, is at her car.

He hopped the shuttle heading back. As they neared the common, something caught his eye. Behind an open-doored ambulance sat a white tent. Stuck in the ground nearby was a two-by-four with a huge red cross nailed to the top. A sign outside read "First Aid Station." *Of course.* How had he missed that before?

"Stop! I need to get out here!"

The driver slammed on the brakes. "Suit yourself, buddy."

He raced to the tent and pulled the flap open.

A woman in a ballcap stood with her back to him. "Carley?"

The woman turned—the same one who'd been driving the golf cart. "'Carley?' I'm sorry, I don't know anyone by that name."

"Oh, I thought maybe ... never mind." He left the tent and walked toward the road leading to the Park & Ride.

The woman followed him. "Excuse me, sir, what did you say your name was?"

Did I hear her right? "Sorry? My name?" Before he could answer, a flash of red drove by. "That's her!" Harrison took off running.

CHAPTER FORTY-TWO

GENEVA: PRESENT DAY

"Wait, Geneva! Wait!"

Geneva stopped. *What imagined emergency does Wilda have now?*

Wilda skidded up alongside her in the golf cart and practically fell out. "Where's Carley?"

"She's on her way home. Why?"

"That man!" Wilda pointed. "The one running toward the Park & Ride." She panted. "He's been sniffin' and nosin' around all morning. Told me he was looking for a friend ... not a *he* but a *she*. He's after Carley!"

She sighed. "What makes you think his *she* is Carley?"

Wilda gulped air. "When he saw her red VW bug go by, he yelled, 'That's her!' and took off down the street."

Pulse racing, Geneva lunged for the golf cart. "Let's pray the traffic slows him down." She took off, calling over her shoulder. "Wilda, find Vern and tell him to meet me at the house!"

Her skin prickled. Geneva would never forgive herself if something happened to her niece. She cut through yards, crossed over fields, then headed down a secondary road until she found the fire roads behind her property. She thanked God for Dubber and Warren. Without all the work they'd done, she wouldn't stand a chance of getting to Carley in time.

In time for what? She wasn't even certain who this guy was, but an uneasy feeling grew.

When she exited the woods to her backyard, no vehicles were in the yard. *Phew.* She drove up close to the house, charged through the backdoor, and bolted for her Winchester hanging on the fireplace. Through the open windows, she heard a car drive in. *Carley.* Before she could check to see if the rifle were loaded, a second car pulled in.

A man got out and closed his door. "Ms. Jantzen! Carley!"

Her niece froze in mid-step. "Dr. Nichols? How did you know where to find me?"

"I followed the breadcrumbs." He shrugged. "You downloaded your directions." He took a step toward her. "Look—"

Geneva threw the front door open and raised her rifle. "Stop right there!"

Carley started, then clutched the porch railing. "I warn you, doctor, my aunt is a crack shot. Now, what do you want?"

"I need to talk to you."

"What is there to talk about?" Carley's voice trembled. "Obviously, you know what I've done, or you wouldn't be here."

He took another step toward the house.

"Apparently, you didn't hear me." Geneva measured her words. "I said, 'Stop ... right ... there.'"

He raised his hands and took a few steps back. "Sorry."

A second later, Vern pulled in and snugged his car up alongside Carley's VW. "Everything all right here?"

Geneva dipped the nose of her rifle. "I've got the situation under control."

"I can see that." He got out and walked toward the doctor. "What's going on here?"

Her niece pointed. "That's Dr. Nichols. He was about to tell me why he's here."

The doctor moved a step closer. "I want to see what I can do to fix things."

"You can't *fix* fraud!" She glared at him. "Anyway, it's too late. The whistle's been blown."

He squared his shoulders. "What if I could un-blow that whistle?"

"Even you're not that powerful." She shook her head. "Tell me, why did you do it?"

Dr. Nichol's brow wrinkled like he was in pain. "I don't know, maybe I'd had enough of their greed or arrogance or flagrant disregard for anyone except themselves."

Flagrant disregard? Huh? Geneva searched Vern's eyes. They held confusion too.

Nichols raked his hands through his hair. "What I don't understand, Carley, is why or how you got involved?"

Her niece crossed her arms. "I got involved because it was the right thing to do!"

He gaped at her. "When is fraud ever the right thing to do?"

What was Nichols saying?

The doctor's eyes flamed. "There has to be something I can do to help you."

Carley crossed her arms. "Help *me*?"

Something's off. Geneva asked, "What do you mean *help* her?" She lowered her rifle. "Vern, are you hearing this?"

Vern scratched his head. "What I'm hearing seems to be different from what these two are hearing."

Carley opened and closed her mouth. "What's going on?"

Nichols's face was blank but for the dark circles under his eyes.

Vern put a hand on Dr. Nichols's back and led him to the porch. "Sounds like you two need to talk."

Carley backed away as the doctor stepped onto the porch.

Geneva motioned to the rocking chairs. "You two, sit. You're both talking but neither one of you is listening."

Vern's phone buzzed. He rolled his eyes. "It's another frantic text from Wilda." He handed Geneva his phone. "Neva, maybe you could call her back to put her mind at ease?"

She sighed. "I suppose I owe her that much. I'll leave you to referee these two." She stepped over the threshold. "I'll be right inside if you need me."

CHAPTER FORTY-THREE

CARLEY: PRESENT DAY

Still shaking-mad, Carley sat in the rocker and called to her aunt through the living room window. "Aunt Neva, keep your rifle handy. I don't trust Dr. Wolf-in-Sheep's-Clothing here." She sputtered. "Let me guess, you figured this all out with the help of my software training?"

He dropped his head. "Yes, that helped."

"I bet it did!" Carley's anger was building again. "Do you even care about how many lives you have messed up?"

He gripped the arms of the chair. "Don't you think I know that? This hasn't been easy on me."

"Easy on *you*?" She couldn't believe he'd said that.

"I'll take the blame for ruining the practice, but I won't take the blame for committing fraud. That's all on the others and you."

"*Me*? You must be joking." Carley felt the heat rise. "What are you trying to pull? I'm the one who blew the whistle on you!"

"On *me*? Why would you do that?" Dr. Nichols returned her glare. "I reported my suspicions about Bryce and Peter way back in April." He drew in a ragged breath. "I didn't know you were involved until last week."

A black Suburban pulled into the driveway.

Ha! Carley smirked and pointed to the SUV. "You can tell your story to the FBI."

His brow furrowed. "When did you call the FBI?"

She folded her arms smugly. "I didn't, but somebody must have."

Two men got out of the black vehicle.

Vern craned his neck. "Carley, are these the agents you spoke with at the library?"

"Yes, the very same. The tall one is Special Agent Unser. I didn't get the shorter one's name."

Dr. Nichols groaned. "Then we're all in trouble. These two goons are in cahoots with Bryce and Peter. I've seen them hanging around the office at odd hours."

Carley stiffened. "What do you mean?"

He mumbled. "Suffice it to say, Carley, they're *not* FBI."

Unser stopped at the edge of the porch. "Hello again, Ms. Jantzen. Hey, Nichols. Nice of you to save us some trouble." He narrowed his eyes at Vern. "And who do we have here?"

Vern stopped the swing. "Beckham. Friend of the family."

Carley blurted, "Is it true you're not FBI?"

Unser ignored her. "Anyone else here?"

Vern leaned back. "No, just us."

Unser walked around the front of the house. "Now what's wrong with this picture? We've got three individuals and four vehicles."

Carley measured the pace of her response. "The pickup belongs to my aunt. We rode into town together this morning. She stayed to help close things up at the fair."

"You don't mind if we check inside, do you?" Unser chin-nodded to his partner.

"Yes, I do mind." Carley began to rise from the chair. "We told you, no one is here besides us."

Dr. Nichols tugged on her hand to lower her back down.

"If you're not the FBI, how did you find me?" Carley tried to distract them but failed.

Silent-man unholstered his gun and charged past them to the door.

Unser sneered. "For starters, your lawyer has a big mouth and a bug in his office."

Dr. Nichols leaned back and crossed an ankle over a knee. "I see Bryce and Peter have you doing all their dirty work, huh?"

"Those two clowns?" Unser sneered. "Hardly."

"What do you mean?" Dr. Nichols asked. "Who else is involved?"

Unser smirked. "Let's just say there's more than one clown car full of doctors under the circus big top, all performing for their cut of the gate."

Silent-man exited the house. "All clear."

Way to hide, Aunt Neva!

Carley put on an I-told-you-so face, but her bravado didn't last long.

Unser showed his gun. "You three, off the porch and over to my car—now!"

A rushed whisper came through an open window. "Vern, on your signal, I'll take the tall one, you take the other. Stall a bit. I'll have a better shot from upstairs."

Vern stayed seated. "Mind my asking where you're taking us?"

Unser waved his weapon. "I said get moving!"

Dr. Nichols whispered to her, "Stay close to me, as far away from them as possible."

"Okay." Without thinking, Carley looped her arm around his.

Unser growled at Vern. "What's the matter, old man? Been sitting too long?"

"Arthritis is all." Vern pulled himself up off the swing and steadied himself against the porch rail. "Joints don't work as well as I need them to."

Carley and Dr. Nichols descended the porch steps together, while Vern half-stepped his way, one tread at a time.

Unser circled behind the trio, pointing his gun. "Keep going!" He barked orders to his partner, "Cuff 'em and put 'em in the back."

Silent-man holstered his weapon and reached for his cuffs.

Unser walked around the front of his car toward the driver's side.

Vern signaled with one sharp nod.

A shot rang out.

Unser grabbed his arm and dropped his gun.

The doctor pulled Carley down and off to the side.

Then Vern flipped Silent-man on his back and secured his weapon. "Hand me those cuffs, Doc." Vern cuffed him and turned him face up.

Aunt Neva shouted from the upstairs window. "I've still got a bead on you, Unser. "Move an inch, I'll shoot you again."

Vern ordered, "Someone check him for a second weapon. I found one on this guy."

Dr. Nichols discovered Unser's ankle holster and another loaded gun.

Rifle in hand, Aunt Neva joined them. "You okay, Carley?"

"A little shook up, that's all."

Vern pretend-pouted. "Hey, what about me?"

Aunt Neva shrugged. "I wasn't worried, not with Vern the Valiant here to save the day."

Dr. Nichols examined Unser's shoulder. "I need something to stop the bleeding."

Carley sprinted to the house for supplies. By the time she returned, a posse of sheriff's cars had arrived with Leo and T-bone in the ambulance behind them.

Before Leo could come to a complete stop, T-bone was out the passenger door, going from one to the other. "Miss Neva? Carley? Vern? You okay?"

"Not us you have to worry about." Aunt Neva pointed. "Check that one over there."

Glancing at the patient, then back at Aunt Neva, Leo waved his hands around and shook his head. "You had to go and shoot someone bloody, eh? Couldn't have held off until our magnificent rig here was at least a week old?"

"Sorry," Aunt Neva said. "Could have been worse though."

A grin slipped out the side of Leo's mouth. "We're sure glad it wasn't, eh, Miss Geneva?"

They loaded Unser into the back, where T-bone attended his wound. Before Leo closed the doors, he fitted Unser with a pair of blue booties. Siren blaring, they took off on their inaugural run to Rumford Hospital, a sheriff's deputy following close behind.

All the weapons were confiscated, including Aunt Neva's Winchester. Deputy Sturgis read Silent-man his rights and handed him off for transport. Then, he took statements from the four of them.

"I freaked out when that guy went into the house." Carley clung to her aunt. "Where were you hiding?"

She shrugged. "In a closet."

"I've seen your closets. Everything has a place, and everything is in its place. He must be half-blind." Carley asked. "And when did you have time to call 911?"

"I didn't. I thought one of you did."

Sturgis chuckled. "Your Wilda Weikert's the one who called. Fortunately, we had units in the area because of Olde Home Days."

Carley was confused. "Why would Wilda call?"

The deputy smirked. "Miss Weikert ... in her own words." He pushed a button on his phone. "When I saw the US Marshalls driving by the common—or who I *thought* were the US Marshalls—I flagged them down to tell them Carley was being chased by the cartel and needed their help. The man who was driving made a call on his cell, which was the same exact burning phone my cousin's brother-in-law wanted to sell me—for a discount price, of course—from the Radio Shack he manages over in Hillsboro—that's Hillsboro, New Hampshire not Hillsboro, Maine. I asked myself, 'Would US Marshalls be using phones from Radio Shack when there's not too many of those stores left in the country?' I answered, 'No, Wilda, they would not.' That's when I called you."

Carley winced. "I think I may have misjudged Miss Wilda."

Aunt Neva dipped her head. "I think maybe we all have."

Another two hours passed before all the various law enforcement personnel departed.

Still numb and confused, Carley plopped down at the kitchen table with Aunt Neva, Vern, and Dr. Nichols. "How do you thank someone for saving your life?" Carley shook her head. "If it weren't for you, Aunt Neva, and you, Vern, I don't know what would've happened."

Dr. Nichols added. "I'll never be able to repay either of you."

"Oh, please, we're not that selfless," Aunt Neva said. "Our own hides were at risk too."

"If Neva hadn't come up with the plan, I couldn't have done a thing," Vern said. "Besides, Carley, your doctor here played his part in getting you out of the way."

Before she could react to his comment, T-bone showed up at the back door. "Anyone hungry? I've got a whole pan full of sausage and onions and peppers here."

"Are you kidding?" Vern stood. "I'll get the plates."

Aunt Neva produced a bag of rolls from the breadbox.

"If the sausage tastes as good as it smells, I'm in." Dr. Nichols rubbed his hands together. "Um, that's if you don't mind?"

Carley passed a plate down to him. "Help yourself."

T-bone stuck out his hand. "Dr. Nichols, I don't believe we've been introduced. Adam Stakes, but folks around here call me T-bone."

"Pleasure to meet you. Call me Harrison, please."

Oh, sure, T-bone gets to call you Harrison.

As one might expect, the conversation over sausage and peppers was limited and informal.

Dr. Nichols took a bite. "Mmm. The first thing I've eaten today, but worth the wait." He swallowed. "So how did your patient do on transport?"

T-bone shrugged. "Complained a little about the accommodations, but I told him not to worry because they'd only get worse."

Aunt Neva chuckled. "Has Leo forgiven me yet?"

"Might take him a while." T-bone grinned. "He's back at the stationhouse detailing the rig again."

Though thankful for the breathable moments of normalcy, Carley sensed they were fortifying themselves for the conversation ahead—and she wasn't wrong.

After the table was cleared, Vern broke the silence. "Seems we have a tangle of loose ends to sort through and tie up. Who wants to start?"

Dr. Nichols cleared his throat and wrapped his hands around his mug of coffee. "I guess I will. Carley, I'm sorry for ever thinking you were mixed up on the wrong side of this. Bryce and Peter can be convincing. I should know."

Her voice rose an octave. "And, on that basis, you went directly to me being *in* on the fraud?"

He hung his head. "No, not until I overheard Roxanne talking to you and discovered you'd lied about being in La Paz. Then I found those documents on your computer."

"I thought you trusted me." Even saying the words hurt. "Dr. Nichols, why didn't you tell me what was going on when this all started?"

"*Harrison*, please." He gave her a side glance. "Tell me, Ms. Jump-to-Conclusions, what made you assume *I* was defrauding the government?"

"Fair enough, *Harrison*." She breathed a little easier. "I found evidence of upcoding and referrals on your server that didn't coincide with our records."

He nodded. "I found them too. When I reported the discrepancies to the FBI, my contact told me to leave everything as I found it so as not to tip off whoever was involved." He stared past them. "I knew what would happen to the patients, to the staff, to the practice when the truth came out. While I was praying for an alternative solution, I think I got stuck in denial."

Carley's hands shook. "I need to call Roxy."

Harrison's forehead wrinkled. "How much did you tell her about all this?"

"You know Roxy. I didn't dare tell her a thing. She would've acted impulsively."

"Impulsively?" He grinned. "You mean like the two of us did?"

She tried to tuck her hair behind her ears. "Maybe."

Vern cleared his throat. "Now that you two have stopped pointing fingers at each other, do you have any idea when this whole mess will come to a head?"

Harrison lifted his chin. "Let me call my FBI contact to see what he knows."

Aunt Neva refilled his mug. "Dr. Nichols, perhaps putting your phone on speaker would save you some repeating."

He shrugged. "At this stage, I don't see why not." He dialed the number.

A man answered. "Nichols, glad you're okay."

"Then you've heard?"

"The Oxford County Sheriff's Department did an excellent job relaying everything to our field office in Boston."

"What does that mean for the case?" Harrison massaged his forehead.

"The Bureau had to expedite the operation. A multi-state-wide dragnet is underway now."

Harrison raked a shaky hand through his hair. "What about our ... the patients?"

"As of now, no one is allowed access to the offices or the medical records. When the staff shows up for work tomorrow, a guard will be there to turn them away."

"I see." He slumped in his chair. "Will you let me know when you take Peter and Bryce into custody?"

"I won't be able to tell you anything until after *all* the arrest warrants have been executed."

"How many arrests are you looking at?"

"Again, I can't say."

Harrison nodded. "Of course, I understand."

They hung up.

T-bone folded his hands on the table "So, what's the next step?"

Carley addressed Harrison. "I should probably wait to call Roxy until you hear back from him."

"Might be best." Harrison scrubbed his face with both hands. "You know, I knew this day was coming, but I thought I'd have enough time."

"Enough time for what?" Carley asked.

"I'd hoped to refer my patients to reputable physicians to avoid lag time in their care. I managed to collect their contact info and medical records on a thumb drive, but I don't know if I'll be allowed to reach out to them now."

Vern spoke up. "I may be able to help you with that. Let me see what I can find out from one of my friends who specializes in this type of law."

Surprise crossed Harrison's face. "Why, thank you, sir. I appreciate that."

Carley asked, "What are you going to do now?"

Harrison checked his watch. "Since I missed the last flight to Philly, I'm not sure." A weary sigh slipped out. "I should probably contact the car rental company before they put an APB out on *me*."

"Why don't you bunk over at my place?" Vern asked. "We can get started on your legal matter in the morning."

"That's very generous of you, sir," Harrison said, "but I should probably get a hotel."

The others chuckled.

"But you won't." Carley shrugged. "Not in Andover anyway."

CHAPTER FORTY-FOUR

GENEVA: PRESENT DAY

Harrison left with Vern around ten, and T-bone wasn't far behind. Geneva and her niece tidied up the kitchen. She washed, Carley dried.

"Tell me, dear, what's going on in that pretty head of yours?"

"A lot." Carley plucked a mug from the dish drainer. "I can't believe how many people are involved in this whole Medicare fraud ring."

"Terrible."

"Roxy will be a mess—not to mention out of a job." She continued drying the mug. "I've told you how she helps her sister and brother-in-law with Hunter's medical expenses, haven't I?"

"Yes, you have."

She put the mug in the cupboard. "This is going to be tough on everyone—staff and patients alike."

"Indeed, it will."

"My lawyer's not going to be happy. Since I blew the whistle on the wrong party, my testimony's not worth the paper the False Claims Act Form was printed on." Carley chuckled at the irony. "Tell me, Attorney Yeager, how much is thirty-three percent of zero?"

Aunt Neva nodded. "'Don't count your chickens,' as the saying goes."

Carley reached for another mug. "And what's going to happen to all the equipment and office furnishings?"

Does she hear herself? Geneva doubted equipment and office furnishings were uppermost in her niece's mind. "Not to mention all those issues of *Yachting, Highlights,* and *People* in the waiting rooms."

Carley shook her head. "I know, right?" Then she put the mug she'd already dried back in the dish drainer.

She took the dish towel from her niece's hand. "Let's sit for a minute. We need to talk."

Carley followed her to the table. "About what?"

"Oh, I don't know. Perhaps we can start with the topic of avoidance. I read somewhere there are multiple types. Situational. Cognitive. Protective. Which one are you experiencing now?"

"I don't know what you mean." Her niece crossed her arms.

"My guess is cognitive." Geneva leaned on her folded arms. "In all your concerns for the future, you have not mentioned your doctor once."

"I was ... I mean ... well, so many people will be affected by this."

"And *you* are one of those people, dear. Tell me what's going on, not in your pretty head, but in your heart."

Carley squirmed in her seat. "I'm not sure. Everything happened so fast I haven't had time to process the facts, let alone my feelings."

Geneva nodded. "Fair enough."

"Even though I know Harrison is innocent, my feelings haven't caught up yet. I was so sure he was involved."

"Like a bruise that follows a punch. No matter the cause of the injury, the bruise still hurts."

Carley agreed. "Yes, sort of like that."

"I'm sure you will agree I'm an expert at avoiding romance." She winked. "Let me run this by you. You told me you've never had a serious relationship. Yet when you found yourself attracted to Harrison, you did nothing about it. Could fear of commitment have triggered your reaction and swayed your opinion of his involvement?"

Her niece sat quietly for a moment. "Oh, dear Lord, I hope that's not what I did."

"Start with being honest with yourself. God will show you what you need to do."

"But I have no idea how Harrison feels about me."

"Oh, please. He risked his life to get you out of harm's way." She laughed. "You should have seen the look on his face when T-bone plopped down next to you at the table tonight. The guy couldn't take his eyes off you the whole time."

"Really?" Her niece blushed. "Speaking of eyes, did you see them? Sea-green with little specs of gold."

"How could I"—she huffed—"when he only had eyes for you?"

Carley sighed. "Even if everything you say is true, he lives in Philadelphia, my home is here. What kind of relationship can we have when we live so far apart?"

"Your home is *here*?"

"In Andover, yes." Carley's eyes brightened. "I can't think of any place I would rather be than with family."

Geneva hugged her. "So glad you feel that way."

"So, romance aside, the next item on my to-do list is to find a job."

"You might want to hold off job hunting for a bit. Vern and I have an idea, but we need to work out some details."

"Well, I can't mooch off you forever."

She backhanded her niece's comment. "Nonsense. You've earned your keep and more."

"Really?" Carley leaned in. "Then could I ask you for one more favor?"

"Anything, dear."

"Will you let me take you wedding dress shopping?"

Geneva laughed. "You snuck that one in, didn't you? I still think the dress I have is perfectly suitable for a wedding."

Carley rolled her eyes. "Yes, but not for *your* wedding."

Chapter Forty-Five

Harrison took Vern Beckham up on his offer of a room for the night.

"Excuse the mess," Vern said as then they entered the house. "I've got some work being done. All I can promise you is a bed with clean sheets."

When Harrison asked about the project, Vern smiled. "After Neva and I are married next month, Carley's moving in here."

Had she ever intended to return to Philadelphia?

After an hour of wrestling with himself and God, he managed a few hours of sleep.

Early the next morning, he and Vern adjourned to the law office. They were into the final draft of a letter to his patients when his FBI contact called.

"Yes?"

"Stryker and Reinhart were picked up at their homes around five a.m. Including the two thugs in Maine and a few ancillary characters, thirty-nine arrests were made. Those taken into custody represented seven medical practices in Pennsylvania, New York, and New Jersey."

"I had no idea the scale was that large. Thanks for letting me know." Harrison wasn't sure if this was the end of a nightmare or the beginning of another one. Before he could relay the conversation to Vern, Carley and her aunt walked in with coffee and pastries.

"Hear anything yet?" Carley handed him a cup. "Milk, no sugar."

She remembers how I take my coffee. "A minute before you came in." He told them what the agent had said.

"Thirty-nine?" Carley's frown deepened. "Sad on so many levels—patients, families, staff. And a big, fat, black mark on the medical community's reputation."

"There's one more thing," Harrison added. "The federal prosecutor wants me on the first plane back. I have to leave here in about a forty-five minutes to catch a flight out of Portland."

"Vern, I need to show you something." Miss Geneva dragged Vern into the next room.

Harrison joined Carley on the leather sofa in the anteroom. "I like your hair." *That's all you've got, really?*

"Thanks."

The air seemed to crackle with unspoken words … and feelings? But were the feelings only his?

Harrison cleared his throat. "I need to expand on something I said yesterday." His eyes held hers. "Carley, other than my patients, you were the only person whose respect I believed I had earned. After I was duped by my partners, I worried you'd think I was a fool or a failure or even a rat for turning them in. I wanted to avoid that for as long as I could."

A softness replaced her nervous expression. "When I thought I found evidence of fraud on your tablet, I felt stupid for having believed you were a tender, kind, and noble person. Feeling stupid made me angry, mostly at myself."

"'Tender, kind and noble?' Really?"

Her face turned a pale shade of pink. "Did I say that?"

He shrugged. "I could be wrong ... but I'd sure like to be right about one thing."

"Would make for a better story, huh?"

She's smiling, that's good.

"Speaking of stories, tell me about this T-bone guy."

Smooth segue, idiot.

"T-bone?" She tilted her head and seemed pleased he'd brought the guy's name up. "You mean Andover's favorite son?"

"I guess." His hopes took a dip in the road.

"He owns his own business. Volunteers as an EMT and a firefighter. Loves animals and even assists the local vet. If that isn't enough, he recently won a bunch of awards for his writing. Pretty impressive, right?"

"Right, impressive." His heart flopped.

"Oh, and one more thing, you know the sausage and peppers he brought over last night?"

"Don't tell me the guy cooks too." *I sound like a jealous eighth grader.*

"No, but his girlfriend does."

"Girlfriend?" His eyes widened before he could stop them. "He has a girlfriend?" *Could I be any more obvious?*

Carley grinned. "I even played matchmaker."

Awkward seconds ticked by while he searched her face for the meaning behind her words. *Why am I so awful at this?*

She whispered, "Harrison."

He couldn't take his eyes off her. He gulped. "Yes."

"Are you going to keep staring at me, or are you going to kiss me?"

He parted his lips to answer.

"Shh." She lifted his chin with one finger and closed his mouth. "*Now* would be good."

They kissed. She was right. It *was* good.

Chapter Forty-Six

Carley: Present Day

Roxy shouted, "I can't believe you knew there was fraud going on the whole time and didn't tell me!"

Carley held the phone away from her ear and stepped outside to sit on the porch swing. "I'm sorry, but can you understand why the FBI forbade me to say anything?"

"Maybe." Roxy cleared her throat. "In keeping with full disclosure, I have something to confess. The doctor who bungled my nephew's delivery was none other than Bryce Reinhart."

"I can't believe *you* knew the whole time and didn't tell me!" *Payback.*

"Funny. After my sister's malpractice lawsuit against him was dismissed, I took the position at Key State Medical hoping to trip him up."

"And did you?" Carley sat on the swing.

"No proof, but I heard rumors he'd been drinking an hour before he entered the delivery room. I know the plans the government has for him now should satisfy me, but that won't help Hunter get better or his parents cover his expenses."

Carley sighed. "I know."

"Anyway, I'm just happy your Dr. Nichols wasn't mixed up in all this."

She stopped the swing. "Speaking of Harrison ..."

"Oh, it's *Harrison* now, is it?"

She couldn't help but smile. "Remember that unexpected trip he took? He was here with me."

"Harrison? With you? In Maine?"

"Yes. By the way, I'm fine with you calling him *my* doctor now."

"What? Carley!"

"You'll have to wait to hear the whole story until I can see you in person. I just wanted to make sure you were okay."

"Well, if okay means being out of a job but *not* in jail, then I'm doing great."

"I promise, Rox. We'll figure something out."

Aunt Neva and Vern sat head-to-head in the library.

Carley peeked in. "What are you two conspirators up to? Choreographing a new routine for your first dance as husband and wife?"

Vern scoffed. "We've don't even know any *old* routines!"

Her aunt waved her in. "Did Harrison call to say he got in?"

"Yes. He was on his way to the prosecutor's office."

"The sooner this matter is settled the better." Her aunt motioned to a chair. "Sit with us, dear. We'd like to discuss something with you."

"What's up?" Carley scrunched her face. "And why so serious?"

Vern smiled. "Don't worry, it's a good serious."

Carley sat. "You certainly have my attention."

Aunt Neva folded her hands. "Before we have this discussion, we need your word that you will never—and we mean *never*—divulge any part of what we say here today to anyone."

Carley held up her right hand. "I solemnly swear not to tell a soul."

Aunt Neva said, "Other than Vern and me, you will be the only other person who holds this information."

"Okay, now you're scaring me." Carley looked at one, then the other. "Not even T-bone?"

"No, and we have our reasons." Aunt Neva nodded to Vern.

He went over to one of the bookcases, pulled a small lever, and stood aside as the bookcase opened like a door.

"What on earth?" Carley stood. "It's a closet. Wait. This is where you were hiding when that man searched the house, isn't it?"

"Yes," her aunt said. "This closet is where we keep the records of our ministry."

A secret closet seems like a lot of trouble to go through just to keep track of donations.

Carley tilted her head from side to side. "Ministry?"

Aunt Neva nodded. "We call what we do ministry because the Lord called us to it."

"Like my dad's call to the mission field?"

"Exactly." She paused a moment. "As a young woman, God prompted me to perform various acts of giving anonymously. Of course, Otto knew. Later, we included Vern as our legal advisor."

Carley asked, "What's the advantage of a ministry remaining anonymous?"

"Don't misunderstand us, we believe it's important to give openly, too, mainly to model obedience and show others how God will provide." Her aunt tapped the table. "However, anonymity has some advantages. I know from experience being on the receiving end of charity makes some people feel uncomfortable. The other side of the coin is some feel entitled and would try to influence us."

Vern nodded. "Anonymity can be a safeguard against pride too. The Bible says, 'But when you do a charitable deed, do not let your left hand know what your right hand is doing.'"

Her aunt continued. "For years, I ran my decisions by Otto, and we both had Vern to counsel us. When Otto passed, I felt a bit wobbly. Vern and I have been managing, but when he found you on that ancestry site, we thought you might be the one to fill the void."

"You picked me out of all your relatives?" Carley's heart swelled for having been chosen.

Her aunt tilted her head. "There is a tiny detail we may have neglected to tell you. Turns out you're my *only* remaining relative."

"Oh." Carley stumbled over a speedbump of pride. "So, you had no other choice?"

"That's not true. We could have chosen *not* to contact you. But we liked what we learned and wanted to meet you. Then Vern and I figured the Lord's hand was all over this. If there had been others, we might have chosen incorrectly." Her aunt smiled. "God made it easy for us."

"But how can *I* help you?"

"You already have, dear. You nursed me back to health after my fall. I was praying for a way to help the sisters when you came up with an ideal solution. I've been doing my best to encourage T-bone in his writing, and you helped with that."

Carley shrugged. "Anyone can do that."

Aunt Neva nodded. "Yes, but there's a difference between doing something because you *can* and doing something because you're *called*. Vern and I believe you're called."

"Maybe, but without a job, I can't offer much in the way of financial assistance."

"As you've witnessed, not all giving involves money," Vern said.

"How do you decide who to help?"

Vern said, "After a few poor decisions, we learned to wait on the Lord."

Carley frowned. "How could trying to help people ever be a poor decision?"

Aunt Neva tilted her head. "Sometimes the *good* we mean for others is not always God's *best* for them. Take Dubber and Warren for example. Tell us how you would help them."

Carley folded her arms. "Well, if I had the money, I'd build them a big building to store their inventory." She chuckled. "Maybe buy them each a John Deere tractor."

"They'd love that, wouldn't they?" Her aunt smirked. "For about a week."

"Huh?" Carley was puzzled. "What do you mean?"

"Vern and I have watched those brothers operate for decades. They love to barter, haggle, salvage, and get dirty putting in a full day's work. They take pride and pleasure in doing a job for a fair price—even if they get paid in manure or firewood."

Vern shook his head. "They've come up with some ingenious ways to meet their needs and those of others. You were on the receiving end of their charity yourself after Neva's fall when they cleaned up the basement and set up that pulley system. Tell me, would you want to rob them of those blessings by handing them a spanking new building and a few shiny tractors?"

Carley thought before she answered. "Now that you mention it, their secondhand inventory would be out of place in a brand-new building, wouldn't it?"

Vern laughed. "There's that too."

"Over the years, Otto, Vern, and I agreed on a few guidelines. Whatever we do has to line up with the Word. We bathe every decision in prayer and never move forward without sensing God's peace. If we can't decide, we vote and the majority wins."

Carley sighed. "I'm still not sure why you need me."

Vern said, "Like the King James says, 'a threefold cord is not quickly broken.' Not to mention we need a tiebreaker."

Aunt Neva added, "Come alongside us and listen for God's voice. If you believe he's given you an idea or you've found a candidate in need, run it past us."

"What about cost? Is there a limit?"

Aunt Neva shook her head. "When the Lord shows us whom to help, he provides everything we need—money included." She pointed to the embroidered sampler on the wall. "Based on this verse in Matthew 25, we call our foundation The Least of These."

Carley's memory clicked in. "Hey, the organization that donated $10,000 to my father's mission fundraiser has that same name."

Silence. No reaction from them whatsoever.

Carley joked, "I suppose that was you, huh?"

Vern shrugged. "We're often called to donate a portion of a need, so others can make up the difference and receive part of the blessing."

"That *was* you?" Carley's mouth dropped open.

Aunt Neva ignored her. "Vern, please get the ledger down."

He lifted a thick book off the top shelf in the closet. "We've transcribed everything to a spreadsheet on our hard drive, but we like to keep a written ledger for quick access." He handed Carley the book.

Aunt Neva said, "Our ledger has become more of a journal. We often go back and read about all the times God blessed us and, in turn, enabled us to bless others. Thumb through the pages to get a feel for what we do and trust God to lead you."

For the next few hours, Carley perused forty years of giving. The ledger's first entry, recorded on May 18, 1981, was for the purchase of a prom dress in the amount of $58.00 for Eliza Emerson's classmate. In 1984, Faith Lankford's $1,150.00 tuition balance due to the Culinary Institute of America was paid in full. In the winter of 1989, a $750 payment was made to a private transport company to bring a dialysis patient to and from his treatments in Rumford.

Flipping through the pages, she found every kind of entry from Eagle Scout camping supplies to a new roof on the town hall; from new saddles for two Ellis River Riders to a used van for the Millers and their eight kids; from false teeth (uppers *and* lowers) for a man named Upton to an emergency flight to Mass General Hospital in Boston for Del Stakes.

Mixed in with bookbags and school clothes were construction funds for a library addition to an elementary school in Kentucky. Two cows and six goats given to a local farmer. Tractor trailers full of food and supplies for victims of hurricanes over the last twenty years. Local churches and their foreign missionaries were not forgotten either.

Real estate purchases were made, and scholarship funds set up at Haven Academy and another for Adam Stakes at Bowdoin College. In addition to the many onetime recipients, there were yearly donations to the Andover Fire Department, the Oxford Sheriff's Department, and Rumford Hospital. A recent line item made her smile. "Stamp collection display cases for the Antoine sisters."

The entry that really caught Carley's attention was the "$1,000,000 grant to Oxford County for six new ambulances."

Near speechless, she found Aunt Neva and Vern out on the porch. Pointing to the entry, she said, "One question. How?"

Her aunt shrugged. "You've seen the books on investing in my library, haven't you? Turns out 'the tenor of my way' lies in making profitable investments. Since Otto's income took care of our personal expenses, I was free to reinvest my earnings and put them to good use."

Vern asked, "So, Carley, what do you say? Are you in?"

"Remind me again how this works. We bring an idea forward, we vote, and the majority rules?"

Aunt Neva said, "Well, it's a little more involved, but that's the gist of it."

"Then I'm in. The first item I'd like to vote on is Aunt Neva splurging on a new wedding dress." She turned to Vern. "All in favor say aye."

Chapter Forty-Seven

CARLEY: PRESENT DAY

Though Carley remained in Andover, her mind was on Harrison in Philly.

Aunt Neva and Vern's wedding preparations were moving along. Faith had full charge of refreshments, Izzy the décor, and Linda the big day's agenda. Carley's main job was to smooth communication between all the parties.

The bride-to-be may have balked at buying a new dress, but for as many times as Carley had seen her gazing at the long-sleeved, lace creation hanging on her closet door, she knew Aunt Neva was pleased. The ice blue color of the dress set off her crystal blue eyes and brought out the silver in her dark hair.

Carley had reminded her, "Aunt Neva, it's not the dress, it's *you* in the dress that makes it beautiful."

Aside from wedding plans and everyday chores, Carley squeezed in a few hours to help paint her soon-to-be living quarters. Under Izzy's tutelage, she learned to repurpose and restore furnishings—some pieces to go with Vern, others to stay with her. No matter what, her move would be complete before the newlyweds returned from their honeymoon.

Though Carley had tabled her job hunting for the time being, she'd spent considerable time contemplating her role in The Least of These Foundation.

Aunt Neva had reassured her. "Don't worry, dear. If the Lord has something for us to do or someone for us to help, he has a sure way of getting our attention."

Though Carley and Harrison spoke often, they had no idea when they would see each other next. The federal prosecutor had insisted both Harrison and Roxy stay close by in Philly while he built his fraud case for the government.

Harrison had explained, "Even though Roxanne didn't have direct contact with the patients, she knows more about billing codes and office procedures. They want me around to interpret diagnoses and treatments."

"I understand." Carley had sighed. "They can't take forever, can they?"

"No, but it sure seems like it some days."

She'd sighed again, too loudly.

"Carley, I don't believe God brought us together after all this time just to separate us for good."

"Perhaps you could mention that to the prosecutor? Tell him I miss you."

Harrison whispered. "Don't stop, please."

"Not possible."

Three weeks into their separation, Harrison called with an update. "You're not going to believe this."

"What?"

"The FBI had an agent working undercover on the fraud case for almost ten months. Care to venture a guess as to his identity?"

"No idea."

"Special Agent Fabian Yanni, the one you nicknamed Silent-man."

Carley gasped. "The short guy with Unser?"

Harrison chuckled. "One and the same."

"Sheesh. He's lucky Aunt Neva didn't decide to shoot *him!*"

Carley loved the sound of Harrison's laugh.

"Agent Yanni explained a little about the pattern of escalation in this case. Professional courtesy referrals turned into paid referrals, which led to incentives, to kickbacks, to bribes. When that wasn't enough, upcoding Medicare patient records was introduced, which eventually led to blackmailing those who refused to participate. They believe a plastic surgeon from Morristown, New Jersey was the ringleader."

"When will the case actually go to trial?"

"The courts are backed up, so probably not for a year or longer."

"Oh." *What does that mean for us?*

"You'd be proud of Roxanne. When the prosecutor complained he couldn't find a link to connect the multiple defendants, she suggested he check college fraternities. Turns out the majority of those involved are members of the same fraternal order—along with the judge who dismissed Roxanne's sister's malpractice case four years ago."

"Roxy knew something fishy had gone on," Carley said. "I confess, I didn't always believe her."

"The prosecutor put Roxanne's sister in touch with a new attorney."

"Does that mean they'll get a chance to present their case again?"

"Looks like it." Harrison cleared his throat. "Sorry this is taking so long. In addition to the legal matters, I've had some personal and professional decisions to make. I'll let you know more when things settle down."

"I understand." *Do I really?*

Aunt Neva and Vern's intimate rehearsal dinner at the house turned into a party for twenty of their closest friends. As Carley meandered among the guests, many of them couples, her longing for Harrison took a turn toward self-pity. *Stop! Tonight is not about you.*

A knock at the door brought her back to the moment. "I'll get it." She swung the door open.

"Hi."

"Harrison! Why didn't you tell me you were coming?"

"Then it wouldn't have been a surprise."

She stepped out onto the porch and into his arms.

He held her tight. "You know, whenever I used to imagine holding you like this, I'd stop myself."

"Why is that?"

"Not in a zillion years did I ever think it would happen, and it hurt too much to think about it."

"Yet here we are." She could not stop smiling.

"So I see." He moved an errant strand of hair out of her face. "I would have been here weeks earlier, but I had to sell my condo in the city and find an apartment I could afford."

"Oh?" Her heart sank. Knowing the question had to be asked, Carley prepared for his answer. "How long can you stay?"

"Well, I don't want to outstay my welcome." His lips brushed her ear as he whispered. "Is forever too long?"

She melted into his arms. "Just long enough, I'd say." She pulled back. "Wait. Didn't you say you rented a new apartment?"

"I did—sight unseen, but the location can't be beat. About a half mile from your new place above the Sawmill Market. The owner's brother—a tax attorney, I think she said—recently moved to Florida."

Tax attorney, taxidermy, should I tell him? "You'll love it."

They moved to the swing. He put his arm around her.

"Harrison, you're staring at me again. Remember what happened the last time you did that?"

He nodded. "Yes, I got to kiss you."

"Well?"

He leaned in and pressed his lips to hers.

Carley caught her breath. "Next time you don't have to wait for an invitation."

"Good to know." He kissed her again.

Once she regained her poise, she said, "Now that we both have a place to live, all we have to do is find gainful employment. Any ideas?"

He cleared his throat. "That depends. How would you like to work together again?" He pulled out a brochure from his pocket. "I got this in the mail a few weeks ago. My research tells me this concept could meet a real need around here. What do you think?"

Printed under a photo of a large mobile clinic were these words: *Fully equipped mobile clinic available in Oxford County, Maine. Ideal for less populated areas. Zero percent financing available. Contact us to see if you qualify for a partial grant.*

Her jaw dropped, her hands shook. She cut her eyes to the window and found her co-conspirators staring back.

Aunt Neva smiled and Vern winked as they raised flutes of blueberry lemonade in a toast.

Carley traced Harrison's jawline with her fingertips. "I think your idea is perfect."

ABOUT THE AUTHOR

Clarice G. James writes smart, fun, relatable contemporary women's fiction, woven together with threads of humor, romance, faith, and mystery. To date, her novels published by Elk Lake Publishing, Inc. include *Party of One, Doubleheader, Manhattan Grace, The Girl He Knew*, and her latest, *The Least of These.*

Clarice grew up on Cape Cod. She also raised her three children there. Eight years after she was widowed in 1998, she was blessed to remarry (Ralph) David James. She and David now live in southern New Hampshire. Between them, they have five children and ten grandchildren.

David, a short story writer, and Clarice both enjoy the writing process. When she's not writing, Clarice is reading, encouraging fellow writers, or giving author talks around New England.

How to connect with Clarice:

Email: cjames@claricejames.com
Facebook: https://www.facebook.com/clarice.g.james
Twitter: https://twitter.com/ClariceGJames
Website: http://www.claricejames.com

A Special Request from Clarice: "If you enjoy reading my books, I would be so pleased if you would help get the word out by writing a review on www.amazon.com or www.goodreads.com. Thank you!"

Party of One (Elk Lake Publishing, Inc., 2017): Risking her privacy, widow Annie McGee founds Party of One, a communal table for single diners, where she meets an electric mix of colorful characters who cause her to confront her fears, question her beliefs, doubt her self-assurance, and take another chance on love.

Doubleheader (2nd Edition, Elk Lake Publishing, Inc., 2019): Casey Gallagher credits a carefully crafted game plan for her wins: her solid marriage, her lucrative marketing career in Boston, and her popular sports column, Doubleheader. When Casey discovers that her late father, the one man she idolized, had an affair which produced a son he never knew about, she's determined to identify this so-called brother before he sullies her father's reputation.

Manhattan Grace (Elk Lake Publishing, Inc., 2018): When a door opens for Gracie Camden to leave Cape Cod and move to Manhattan as a nanny for a Juilliard drama instructor, she fully expects God to use her acting talent to launch her to stardom. It's been six months. What's taking him so long?

The Girl He Knew (Elk Lake Publishing, Inc., 2019): When Juliette Dawson, a health-conscious triathlete, drops dead during training, her husband Charlie needs to find out why before he loses the girl he knew forever.

Ask for Party of One, Doubleheader, Manhattan Grace, The Girl He Knew, and The Least of These at your local bookstore or go online to www.amazon.com.

If you enjoy Clarice's books, please help spread the word by writing a review on www.amazon.com or www.goodreads.com. Thank you.

DISCUSSION QUESTIONS

(Spoiler Alert!)

1. Why was Carley Jantzen conflicted about reporting the Medicare fraud in the medical practice where she works?
2. If you discovered your employers were committing any kind of fraud, would you report them to the proper authorities—even if it meant people would lose their jobs?
3. What first impressed Harrison Nichols about his fellow medical school students, Peter Stryker and Bryce Reinhart? Have you ever been impressed by someone for the wrong reasons? Has anger, a lack of self-worth, or jealousy ever tainted your decision-making?
4. The theme running through this book is doing for the least of these. How do the characters in the story provide for the least of these? Geneva? Carley? Carley's dad? T-bone? Geneva's employer, Mr. Emerson? Otto? Vern? Dubber and Warren? Frank and Linda?
5. What reasons did Geneva and Vern give for keeping The Least of These Foundation a secret?
6. Other than helping financially, what are some ways you can help those in need?
7. Roxanne Ingram's nephew's birth had been botched by Dr. Reinhart. Roxy had a hard time letting go of her

anger and resentment. Was she justified? Did her anger help?

8. Vern had been best friends with Geneva and her husband Otto since they were teens. Do you think it's possible for friends to fall in love after years of friendship? Has that happened to someone you know? If it happened to you after you were widowed, would you feel guilty?

9. Have you ever jumped to conclusions about someone's behavior? When you learned the truth, did you apologize, rationalize, or pretend it never happen?

10. Judging the lifestyle of Dubber, Warren, and Quonset (the man who lived in the rundown trailer) is tempting. What is your first reaction?

11. What are the differences and/or similarities between small town and city living? Which do you prefer and why?

12. Moving forward, what are some of the ways you could help those around you? Would offering help anonymously work for the situation?

AUTHOR EVENTS

Meeting my readers and aspiring writers at various events is such a pleasure. Check my website at https:// claricejames.com to see where I'll be next.

If you or your group would like to host an author event, these types of venues are an ideal fit:

Book Clubs: If you're in my area of the country and your book club selects one of my books, I can join you to discuss it—either on video chat or in person.

Bookstores: I love to support small, locally-owned bookstores by doing author talks.

Cafés & Coffee Houses: Chatting about books is always better over coffee.

Family-style Restaurants: I'd be happy to set up a table in a private room or the foyer.

Ladies Church Groups: My books, *Party of One*, *Doubleheader*, *Manhattan Grace*, *The Girl He Knew*, and *The Least of These* are written with women readers in mind. Themes include forgiveness, grief, loneliness, pride, surrender, charity, mercy, and discerning God's purpose for your life. I'd be pleased to speak on those topics.

Over 55 Communities or Senior Activity Centers: Invite me, and I will come.

Private Author-in-the-House Parties: Host an Author-in-the-House home party (local to me). This venue gives readers and authors the chance to get to know one another better.

Call or text me at 603-689-8945 if you live in the New England area and want to hear more about the interactive Lessons Learned on the Way to Publication Writers Workshops for new or pre-published writers. Attendees are encouraged to come armed with curiosity and questions. Here are just some of the topics covered:

- How to know if you're a "real" writer
- Being professional before you're published
- Step by step guide through the writing and publishing processes
- Editing your own work
- Finding the right kind of agent, editor, and publisher
- Things to do before you submit a manuscript to an agent or publisher
- What to include in a query letter and book proposal
- Reasons why your submission may have been rejected
- Pros of both self-publishing and traditional publishing

Call or text me at 603-689-8945. If you prefer, email me at cjames@claricejames.com. Thank you.

REFERENCES & RESOURCES

(BY GENRE, IN ORDER OF APPEARANCE)

Bible:
Scripture taken from King James Version (KJV) of the Holy Bible and the Darby Translation (DARBY), both in Public Domain.
Prologue: Matthew 25:40 (KJV)
Ch 20: Luke 6:38 (KJV)
Ch 21: Matthew 25:40 (KJV)
Ch 24: Proverbs 22:6 (DARBY)
Ch 29: Matthew 25:40 (KJV)
Ch 46: Ecclesiastes 4:12 (KJV)

Books:
Ch 24: "The law of reciprocity is based on the biblical principle of 'Give and it will be given unto you.' The law of use is about using what we have been given for the good of others. The law of responsibility teaches us how to be wise in all we do." Based on principles outlined in *The Secrets of the Kingdom*, Pat Robertson (Word Publishing, 1987)

Poems:
Ch 40: "Bound," Ralph. D. James, 1979

Songs:
Ch 7: "It Is Well with My Soul." Hymnist, Horatio Spafford. Composer, Philip Paul Bliss, 1876.

Made in the USA
Middletown, DE
25 May 2021